THE IRANIAN FIASCO

The Iranian Fiasco

RAY HARTJEN

The Iranian Fiasco

© 2026 Ray Hartjen

All rights reserved. No portion of this book may be reproduced, stored in a retrieval system, or transmitted in any form by any means—electronic, mechanical, photocopy, recording, scanning, or other—except for brief quotations in critical reviews or articles, without prior written permission of the publisher.

First Printing, 2026

Published in Mission Viejo, California by Two Red Chairs Publishing.

ISBN 979-8-9997831-2-7 paperback

ISBN 979-8-9997831-3-4 e-book

Front & Back Cover Photography by:

subinpumsom/iStock

Cover & Interior Design by:

Lori & Ray Hartjen

rayhartjen.com

Dedicated to my loving and supportive wife, Lori, my "rock" and partner for over thirty-two years, and our two children, Olivia and Raymond. Thank you for your unconditional love and support.

Contents

Chapter 1

Tiger Swanson had never been a sound sleeper, and her nights became substantially more restless after she joined the Central Intelligence Agency as an operative in Ground Branch of the Special Activities Center. It was difficult to sleep when your head was turning with thoughts and working for the agency certainly filled one's head with thoughts.

This night was another one of those nights, amplified by the fact that she was in a new house. After years of bouncing from one temporary living space to another, a sort of Airbnb vagabond, she had finally committed to signing a year-long lease, occupying a one-bedroom guest house bungalow of an old manor in Old Town Alexandria, Virginia, tucked along the Potomac River and just a thirty-minute jaunt up the George Washington Memorial Parkway to the agency's front gates in Langley.

Just her third night in her new place, Tiger thought it must be her new environment that was making her restless. After all, she was enduring a patch of relative downtime at the agency, with no active operations on the docket and none visible on the short-term horizon. This should be the time to catch up on rest, she thought, rather than rely on complete exhaustion to set in while in the field.

"I guess that's what adrenaline junkies get," she mumbled as she got out of her brand new, queen-sized Casper bed delivered just a day ago. "Maybe I should try the floor or the backyard?"

She reached down and picked up a folding karambit knife, absentmindedly flipping it open and inserting her index finger in the hole at the bottom of the handle. Karambit knives dated back to the eleventh century, originating in Indonesia and southeast Asia as a curved-edged farming tool. Over the centuries as a tool, it had evolved to much more sinister uses.

Some people had worry stones to fiddle with while in thought. Tiger had a karambit.

Tiger liked to twirl the karambit around as she thought, and this particular knife was a Cold Steel-manufactured Tiger Claw, given to her as a gift by Devin Thomas, the agency's Deputy Director of Operations and Tiger's ultimate boss. When Thomas saw the knife's name, he couldn't resist the gift.

Tiger spun the knife and its razor sharp, plain-edged, three-and-a-half inch hawkbill blade repeatedly as she shuffled her bare feet along the hardwood floors and out of her bedroom. Moonlight slipped in through the back windows that opened out to the Potomac, and guided her through the living room, equipped with one of her very few household possessions, a square throw rug she had picked up from Wayfair.

She leaned onto the counter that separated the kitchen from the living room in the renovated open-space floor plan and debated firing up her most prized of newly acquired possessions, her Breville Barista Express Impress espresso machine. Before pushing the power button, she looked at her watch and saw it was only 3:12 am.

She turned around and leaned the small of her back on the counter, wondering what she should do with herself. "Maybe a drink of water and back to bed," she muttered to herself.

But before she took her first step, movement from outside in her peripheral vision caught her attention. Glancing in that direction, she first noticed the reflection of moonlight off a glass object. In the fraction of a second, she recognized it as a red dot reflex sight mounted to the claw mount atop a Heckler & Koch MP5 submachine gun, carried by a man dressed fully in black tactical gear, including a facemask and a lightweight helmet.

Tiger had seen the man, but the man had not seen her. Her fight or flight instinct kicked in, but for her, it wasn't much of a choice. Fight was in her nature, and she would bet her bottom dollar that the man wasn't working alone—he had at least one colleague covering the front door.

Fight it was.

If she had a gun, she just would have shot the man through the window. But she didn't have a gun, at least not yet. So, Tiger moved to rectify that situation.

As Tiger flipped the orientation of her karambit so that the blade was at the bottom of her closed fist, she crouched and moved stealthily to the right side of the door frame of the back door. Breathing slowly and deeply, she was in position for only five seconds before she could hear the deadbolt lock being picked. A moment later the handle turned and the door slowly opened. She could smell oil being applied to the hinges to silence them as much as possible.

Whoever this was, she thought, they were careful and professional.

When the door opened more, the first thing that entered the house was the suppressor-equipped barrel of the MP5 that first swung away from Tiger to the intruder's right, then back left again toward her. When it did, she pounced.

Taking a quick step to her left, Tiger grabbed the barrel with her left hand and pulled it and the man toward the living room, simultaneously using her right foot to kick the door open more fully. Then with her right hand, she swung her fist upward, striking the surprised man under the chin as he reflexively pulled the trigger, firing suppressed rounds toward the front of the house.

Tiger knew the wound wasn't fatal as the karambit was more of a slashing and clawing knife rather than a stick-and-twist knife. So, she pulled the blade from under the man's chin and dropped to a knee, savagely slicing at the man's femoral artery alongside his inner right thigh.

She then drove upward from the floor to a standing position and slashed the left side of the man's neck, tearing open his left common carotid artery.

The last two cuts were to be fatal, and the man slumped forward as his blood pressure plummeted. On his way down, Tiger grabbed the MP5 with her left hand and freed its sling from his neck while she dropped the karambit. She then knelt down again, grabbed the man by the back of his tactical vest, and pulled him to the side of the open door, rolling him over in the process. As she released the ammunition magazine from the MP5, she grabbed another from the front of the man's vest and slid it into the weapon.

Just as she worked a new round into the chamber, the front door was kicked in and another man in full-black tactical gear, fully alert from nine-millimeter rounds thumping into the guest house's front wall and door, swung into view.

Believing the second intruder to be wearing an armor plate on his chest like the first man, Tiger took aim at his legs, gently compressing the trigger and shooting. The rifle selector switch was on full auto, so she worked the trigger to fire a few shots at a time, sweeping over both of the man's legs, causing him to topple forward in the front entryway.

On his way down, the man fired his own MP5, the bullets tearing through the floor just inches from Tiger and out the opened back door.

Before the man could reposition himself to a firing position from the floor, Tiger carefully lifted her MP5 and peered through the Aimpoint Micro T-2 site she had first noticed barely half a minute before, placing the red dot reticle on the right side of the man's neck. Then she fired a two-second burst that nearly severed his head from his body.

Not wasting a second to admire her work, she again switched out the ammunition magazine and placed a spare mag in the waistband of her pajama pants. Then she stood up and backed her way toward the kitchen, scanning both sides, the front and the back of the house.

This was a professional hit team, she knew, and if it was her operation, she would have sent a team of five—one handling transportation and four handling the hit. It was always better to have redundant capabilities, and there was a definite advantage, most of the time, with numbers.

Always one to enjoy the view of the Potomac out the back, Tiger had left the blinds on the windows along the back of the house open. However, those on the front were closed, so she backed herself through the small living room toward the front, swiveling her head and field of vision from the back windows to the front door.

Once at the left side of the open front door, she looked out to the right and across the yard to the back of the main house. She avoided looking at the house's back patio lights to keep from blinding herself. And knowing that the human eye was better at picking up movement in peripheral vision than objects at night, she actively kept her eyes moving, scanning from side to side.

Convinced no one was lurking out to her right, she quickly swung her head out the door and caught a glance at her left before swinging back in. Having seen no one, she leapt across the doorway and continued her reconnaissance to her left.

Determining that the front was clear, she slowly walked out the front door in a crouched position, the MP5 trained ahead. She turned left and crept along the front of the house, then turned around the corner. As she walked down the side of the house, she noticed a boat without running lights bobbing along the side of the river. Wanting to trust her own eyes rather than the optical scope, she dropped the rifle slightly and continued to walk forward. At that moment, she saw yet another man dressed fully in black move to the helm, fire up the inboard engine, and shift into forward gear.

Still alert for more intruders, she carefully turned around the far corner of the house and saw that the rest of the backyard was clear of threats. Then she ran toward the river, sighted the boat, and squeezed off short bursts of suppressed shots. The rocking movement of the boat caused some shots to miss, but she did rake a patchwork of holes down the starboard side of the boat.

None of her shots, however, apparently hit either the driver or the engine, at least not to the point of incapacitating either. By the time she got to the edge of the river, the boat was effectively out of range.

Tiger ran back up to her bungalow and entered through the open back door. In her bedroom, she grabbed her phone from where it had been recharging and made a call to a familiar ten-digit number. When the call connected, she calmly said, "Swanson, one, zero, two, zero, eight, nine, eight, two, two, two," and hung up.

Ten seconds later her phone vibrated with an incoming call. Upon answering, a female voice on the other end said, "Housekeeping, how may I help you."

"I need a cleanup for a party of two in ZIP code two, two, three, one, four," Tiger said.

After a short pause, the woman said, "We can have a house cleaner there within the hour. Please hold on for an address and a few other details."

Still on edge and scanning the room for threats, Tiger took a deep breath and ran her hand through her hair.

No more rest for tonight, she thought, before she continued with her call.

<h1 style="text-align:center">Chapter 2</h1>

At 4:00 pm next afternoon, Tiger found herself waiting anxiously outside of Devin Thomas's office on the seventh floor of the Original Headquarters Building at the George Bush Center for Intelligence in Langley. To say it had been an eventful thirteen hours would have been an understatement.

True to its word, the agency's cleaners, two women and a single man, had arrived in less than an hour, and they immediately got to work. Working in detached, professional silence, they first unmasked both bodies and took facial photographs, both directly on and from both sides in profile. Then they stripped the bodies and took photos of any identifying marks. In both instances, it meant a cataloging of tattoos. Finally, both bodies were fingerprinted.

With all the work intended to help with identification completed, the cleaners then bagged each body, along with clothing, equipment, and the many soiled laparotomy pads that had been used to mop up the spilled blood.

Less than ninety minutes after their arrival, the cleaners left, having hauled away all evidence of the early morning activities, including the spent shell casings both in the house and outside, in the yard between the bungalow and the Potomac.

What had been left behind was a bullet riddled interior in the bungalow. Luckily for Tiger, no windows had been broken, and no bullet holes pierced the exterior of the guest house. From the main house, her landlords, a retired lobbyist and his socialite wife, would be none the wiser of the night's events. She just hoped they didn't come down and pay her a visit anytime soon.

After the cleaners vacated the premises, Tiger drove her 2025 Chevrolet Tahoe, borrowed from the agency's motor pool, to Langley, where she immediately engaged the overnight staff of the Office of Security, part of the Directorate of Administration. Her detailed debrief of the attack, recorded on video, took longer than the event and the cleanup combined. Dawn had long broken on a warm June day by the time Tiger had an opportunity to visit the cafeteria and dining room for breakfast.

The rest of Tiger's day had been spent trying to make heads or tails of the attack. It had been completely unexpected, so much so that she had been caught off guard without a firearm for self-defense. If it hadn't been for the karambit ....

Thomas's office door opened, and as Tiger rose from her chair, he said, "Well, Tiger, I understand you've had a bit of a day thus far."

"I have indeed, sir," she replied as she followed his outstretched arm into his office, "but it's been a much better day for me than for my uninvited guests who deigned to interrupt my night."

Thomas chuckled and closed his door, then led Tiger over to a table with four chairs next to the left most of the three windows that lined the side of his office, at the far end from his desk. On the table was an unmarked manila file folder.

Tiger took her customary spot with her back to the window, with Thomas directly across the mahogany table. Once seated, Tiger asked, "Has any intel come back from this morning?"

"We're piecing it together," Thomas replied as he opened the file folder and spun it around so that its contents were legible to Tiger. "Your first assailant, the man who came in the back door, has not been identified. He's not in the system, either fingerprints or facial recognition. We're still working on him."

"And the other?" Tiger asked.

"With the second perp, we were aided greatly with this," he said as he slid over an up-close photo of a tattoo on the man's right forearm, a red star on a black background with feathered edges, with negative space in the middle depicting a fist tightly coiled around a black submachine gun, itself framed by negative space. "It's a tattoo favored by Spetsnaz operators, not to mention a whole lot of wannabes too," he said with a smirk.

"Russian special forces?" Tiger asked, her brow wrinkled in confusion.

"*Former* Russian special forces," clarified Thomas. "Using the tattoo as the lead, the team followed a trail that ended up positively identifying the man as Yuri Konstantinov, a fifty-three-year-old from Novosibirsk in Siberia, and a twenty-plus year veteran of the Russian Armed Forces, last dozen as a Spetsnaz operator. That is until he vanished seven years ago, falling completely off the grid."

Tiger was silent for a moment as she let that information sink in. "So, he's a mercenary, a private gun for hire?"

"That or he's part of an organization that knows a thing or two about keeping a secret and being off the books."

"And the boat?"

"Most likely stolen and sitting at the bottom of the Potomac right now. No boat has been reported stolen thus far."

"Pretty thin," Tiger responded. "Three perps, one a former Russian soldier. But the thing that's been bothering me all day, sir, is why me, why now, and how the hell did they even find me? I moved in four days ago, for crying out loud. That's not long enough to recruit hired guns and plan, equip, and activate an op."

"The working theory is that you've been targeted for a while, Tiger, and that last night was the first best opportunity to execute. Where were you prior to Old Town?"

"I've been bouncing around short-term rentals forever," she moaned, seeing the logic play forth in front of her.

"And you didn't notice any surveillance?" Thomas asked.

"No sir, I did not," she replied. "Although stateside, as you know, we're not in the practice of running extensive surveillance detection routes."

"Yeah, well I'd recommend you start exercising more caution with SDRs for now on, particularly in the short-term," he said with a tilt of the head and a rather pedantic tone. "In the meantime, we'll continue to investigate, pull on some strings and see which ones lead, ultimately, to you."

"Sir, I'd like to be involved with the investigation," Tiger added.

Thomas drew a deep breath, clearly in deep thought. After a moment he said, "Tiger, ordinarily we frown upon agents investigating their own situations. There's often a strong bias because of proximity, from simply being too close to it all. But in this case, your case, looping you in might be the best course of action. You've had all day to think about it—where do you think this came from?"

"Well, the Russian merc is a red herring. I can't see any reason why Russia would risk a hit on US soil on account of lil' ol' me. Russia is a non-starter. And while I've been working in Afghanistan the past couple of years, Tali wouldn't have the reach to come to our shores. The only thing I can think of is me being persona non grata in Taiwan after the Hualien thing last year."

"My thoughts exactly, as well as that of the team," Thomas agreed. "Taiwan might not want you to visit again after last year's op on their soil, but they certainly wouldn't come after you. But a leak revealing your identification to the People's Republic of China can probably be thought of as being inevitable. And China, or rather a particular high-ranking individual in the

Chinese Communist Party, would have a great deal of interest in your whereabouts."

"Zhau Xiang," Tiger nodded in agreement. "I suppose he still leads the Ministry of National Defense?"

"Yes, he does," confirmed Thomas, "reporting directly to the General Secretary. And with the loss of his son, Zhau Ming, killed tragically in an IED explosion in Afghanistan this past winter, he has a significant amount of skin in the game."

Tiger pursed her lips in resigned agreement and nodded her head. "Strictly speculation thus far, sir, but I'd like permission to engage with Collett on the China desk and dig a little deeper."

"I've already paved the way with the Directorate of Analysis," Thomas replied, "and they're already building a framework to gather intel. They're expecting your forthcoming visit."

Tiger slid back her chair and began to rise. "If that's all, sir, I'll let you get on with bigger matters in your day."

"Just one more thing, Tiger," Thomas said as he, too, rose from his chair. "I know this isn't your first rodeo, but you've been through a traumatic experience. It might take a little time, but the trauma will, eventually, catch up with you. Do you think you could benefit from talking to someone about it?

Tiger's lip stretched wide in a tight, humorless smile. "Yes, sir, I definitely need to speak to someone. And a very particular someone at that."

Chapter 3

Cal McHenry pulled off his sweat-soaked, sun-bleached, burnt orange Texas Longhorns cap and wiped his brow with his right sleeve. It was late afternoon, close enough to quitting time to not have to think about any additional chores, and the season's second cutting of hay had been bailed and now, finally, put in the barn. Yeah, McHenry thought, it was about time to pay a visit to the old refrigerator in the shop and liberate a cold Shiner Bock from captivity.

He ran the fingers through his wet, shaggy brown hair and placed his cap back on. With his hands on his hips, he arched the small of his back, stretching out a bit of the aches, pain, and fatigue of his fifty-eight-year-old body. As he did so, he looked out the barn and saw a red, late-model sedan slowly descending from the hill near the front gate, dust belching from its tires as it navigated the dirt path toward the main house and its immediate outbuildings.

"Hmmm, it looks like the ranch has a visitor," McHenry mumbled as he began to walk out in greeting. "I hope they had the courtesy to bring along some beer."

He got to the front of the garage, a standalone structure off the main house that had space for five vehicles and a complete shop, at the same time the sedan, a Toyota Camry in supersonic red, pulled to a gentle stop. McHenry abruptly halted his gait, put his hands on his hips, and smiled as he recognized the driver, none other than Lilly "Tiger" Swanson.

As she opened the door and put her left shoe on the ground, he said, "Well I'll be damned if it ain't my good friend, Tiger."

"Are we still good friends, Mac?" Tiger asked in return, shielding her eyes from the still blazing sun with her right hand.

"'Course we are, Tiger. Now why would you say that?"

"It might have something to do with you ignoring my phone calls, Mac, my repeated phone calls, I might add."

"I ain't been ignoring your calls, Tiger," McHenry responded. "Truth be told, I'm not entirely sure I know where my phone is. So, if it makes you feel any better, I imagine I've missed more calls than just yours."

Tiger shook her head and rolled her eyes. "Now why wouldn't you keep your phone with you?"

"Well, Tiger," he said as he approached her to give her a hug, "I got around to figurin' my phone would be best served to allow me to call and interrupt others rather than others to call and interrupt me."

The two shared a strong embrace then separated. Tiger then put both her hands on McHenry's shoulders and looked him in his eyes.

"Well, you big lug, because of your ... eccentric behavior ... and my need to speak with you, I had to fly into Austin-Bergstrom and then drive all the way out here, just hoping you'd be around."

"And look at your luck," he replied with a grin, "I am indeed around. Ain't been anywhere else for months now."

Tiger looked around to see if anyone else was in hearing distance. Seeing that no one was, she said in a low voice, "Look, Mac, I had three unexpected visitors drop by two nights ago, and the working hypothesis is that it was payback to avenge the Zhau thing."

"Hmm, I see," McHenry responded, scratching his week-old growth of beard in thought. "Hey, let's take a ride. Pops, Ma, and a few others are in the house, and some hands are around, in the barn and the shop." Pointing away from the barn he said, "We can talk more freely out there."

Needing to ride the fences later in the week anyway, McHenry took Tiger out in the ranch's John Deere XUV835M Crossover Utility Vehicle, the modern age's replacement for yesteryear's horses. Of course, at a sticker price of over $20,000, the vehicle was multiples more expensive than any of the horses McHenry had grown up riding. Then again, everything was multiples more expensive than they had been back then.

They drove slowly west out a dirt service road splitting the herd field from one of the farm fields, each looking for any needed fence repairs on either side of the service road. Once they got to the edge of the property, they turned north and followed the perimeter to the main road. A well-maintained operation over the decades, McHenry only twice had to make notations of post repairs in the Garmin GPSMAP 67i handheld unit that was kept in a pocket in the dash of the XUV.

"So, Tiger, thus far all you know of your perps are that one was Russian, former spec ops, and two John Does, one deceased, one most likely still breathing?" McHenry asked in summation.

"Yeah, Mac, not a lot to go on."

"Something interesting is that the agency hasn't had anything pop on the Russian or the other KIA through facial recognition at the border. That means they've been in the US for a while, or they came in through another means, like from Canada or Mexico," McHenry said.

"Or from the Pacific, Atlantic, or the Gulf of Mexico," Tiger added.

"I guess that doesn't narrow it down much, but you can still splinter off an arm of the investigation to look at like ops on US soil since the Russian has been off the grid. Any clues from similar, unsolved ops might lead you somewhere productive."

"Yeah, that's a good idea, Mac," she replied. "I'll pass that along to the team. It will require assistance from our domestic agencies like the Bureau, and maybe even the NSA."

"Oh yeah," McHenry said sarcastically. "That sounds like a bureaucratic good time right there."

Tiger just smiled in resignation. He was right—the typical challenges of interagency cooperation were something only a politically-minded bureaucrat enjoyed.

Just then, McHenry slowed the XUV considerably and pointed up ahead to a late-model GMC Yukon sport utility vehicle parked off the two-lane road, two hundred meters shy of the driveway leading to the McHenry ranch, and nestled in behind a grove of Ashe Juniper trees.

"You didn't come with anyone, did you, Tiger?" McHenry asked.

"No, Mac, I didn't," Tiger responded.

Nodding toward the vehicle and its Texas license plates, he added, "It could be a stranded motorist, but all four tires are up, the hood is down, and the hazard lights aren't on. Still, the car being right here at the ranch is a bit of a coincidence, don't you think?"

"Yeah," Tiger followed, "and we've been in this business a bit too long to believe in coincidences, huh?"

McHenry pulled the XUV off the road as far as he could, leaving just enough room for Tiger to get out along the property's fence. He motioned with his head toward the back of the XUV where they met, still looking at the Yukon and scanning the immediate vicinity.

Reaching into the top tray of the sport accessory rack on the rollbar at the back of the vehicle, McHenry opened a small toolbox, removed a foam cover, and withdrew a Taurus Judge Executive Grade handgun. He opened the cylinder of the revolver and checked to ensure all five chambers were loaded, snapped it closed, rotated it in his hand, and extended the weapon, handle first, to Tiger.

"What the heck is this thing?" Tiger asked.

"That's a snake gun, Tiger," he responded, "a person's best friend when stumbling across a rattlesnake. It's loaded with .410 shotshell and has an effective range for small game at twenty to twenty-five meters. For bigger threats on two legs, that range goes down to just three to five meters."

After transferring the handgun to Tiger, McHenry reached into the bed of the truck, unfastened two bungee cords, and freed a black plastic Pelican rifle case. Opening it, he withdrew a Winchester Model 94 Trails End Takedown rifle.

A modern manufactured rifle, it showcased John M. Browning's original takedown design for a rifle that comes apart quickly for easy transporting. With its two components already attached to one another, McHenry lifted the rifle, quickly checked to see it was loaded with .30-30 cartridges, and carefully started walking toward the Yukon.

McHenry walked with his right hand inside the lever-action handle, his left hand gripping the wooden stock on the underneath side of the twenty-inch barrel, and the business end of the rifle pointing down and to his left. It was a safe, non-threatening way to carry a weapon, but one that could quickly be brought into a ready-to-fire position.

At the front of the Yukon, McHenry saw a small Hertz Car Rental sticker on the low corner of the windshield on the driver's side.

"It's a rental, Tiger. Watch my back for a second."

"Copy that, Mac," Tiger responded, her eyes scanning forward to the ranch's driveway and back along the fenced and tree-lined perimeter to the car.

By the driver's side front tire, McHenry dropped to knee and unzipped a small hidden-zipper pocket in his AKOVA all-purpose pants, withdrawing his Benchmade Bugout folding knife. While his left hand worked free the plastic valve stem cover of the front tire, his right hand flipped open the knife's three-and-a-quarter-inch blade. He then pressed the tip of the blade on the core tip of the valve stem, depressed it, and started to release the tire's air. Less than two minutes later, the tire was flat, the weight of the front left of the car resting completely on its steel wheel.

"There," he said, "that will ensure that we at least get to have a conversation."

Their first task completed, McHenry then led Tiger along the side of the fence, carefully positioning his boots to be as quiet as possible, with Tiger following one meter behind, literally in his footsteps. Seventy meters down, his trained eye saw where at least somebody had placed a boot on the bottom rail of the fence and hoisted themselves over the top, breaking through an overgrown strand of Whitebrush. For McHenry, it was a clear sign that their visitor or visitors had less than honorable intentions.

Alert and rifle-ready, he climbed over the fence with the practiced familiarity from having grown up on the ranch and, crouching, slowly worked his way through the scrub brush, moving from tree to tree in cover. Tiger, herself a highly experienced field operative, crouched and followed five meters behind.

Nearing the edge of the trees and a clearing that stretched to the main house and its outbuildings, McHenry threw up his left fist, signaling Tiger to stop. He then dropped to one knee, training his rifle to his left.

While his Model 94 was drilled and tapped at the factory for scope mounts, he had never bothered outfitting the rifle with a scope. He kept it in the XUV strictly as a hog hunting gun when opportunity presented itself. Now a different type of prey was in his sights.

Still gripping the rifle with his right hand and sighting through his dominant right eye, McHenry raised two fingers on his left hand and then pointed to his front and left, signaling to Tiger the general location of two targets. He then pushed his palm toward the ground and back three times, then slowly swept his palm forward, toward his side.

Being extraordinarily careful and silent, it took Tiger over two minutes to close the five meters to McHenry's side. Her voice a barely audible whisper, she asked, "What do you see?"

"Two tangoes, twenty-five meters out, laying prone by the edge of the trees," he whispered back. "One's got a sniper rifle. The other's his spotter."

"Can we take them alive?"

"With the tools we have, not both of them. One, at best."

"What's the move?" she asked.

"I'll take the shooter out. On the shot, you take off to the left, out of my line of sight, and close the distance to number two. Use that serpent gun to get his further attention."

"Copy that, Mac. Ready at your mark."

A forty-year veteran of both the US Army and the agency, McHenry was as experienced as they came, and he was already calm. Still, he slowed his breathing even further and nestled the stock of his rifle into his right shoulder. Inhaling, he methodically leveled the rifle's Marble Arms front sight and adjustable semi-buckhorn rear sight. Holding his breath for a one count, he slowly pulled the brushed polish trigger.

The rifle blasted out its .30-30 slug with a roar, and the sniper's head jerked violently forward and to the left, coming to a rest on the ground behind the retractable stock of his M2010 sniper rifle. At the shot, Tiger bounced over shrub bush in a forty-five-degree angle away from McHenry, and fired two shots in the general direction of the targets.

Stunned, the spotter got to a knee and spun toward McHenry and the direction of the shot that had felled his partner. In the process, he had dropped his binoculars and grabbed the pistol grip of a M4A1 assault rifle.

With the tango now visible to her, Tiger stopped and leveled her pistol, even though she was still out of effective range. "Don't move," she yelled. "Don't do it."

On instinct and out of trained reflex, the man turned his rifle toward her. At that threatening move, McHenry fired again, hitting his target center mass in the chest, dropping him instantly.

Tiger and McHenry each closed the distance to the two fallen targets and when they arrived, it was clear that the sniper was dead. The second man, the sniper's spotter, was in obvious distress, clutching a wound on his chest and gasping for breath, blood dripping from the corners of his mouth and spraying into the air with each exhale.

Bending over, Tiger grasped the barrel of the M4A1 and tossed the weapon to the side, out of reach. While McHenry continued to train his sights on the man, she ensured his hands were empty of any weapons. Then she knelt and pressed her hands onto the man's hands, in what was to everyone present a clearly futile effort to staunch the bleeding. Still, they tried.

"Who sent you? Who do you report to?" she asked.

The man's lips moved, more out of trembling than an effort at speaking. Then as he spat out a mouthful of blood, his head, with eyes wide open, fell to the dry Texas dirt as life left his body.

After a moment, Tiger turned and looked up at McHenry. "Mac, I'm sorry I brought this to your home."

McHenry lowered his weapon and looked around at the scene. "That's alright, Tiger. We can take care of ourselves. Heck, we got more guns and ammo down at the house than Canada," he said with a smirk. "Still, you can do me a favor."

"What's that, Mac?"

"How 'bout you give Sami and JV a call and warn them they might be receiving some unwanted visitors."

"Shit, Mac, I did that yesterday. You're the off-the-grid guy I needed to track down and warn!"

Chapter 4

Well outside of the home court proximity of the agency, it took sixteen hours for a two-person team of cleaners to arrive at the McHenry ranch, where they wrapped up their work on property in less than fifteen minutes. Nobody at the ranch was any wiser for what happened as the incident happened at the end of the day and just a few hours before nightfall. The gun shots were explained as missed long-distance shots at a feral pig. For that, McHenry received a good amount of grief at the dinner table that night, particularly from his father.

After a few chores around the ranch the next morning and a big farmer's lunch, Tiger drove the two to Austin-Bergstrom International Airport, southeast of downtown Austin. After returning her rental car, the two caught a shuttle bus to Signature Flight Support, a fixed base operator in the south terminal, where they met a two-person crew from Air Branch, the aviation wing of the agency's Special Activities Center's Special Operations Group.

Within thirty minutes, the crew had a Gulfstream V wheels up and headed to Pope Army Airfield at Fort Bragg, northwest of Fayetteville, North Carolina and 125 miles east of Charlotte. The only passengers in a cabin outfitted to seat twelve, McHenry and Tiger sat across one another in the four-person club seating area in the middle of the fuselage, a highly polished oak table between them.

"So, Mac, Bragg represents something of a homecoming for you, huh?" Tiger asked.

"Yeah," he replied with a sigh. "I spent nearly twenty years with the 1st Special Forces Operational Detachment-Delta, damn near all of them with B Squadron. The last eighteen months with Delta I was part of G squadron."

He chuckled. "Of course, you knew the G squadron part as that's where I was when we met a little over six years ago."

"Ah, yes," she replied with a smile, "and the eventual extension of my offer you couldn't refuse."

"Oh, I could have refused it alright," he said with a broad smile. "But I figured it would not only be an interesting change of pace, but it would also allow me to help do more good for the country more often."

He turned his head to the side and looked out the window, his smile fading as he fell into thought.

After a moment or two, Tiger asked, "You thinking about Five?"

Five had been the call sign of Taylor Gentry, a former Green Beret who McHenry recruited into Tiger's four-person quick reaction force. Late the year before, Gentry had been hit during an operation in Haulien, Taiwan. While the op was considered a success by the brass at the top of the agency, it became an immediate and unequivocal failure the moment Gentry died in surgery.

"Yeah, I think about him almost every day," he answered. "And when the rare day goes by that I don't think about him, I feel guilty for it."

"I hope you're not going through some daisy chain thought of, 'If I had turned Tiger down, I never would have recruited TG, and therefore he never would have been in Taiwan that night.'"

"I've always known you're smart as a whip," he replied. "Didn't know you had an aptitude for mind reading, too. But I know what happened in Hualien coulda happened anywhere. Firefights are occupational hazards for soldiers, Tiger. But losing a brother, or a sister," as he nodded toward her, "never gets easier. Never comes without regrets."

"No, it doesn't, Mac. Coming home alive and healthy is always objective number one," she replied. "Just know that I will never sacrifice a single operative for the success of the mission. We're not in those kinds of fights."

"I know, Tiger," McHenry responded, reaching over the table and patting her hand. "And I appreciate your leadership. It's why I've stuck by your side for six years," he added with a smile, trying to lighten the mood a bit.

Rising from her seat, Tiger looked back toward the galley and asked, "What do you say we find out what kind of bourbon they may have stashed away on this plane?"

"Ah, that's music to this ol' cowboy's ears," McHenry said with a grin.

Soon after they had sipped their way through a healthy tumbler-full of Woodford Reserve Double Oaked, the Gulfstream touched down gently on runway 5/23, the 7,501-foot primary at Pope Army Airfield. From touchdown, it was a short taxi back to the southwest end of the runway and the Green Ramp, where a 2025 Lincoln Navigator Reserve, flawlessly painted in infinite black metallic with darkly tinted windows, awaited them.

Looking out the window, McHenry asked, "Tiger, just once, wouldn't it be nice to have a car that wasn't painted black? I mean, the blacked-out SUV borders on the cliche now, doesn't it?"

Tiger laughed. "That it does, Mac, that it does. But if the government wants to fund Detroit by buying luxury SUVs all murdered out in black, who am I to offer up an opinion otherwise?"

As each slung a small backpack of gear over their shoulders and made their way down the Gulfstream's built-in airstair, two familiar faces emerged from the front seats of the Lincoln. James Villapiano and Samir Hadid, the other two members of McHenry's quick reaction force, were there to pick them up.

"Well, ain't this a sight for sore eyes," McHenry bellowed with a smile as he strode across the tarmac. "It sure is good to see you two!"

McHenry dropped his back and gave each man a hug, clasping his hands on both shoulders after each hug and maintaining eye contact, each man nodding ever so slightly in acknowledgement that all was good.

"It seems you boys were a bit ahead of the game in finding out that the team might be under threat," McHenry said. "Everything alright with you and yours?"

"I don't know if we were so much ahead of the game as you were behind the game, Mac," Hadid replied. "What, you using smoke signals now to communicate, old-timer?"

McHenry chuckled and ran his hand over his chin. "Well, you might have me there. I've been a bit ... how y'all say it, 'Off the grid?'"

"You look good, Mac," Villapiano chimed in. "Ranch life out in the boonies seems to suit you. And to answer your question, all's good at home. We're here as a precaution. Neither one of us has seen anything out of the ordinary."

"That's good to hear, JV," McHenry said with a smile. "Better to settle our squabbles on their turf, not at home on our turf."

"Seriously, Mac, how you holding up after Taylor's death?" Hadid asked. "I know how close you were."

"I'm getting along okay, Sami," he replied. "I miss him, 'course, but I'm hanging in there. How 'bout you two?"

"Same, Mac," came the reply from Villapiano, as Hadid nodded in agreement. "Dealing with it daily on the reg, but as Taylor used to say, 'We don't get PTSD, we deliver it.'"

The group laughed in remembrance of their fallen comrade and one of his oft-used expressions.

"What do you say we get out of here and tip back a glass or two in Taylor's honor?" McHenry asked as he and Tiger threw their packs in the back of the Navigator. "First round—and maybe even the second—is on Tiger."

Chapter 5

After a night of revelry and getting caught up at the Smoke Bomb Grille, a popular pub on 9th Infantry Street frequented by soldiers stationed at Bragg, the team rousted themselves from their rooms at the IHG Army Hotels Moon Hall located on base next to Bryant Hall and the JFK Auditorium. They ate a leisurely breakfast, at a civilian-like pace, in the dining room before piling into the Navigator and taking a very short drive to the Joint Special Operations Medical Training Center Building, just off Bastogne Street and just about a half mile as the crow flies from their hotel.

Ensconced in a sensitive compartmented information facility, or SCIF, the team sat as one for a briefing. Ordinarily Tiger took the briefings with Langley and then passed any needed information down to the team. Today, they decided it was best for all to hear the latest at the same time.

The twenty-foot by thirty-foot SCIF was lined by whiteboard on both sides. At the far end of the door, at the head of a table that could seat eight, were a matrix of four sixty-five-inch 4K displays. On the top left screen was the live video feed from a SCIF in Langley connected over a secured, encrypted connection. Filling that feed was an image of Percy Whiteside, a senior analyst in the Directorate of Analysis.

"Tiger, it's nice to see you again," Whiteside said, "and it seems you brought some friends to the party."

"Yeah, Percy, nice to see you too," Tiger responded. "Team, this is Percey Whiteside, a stand-up guy and straight shooter out of Langley; Percy, this is the team, all stand-up guys as well and quite literally straight shooters."

Whiteside chuckled in acknowledgement, then went straight into the briefing.

"We've got some news for you on the Texas situation," he started as two other screens at the head of the table flickered to life with photos. "The second man, the apparent spotter, has been identified as one James Nelson, or 'Jimmy Nels,' a New York City career criminal with an extensive rap sheet. Of particular import is a long and direct relationship with the White Tiger Triad in the Big Apple. He's been somewhat of an errand boy for them over the years, tied to a variety of less-than-upstanding events."

"Do the White Tigers have ties back to China?" Tiger asked.

"Like every Triad, Tiger, the White Tiger has direct ties to Beijing and the Chinese Communist Party. Those connections almost assuredly include none other than Zhau Xiang of the Ministry of National Defense."

"You think our two most recent misadventures tie back to Zhau?"

"I most certainly do, Tiger," Whiteside responded, "although we lack hard evidence as proof. We're working on establishing that, but then again, we're not exactly a court of law, now are we?"

"No, Percy, we most certainly aren't," replied Tiger. "Depending on the circumstances, our burden of proof is a whole lot lower."

"We like Nelson as the driver of the boat on the Potomac job," Whiteside continued. "He took the Acela train on the Amtrak line down to D.C. almost two weeks ago. We think he met up there with the Russian, Konstantinov, and the John Doe. After your handiwork and his subsequent escape, he then tailed you to Austin, where he met up with this man, the shooter who was positioned up behind the M2010 sniper rifle."

More images filled the screens.

"He has been identified as Edgar Figueroa from Laredo, Texas, a psychopathic former US Marine with ties, after his dishonorable discharge in 2019, to the Cartel del Noreste across the border in Nuevo Laredo."

Both rooms fell quiet as the information set in. After a few seconds, Tiger broke the silence, saying, "So within just a degree or two of separation, we're looking at a high-ranking official of the CCP, a Triad with New York operations, and a narco cartel in Mexico?"

"That's about the state of it, Tiger," Whiteside responded.

"What about our families and homes?" Hadid asked.

"That's a good question," Whiteside responded, "and I have good news on that front. We've co-opted the Bureau to provide surveillance on addresses in Chicago and Carlsbad, California. Nothing unusual to report at either location and we'll probably pull down surveillance within the next twenty-four hours.

"Our lead guy in Taiwan identified the mole within the government who leaked Tiger's name to Beijing. Having put him under extensive interrogation, we're confident he doesn't know anything further about the op in Hualien or the people involved with it. Hell, if it makes you feel better, I don't even know the names of you gentlemen sitting alongside Tiger. Other than numbered accounts in Finance for compensation for services rendered, you all don't exist at the agency—just Tiger."

"Thank you for arranging that surveillance," Hadid replied. "We appreciate it."

The room nodded in silent agreement.

"So, Percy, what are we fixing to do about all this?" asked Tiger. "How can we make a move on Zhau and show him he can't get away with trying to take out Americans on US soil?"

"Right now, Tiger, we can't make a move on Zhau. First, we have no hard proof of his involvement whatsoever. Everything we have thus far is speculative, and we're still working to connect all the dots."

"Oh, for Christ's sake," Tiger interrupted in a fit of frustration. "We know it comes from him. Plus, we're in agreement that we're not a court and don't need a burden of proof beyond a reasonable doubt."

"All that's true, Tiger," added Whiteside. "But the second part of what I was going to say is that Zhau ain't leaving China any time soon. Any op targeting Zhau directly would have to happen in China, and an op like that wouldn't involve you or your team—each one of you would stick out in Beijing like a sore thumb."

"So, we're just going to let him get away with it?" Tiger rebutted.

"No, Tiger, we absolutely fucking won't let him get away with it," Whitside said in exasperation. "What we are going to do is hit him hard, but in a very measured, calculated manner. We gotta do this right, and that means by the book and with complete, unequivocal deniability."

Tiger inhaled deeply and shook her head.

"No, I get it, Percy. I don't mind so much that he moved on me. What I do mind is that Zhau's goons brought the fight to my friend's home," she said while patting McHenry's shoulder twice. "That's got me riled up."

"And I don't blame you," Whiteside added. "We'll get the sonofabitch, and in a lot of different ways at that. We'll look to start at hurting his interests, and his varied interests all lead to one final outcome—China's global governance as the cultural, political, and economic center of the world. That gives us a lot of potential targets."

"Well, we'd sure like to get our hands dirty in anything that gets operationalized," Tiger replied. "Hopefully you'll keep us in mind."

"As a rule, the most appropriate resources are applied to each and every op. You and your team have a well-deserved reputation. I'm certain there'll be a role for you all to take on. We're working day and night to draw hard and fast connections on these attacks to those responsible, and there will be retribution, I can promise you that."

"Thanks, Percy," Tiger commented. "We'll be at the ready."

"There's one more thing, Tiger, and it's problematic," Whiteside added. "Nelson tracked you in two different manners. First, he tracked your phone. We've cloned your phone onto a new device and are shipping it to you today. Destroy your old phone after this call. Secondly, Nelson was on your flight to Texas."

Alert and at the edge of her chair, Tiger responded, "There's only one source for that type of information."

"That's right, Tiger," Whiteside responded. "We've got a leak in the agency."

Chapter 6

Zhau Xiang shuffled across the ornate rug in his office in the Chinese Ministry of National Defense headquarters in the August 1st Building at No. 7 Fuxing Road in the Haidian District of Beijing. He stopped at the shelf along the wall opposite his desk, behind a nine-foot-long antique sideboard cabinet.

There he paused for a moment of quiet reflection before reaching up slowly and adjusting the black lace drapes on either side of a portrait of his only child, his son Zhau Ming, framed in nanmu, a precious wood unique to his beloved China. Satisfied it was perfectly and respectfully aligned, he pulled a lighter out of his right coat pocket and lit the rolled sheet of gold foil-embossed joss paper in his left, then placed it on a small curved ceramic plate in front of the portrait and watched the smoke drift lazily upward.

It was a daily routine of Zhau's, a traditional practice meant to provide ancestors and spirits with material goods and money in the afterlife. Nearly a half year after his son's death in an explosion in the Afghanistan countryside, Zhau was still in mourning.

For the first 100 days after his son's death, Zhau had worn nothing other than white clothing, signifying the mourning of a child, the white color a symbol of purity and grief. Since then, Zhau had worn black, but each day he pinned a small piece of cloth, called a *xiao*, to his left sleeve, the side that represented a male decedent. It too was white to represent the death of a child, his child, his only child.

Zhau Ming had been Zhau Xiang's child, but he was no child. He had been fifty years old at his death, and a high-ranking official of the Ministry of State Security, China's version of the CIA. His untimely death had been a severe blow to the Ministry. But its effects had been felt even more with his father, Zhau Xiang, the head of the Ministry of National Defense and the trusted confidant of the General Secretary of the Chinese Communist Party.

Zhau was more than just in mourning. He was hellbent on revenge. Somebody was going to pay.

Zhau Ming had died in an IED explosion along an unnamed dirt road a couple of hours out of Kabul. Improvised explosive devices were long a calling card of both the Taliban, who controlled the country now, and the resistance. However, Zhau didn't believe for a moment that either had been responsible.

Zhau didn't have any hard evidence that tied back to any responsible party. He felt in his heart, though, in every fiber of his being, that the Americans were to blame. And the only American who made sense to him was Lilly Swanson, the CIA agent who had been involved in a shootout with his son in Taiwan months before the IED explosion.

The Ministry of State Security was either unable or uninterested in helping Zhau extract revenge, so he had taken matters into his own hands. Surely, he thought, his son could rest in peace as the woman agent was undoubtedly dead by now.

Zhau's quiet moment in front of his son's portrait was broken with a knock on his door. Instructing his visitor to enter, he saw that it was Liu Jun Hie, a commissioner in the Ministry's Foreign Affairs Office. Ah, thought Zhau with a slight knowing smile, just the man to provide an update on the Swanson operation.

Walking behind his ornate desk and sitting down in a well-practiced display of positional power, Zhau crossed his hands and laid them in his lap. Expecting good news, he said, "I trust,

Liu, that you've come with a positive report on our mission against the American aggressor. What has been the progress thus far?"

Liu shifted his weight uncomfortably side to side, standing awkwardly in front of Zhau's desk as he had not been invited to sit in one of the two leather upholstered chairs either side of him. After nervously clearing his throat, he said, "We are having difficulty getting information back in the way of progress reports, Minister."

Zhau unclasped his hands and gripped both sides of his chair while his lips pursed in anger. "And what does that mean, Liu?"

"Our asset with the Triad has missed his last three scheduled reports. We can only assume that he has been ... compromised," Liu reported sternly. "Our sources tell us that nothing indicates that the mission against the American target has been successful."

"Well, where is she?" Zhau demanded.

"That, minister, we don't know," Liu responded. "While there are no indications that the target has been hit, there are also no indications of where she might be. If she's alive, she's underground."

"So, she might be dead?"

"Unlikely minister, as the Triad asset hasn't asked for the balance of the payment. There's no proof of death. Without it, we need to assume that the mission has not reached its successful conclusion."

Zhau shook with anger, his lips a tight line across his face, his unblinking eyes staring back at Liu. Finally, after a tense moment of silence, Zhau slammed his right fist on his desk and shouted, "Unacceptable, Liu. You have one more chance to fix this problem before I get someone else to do it for you. Now get out of here and get us our prize!"

Liu, understanding the implied threat, bowed his head, spun on his heels, and quickly made his way to the office door.

Chapter 7

It was a little less than a mile run back to the IHG Army Hotels Moon Hall from the Frederick Performance Enhancement Center at Fort Bragg. It wasn't long enough to make a big separation among team members in a race, but certainly big enough to determine a winner and three losers.

Earlier in the morning, after a light continental breakfast at the hotel, the team had jogged over to the gym at a rather leisurely pace, the run serving strictly as a warm-up for the workout that would follow. At the gym, the level of work effort rose considerably.

The four team members had been away from one another for a few months, and while each had kept up their physical fitness regimens, they still wondered how they compared with the others. Were the others in fighting shape? Were they, themselves, in fighting shape? A hard morning workout at the gym would provide the answers soon enough.

Once at the gym, Tiger led the team to the dumbbell and kettlebell racks on the far side of the FieldTurf away from the facility's collection of barbell racks and machines. She grabbed a twenty-pound dumbbell in each hand and instructed McHenry, Villapiano, and Hadid to pick up thirty-pounders themselves. Then she led them through a five-minute CrossFit routine of increasingly difficult effort.

The routine started out innocently enough with "hammers," where with each arm hanging down by their sides, the team members moved their wrists up and down, like they were hammering nails. After achieving a burn in the muscles of their forearms, Tiger transitioned them to "floor ups."

That exercise had McHenry and the others bend their knees until their dumbbells touched the floor, then straighten up, bringing their dumbbells to their shoulders, then pressing overhead. With dumbbells overhead, they then lifted their heels off the ground to work their calves. Twenty-five repetitions later and with a sweat fully beginning to break out over their bodies, Tiger moved on.

Next up were squats, where with straight backs and bending slightly at the waist they bent their knees until the dumbbells touched the floor. After a short pause, they then stood up to an upright position. Twenty-five reps later, McHenry's legs were burning and his heart was pounding.

He wasn't alone. Three minutes into the workout, Tiger had the entire team working at their maximum effort.

After the squats came fifteen bicep arm curls that, immediately upon completion, transitioned into fifteen overhead presses to work the deltoids of the shoulders and the latissimus dorsi muscles of the sides. With everyone breathing hard, Tiger then led them further into misery.

Next up on the CrossFit menu was a seated squat, where everyone kept their knees at a ninety-degree angle to the floor and back behind their toes, butt low and forearms resting on thighs, the dumbbells serving as counterweights to their bodies. A minute in that position felt like torture.

To much relief of McHenry and the others, Tiger then had them stand, bend slightly at the waist, and do twenty "reverse rows," where they pulled the dumbbells up to their chests, working their rear shoulders and back.

Lastly, Tiger had led the men in a set of twenty "reverse flies," where, after bringing their dumbbells together at their waists, they raised them to their sides.

Six minutes after they started the routine, the four were drenched with sweat. They dropped their weights and walked around with their hands on their hips, breathing heavily.

The break for rest didn't last long. Once their breathing had settled down a little, Tiger led them to weighted sleds at the far end of the open expanse of FieldTurf. There, they split into pairs, McHenry with Villapiano and Hadid with Tiger. They then took turns pushing and pulling the sleds, their partners standing on the sled for resistance, across the forty-meter strip of turf.

The workout was designed for functional strength, conditioning, and flexibility. It worked their bodies to prepare them for the challenges of being in the field. Some people worked out for beach muscles, building muscles for show. Front line, clandestine operatives worked out to build muscles to go.

Seventeen minutes after they entered the Performance Enhancement Center, they walked out the front door to begin their dash back to the hotel. No scrolling through Instagram between sets like civilians at their gyms. It was strictly business.

McHenry's muscles screamed with fatigue, but he felt good with the effort. While he hadn't been into a gym in months, he had been hard at work around the ranch. Plus using the barn and workshop as a sort of parcourse, he had done his share of pullups and other strength exercises during his downtime.

Once they jogged out to Gruber Road and took a right, Hadid took off at a blistering pace. Tiger trailed a few paces behind, with McHenry and Villapiano another couple of strides further behind. While the pace was quick, all four felt that an even faster kick to the finish was coming.

Hanging a right on Rock Merritt Avenue, Hadid, resigned to the fact that he wasn't going to distance himself from the group on the run back, slowed slightly, gearing up for a sprint to the finish. Everyone knew bragging rights were at stake, and in this group, those were no small stakes.

McHenry, as the operations leader when boots were on the ground, had two minds when it came to these physical contests between teammates. If he felt the team needed a comeuppance of sorts, for whatever reasons, he would push to be first, leading by example and demonstrating to the team that if a fifty-eight-year-old veteran could do it, his younger teammates could maybe do it even better.

At other times, McHenry would look to finish at the rear, ideally right alongside the last teammate in line. It allowed him to keep track of how the entire team was performing in the moment, yet at the same time showed that he was still up to the task. That was the approach he chose today, settling in comfortably off of Villapiano's right shoulder.

Turning left on Bastogne Drive and facing the last 150 meters to the hotel door, Tiger took off, hoping to catch the others sleeping. She didn't.

Hadid quickly caught up with her, dragging Villapiano and McHenry along as well, still five meters behind. About twenty seconds later, that's how they finished, Tiger and Hadid side by side, slightly ahead of both Villapiano and McHenry.

Thoroughly exhausted after their high-intensity workout, the four walked around in front of the hotel, gasping for breath with hands on their hips. With their bodies desperate for oxygen, no one spoke for a couple of minutes. Finally, Tiger broke the silence.

"I see you boys weren't slacking off the past few months," she said.

McHenry smiled, then while still catching his breath said, "The same seems to be true for you, too. I see you haven't grown soft sitting behind a desk."

"Yeah, Tiger," Villapiano chimed in. "You worked us all pretty hard there. That some sort of test?"

"Every workout is a test, JV," she replied. "And I'd say you boys are operationally fit. Now what do you say we go over to the range and see if you all can still shoot?"

Chapter 8

After Tiger washed herself clean with a luxuriant warm shower, she twisted the water valve to full cold, a trick she picked up from Hadid and Villapiano, both former US Navy SEALs. The cold finish to her shower was tolerated—just barely—for a combination of physical and mental benefits. The cold exposure was believed by many, a great many SEALs among them, to improve muscle recovery, reduce inflammation, and increase alertness. Mentally, the torrent of frigid water helped build mental toughness, discipline, and the ability to handle stressful, less-than-ideal situations and circumstances.

If it worked for SEALs, Tiger thought, it's a good enough practice for me to incorporate into my daily routine. Even if she didn't particularly enjoy it.

Finally turning the water off and toweling herself dry, Tiger felt satisfied with a hard day's work. It had been a good day.

After the morning workout, the team piled into the Lincoln Navigator and drove a short five miles to the Rod & Gun Club at Fort Bragg. Once there, they took to the facility's twin 100-meter rifle and pistol ranges with the box of goodies Hadid had brought on the trip—two SIG Sauer M7 rifles, a gas-operated, magazine-fed assault rifle chambered for a 6.8x51 millimeter round, and two SIG Sauer M17s, the full-sized variant of the US Army's standard issue handgun, featuring a 4.7-inch barrel and chambered for the 9x19 millimeter Parabellum round.

To Tiger's eye, the team members hadn't missed a beat all day. They were as sharp as they ever were, and, in her mind, operationally fit. She felt she, too, was fit to step operationally into the field.

Tiger had always been an athlete, and as a senior she had captained Yale's women's hockey team. But it wasn't her athletic talent that had drawn the agency's eyes. What drove the agency to recruit her was a combination of her coursework in pursuing multiple degrees in Middle Eastern religious studies and her natural affinity for learning languages. Going into her final semester, Tiger was fluent in Hebrew, Farsi, and Gulf Arabic. Upon joining the agency after graduation, she spent ninety-six weeks at the Defense Language Institute Foreign Language Center in Monterey, California, where she duly added Dari, Pashto, and Russian to her expansive repertoire.

With her language skills, Tiger knew she could practically write her own ticket with regards to diplomatic positions and even political appointments. But the fierce, athletic competitor in her steered her toward the daunting field of operations. Tiger had actively sought out a role in the Directorate of Operations, and she had steadfastly refused considerations of other functions.

As an operative over the last seven years, she had excelled. The agency always held its collective breath when she was in the field, for she was very much considered a "force multiplier," and the higher ups, including Thomas on the seventh floor, preferred her boots not be on the ground but rather behind a desk. McHenry and the team, they were the force that Tiger's reservoir of knowledge, skills, and experiences multiplied.

But Tiger loved being out in the field. Maybe one day, she thought, she might find satisfaction in a more mundane desk job. For now, though, she relished the time with her team in the field, making a difference so many could not or would not.

It was the "would not" that concerned Tiger as she hurriedly threw on a t-shirt and pants, slipped into a pair of flip flops, and exited her room to meet up with McHenry in the hotel lobby. Now was as good a time as any to see where McHenry's head was.

Fast approaching his fifty-ninth birthday, Tiger knew McHenry had been contemplating getting out of the game. He had alluded as much on a couple of occasions in the past year. Then came Gentry's death in Hualien last November. The two had been close. Hell, the entire team was close, Tiger knew, the byproduct of so much time together in the field.

After Gentry's death, McHenry fell off the grid after he went to the family ranch and farm in Texas. Tiger had given him his space. It was the only thing she could do. McHenry had needed the time and space to think, and Tiger knew she sure as hell wasn't going to be able to influence him one way or another. Moreover, she didn't want to.

This was to be McHenry's call, as it always had been and always would be.

Walking down the steps from her fourth-floor room to the lobby, Tiger thought about her time with McHenry in the field. She had never worked with anyone better.

A long-time Delta operator, McHenry had the sage wisdom that could only be accumulated through a long, distinguished career as a frontline operator. When it came to operations, especially combat operations, McHenry had "been there, done that," and that vast experience was invaluable to the team, both in planning operations and in their execution.

McHenry was also a trusted leader. He led from the front, but was, at the same time, inclusive of his teammates. Recognizing each individual's strengths and experiences, McHenry actively sought out opinions, ideas, and alternatives to plans. It made the team tight, close, and cohesive. The team truly moved as one highly polished, effective, and incredibly lethal organism. Tiger hoped that the team would continue forward under McHenry's leadership and mentoring.

Walking down the first-floor corridor, Tiger spotted McHenry in the lobby and, after catching his eye, gave a small wave. When she drew up next to him, they traded a little fist bump.

"How 'bout a quick little walk?" she asked.

"Sounds good, boss," McHenry replied, "as long as you're not heading us toward the gym. I had enough of that place this morning."

Tiger laughed as they walked through one of the sets of front doors. "No worries in that regard, Mac," she said. "How 'bout we save that for tomorrow?"

"That's a deal, Tiger. Tomorrow."

"Speaking of which, though, what's your assessment of the team and its readiness?"

"From what I saw, the fellas didn't miss a step all day. You either, for that matter. I'd have zero reservations dropping into an op with any of you."

With the two alone on the sidewalk, Tiger stopped walking. In response, McHenry stopped, turned to her and met her eye.

"What about you, Mac? Where are you at?" she asked.

"Heck, boss, you tell me," he replied.

"At the gym and at the range, I saw someone sharp as a razor," Tiger responded. "And at no surprise, I might add. The question is, 'Where are you at up here?'" she asked, tapping the side of her head for emphasis.

"I'm good, Tiger," came his stern reply, his steely blue eyes still in direct contact with hers.

"So, you're in?"

"Heck, Tiger, I've always been in. And it will be that way until I'm not. You and I will know at the same time. When I can't keep up, when I become a liability to the team, that's when I'll be out. 'Til then, I'll walk into anything alongside you and the boys."

Tiger nodded. "I'm glad to hear that, Mac, because Langley has a little something for us to do."

Chapter 9

After another morning workout at the Performance Enhancement Center, Tiger led the team over to a scheduled mid-morning meeting at the headquarters building of the United States Army Special Operations Command on Desert Storm Drive. Responsible for organizing, training, equipping, and deploying Army special operations forces worldwide, the main USASOC building had multiple secured SCIFs in which to confer with Langley.

After depositing their mobile devices into a lockbox outside of the SCIF, the team spread out on either side of an eight-foot by eight-foot workspace with nine chairs aligned in a U-shaped formation, all positioned to face a wall filled by a matrix of four 65-inch 8K super-high-resolution monitors. Each monitor displayed the USASOC's Distinctive Unit Insignia, a stylized spearhead, invoking the spirit of Native American warriors and the command's heritage, a black Fairbairn-Sykes dagger, symbolizing the preparedness and readiness of Army special operations forces, and an Airborne tab, indicating the command's airborne status.

Looking at the vivid images on the monitors, Villapiano whistled and said, "Damn, Tiger, you think you can reserve this room for weekends during the football season?"

"You Bears fans in Chicago still bother watching games?" asked McHenry sarcastically.

"Like you Cowboys fans have any reason to gloat? Aren't they replacing their uniforms with clown outfits?" came Villiapiano's sharp retort.

Not about to let his teammate have the last word, McHenry responded, "Well we do have the Longhorns on Saturday, JV. What do you have on Saturday other than watching paint dry?"

"You just watch out for my Notre Dame Fightin' Irish this year, big fella."

Slapping her palm on the table, Tiger interrupted the revelry and asked, "Are you all about freakin' done? Can we interrupt your football fantasies long enough to talk about threats to national security?"

Chastised, the team came to a silent order. After a pause for effect, Tiger then added, "Besides, everyone knows it's the Patriots' year again."

The room erupted in laughter, with all four of the team talking over one another about the merits of their favorite professional football teams. Unnoticed by the team was the image on the upper left monitor, showing a group of four—two men and two women—seated around a dark square table in a fairly darkened room, the people illuminated by rather harsh track lighting from the ceiling."

"Ahem," came a clearing of a throat from the secured and encrypted video and audio system, mostly unheard from under the din in the SCIF in Fort Bragg. Then, louder, a "Hey!"

Surprised, Tiger, McHenry, and the team turned to the open feed on the monitor and then quieted down. Subconsciously, they sheepishly dipped their heads and avoided looking into the camera mounted at the bottom of the display matrix, a combination of embarrassment and deference to authority.

The clearing of the throat and the loud interjection had come from Devin Thomas, seated on the far right of the group of four on the monitor. Less than pleased, the Deputy Director asked rhetorically, "Are you quite through playing grab ass down there at Bragg?" Then he added, "Shall we commence then with the briefing?"

Ready to move forward, Tiger looked directly into the camera and said, "Yes sir, let's get started."

Looking directly into the camera in his SCIF at Langley, Thomas paused for a couple of seconds and then added, "Let me just go on the record and say the Commanders win the Super Bowl this year."

The mood lightened, and everyone in both rooms allowed themselves to smile.

Thomas then continued, saying. "To my far right is Zeynab Tayebeh, who heads up the Iran Mission Center here at Langley. Next is Joonas Rasmus, a counterintelligence threat analyst in the Directorate of Analysis. He's also one helluva mission planner. Finally, directly to my right is Alison Collett, head of the China Mission Center."

"We have something to move against Zhau?" Tiger asked optimistically.

"Probably not," replied Thomas. "If it is, it's coincidental. Let me have Tayebeh explain."

"Group, as you know," Tayebeh began, "Iran has been enriching uranium for nearly fifty years, beginning clandestinely in the 1980s with equipment supplied by China and Pakistan. In 2002, their main site at Natanz was revealed.

"In 2009, another key site was revealed, this being the Shahid Ali Nuclear Facility at Fordow, twenty miles north of Qom in the Qom Province, featuring an underground facility built into a mountain."

As she spoke, the other three monitors flashed to life with various images of the site, the surrounding area, and topographical maps of Iran.

"Iran, of course, has always insisted its nuclear program was for energy and medicine," Tayebeh continued. "The international community, especially the US and Israel, have been less than convinced that the program doesn't have nuclear weapons as the end goal.

"Highly enriched uranium, or HEU, contains twenty percent or more uranium-235. Weapons-grade HEU is typically enriched to ninety percent uranium-235. Iran currently possesses over 400 kilograms of uranium enriched to sixty percent, and in total, the International Atomic Energy Agency reports that their total enriched uranium stockpile is over 6,000 kilograms."

"So, they have a lot of enriched uranium, but not highly enriched enough to produce a nuclear weapon, at least not yet," Tiger replied.

"Unfortunately, that's not true," responded Tayebeh. "While you would ideally want ninety percent enriched uranium-235, lower enrichments can be used for nuclear weapons. It just requires larger amounts of material, and that makes weapon design much more difficult."

"Importantly, group," Thomas interjected, "Iran's 400 kilos of sixty percent are enough for about ten nuclear bombs."

Silence fell over both rooms.

"Politics is largely to blame for Iran's buildup of enriched uranium. In July 2015, the Joint Comprehensive Plan of Action, also known as the JCPLA or the 'Iran Nuclear Deal,' was agreed to upon by Iran and the five permanent members of the United Nations Security Council—China, France, Russia, the United Kingdom, and the US—along with the European Union. Under the agreement, Iran agreed to constrain its nuclear program in exchange for relief from nuclear-related sanctions imposed by the United Nations, the EU, and the United States. Importantly, the US sanctions unrelated to the nuclear issue, namely Iran's missile program, support of militant groups and terrorist organizations, remained firmly in place, limiting the economic effect of sanctions relief.

"Unfortunately, in 2018 the administration, thinking the deal was a 'bad deal,' withdrew the US, imposing sanctions under what it called its 'maximum pressure campaign,' which applied to all countries and companies doing business with Iran and cut it off from the international financial system, thereby rendering the nuclear deal's economic provisions null and void. Ultimately, that decision backfired. Since the 2018 dissolution of the Iran deal, Iran's stockpile of enriched uranium has doubled."

Thomas lifted his hand and interjected once again. "So, I trust that everyone's respective underside is properly puckered. Any questions from Bragg so far?"

"None so far," replied Tiger.

Tayebeh then continued. "Uranium enrichment is achieved primarily through gas centrifuge technology, which separates uranium isotopes based on their mass. Between Natanz and Fordow, Iran has over 19,000 gas centrifuges. Each centrifuge enriches uranium only slightly, so large numbers of units need to be arranged in complex 'cascades' to achieve the desired enrichment level. That, alone, is a significant operational hurdle to overcome.

"Other hurdles include specialized materials and safety measures to deal with highly corrosive and toxic uranium hexafluoride that's used, along with incredibly precise engineering required for centrifuges to spin at near supersonic speeds to separate uranium isotopes. That last factor leads me to introduce you to Ms. Collett of the China Mission Center."

Before Collett could speak, three images of a young Asian male filled the lower right monitor in the video matrix at Bragg. "This," Collett said, "is Bo Jianguo, a thirty-four-year-old born and raised in Guangzhou, China's southern capital, located northwest of Hong Kong on the Pearl River. He studied nuclear engineering as an undergrad at Tsinghua University, then came to America for his graduate studies, eventually earning a Ph.D. at the University of Michigan in Ann Arbor. By all accounts, he's a brilliant engineer and physicist.

"Bo's been on loan to the Iranians, working on site at Fordow, in the aftermath of the recent Israeli and US missile and bomb strikes against the facility. He's been tasked with getting the facility back online at full capacity. Here's the thing: we'd very much like to talk to him."

Collett let a moment of silence extend for emphasis, she and the rest of Langley looking into the camera, their faces displayed to Tiger and her team.

Tiger was the first to take the bait. "You just want to talk to Bo? Can't you just send one of our in-country assets, either agency or private military contractor, and have that talk? Why are we here?"

"It's an extensive, highly technical conversation," Collett continued. "One that would take multiple days. But most importantly, there's extremely low access to Bo, even from insiders at the facility. There's him, his interpreter, and a handful of Iranians."

"Oh, okay," Tiger responded. "What you're looking at is a good ol' snatch and grab."

Collett simply nodded in the direction of Rasmus seated next to her, giving him his cue to elaborate.

"That's exactly right," he said. "Bo is a world-class engineer and scientist, and he has a strong familiarity with the inner workings of the Shahid Ali Mohammadi Nuclear Facility. Not only would we like to take him off the board for both the Iranians and the Chinese, but we also think we have a strong chance to make him one of ours."

"What makes you think that?" asked Tiger.

"Well, he's treated much like a prisoner at Fordow," Rasmus replied. "He works at the facility and then is taken to his quarters, a trailer, on the grounds. That's it. But there's more. He's got no living relatives in China, he has spent the better part of six years in the United States, and he has a long-distance girlfriend, a woman he met at Michigan, who works at a laboratory in the Bay Area of northern California.

"So, yes, we'd like to have a comprehensive debrief from him. But we'd also like to conclude that debrief with an offer to work with us, here in America."

"All that end goal stuff sounds great," Tiger replied, "but getting into Iran is no easy task, much less leaving again with someone who may, or may not, be willing to go."

"You're absolutely correct," Rasmus said. "Covertly entering Iran is about as difficult as it gets. Iran shares borders with seven countries—Iraq, Türkiye, Azerbaijan, Armenia, Turkmenistan, Afghanistan, and Pakistan. Each of those pose significant challenges for US personnel. There's also over 1,500 kilometers of coastline along the Persian Gulf, but that's not easy pickings either.

"Over land, the best way of legitimately entering the country is in the northwest, via Türkiye, Armenia, and Azerbaijan. It's also highly guarded; you'd never get in.

"That leaves the east, from Afghanistan or Pakistan. Afghanistan would require entry from the north and working your way to the southwest, a long and treacherous trip. Pakistan would require a great deal of subterfuge, as they are, as you know, 'frenemies' at best. Getting caught harboring Bin Laden was all the proof we ever needed that they're willing to play both sides in order to keep things quiet in country.

"Besides, entering Iran from either Afghanistan or Pakistan just gets you into some of the most inhospitable desert on

Earth, where pretty much only smugglers dare to tread, and they do that only out of necessity."

"If it's not patrolled by the Iranian government, we could do that route," Tiger replied. "It wouldn't be easy, but we don't usually do easy."

"The area in eastern Iran is regularly patrolled by drones, both by the government and by several terrorist groups holed up in the region, including segments of ISIS. How they intervene varies," answered Rasmus. "A couple of nomads leading pack horses might or might not be surveilled further, depending on resources and other priorities. A caravan of a couple of trucks or more gets a lot more attention."

"So can we get in by air?" asked Tiger.

"Not undetected," responded Rasmus. "The Iranian air defense system was supplied by Russia, and it is cutting edge. Nothing flies in Iranian air space that doesn't get identified and tracked."

"So, there's no good way to covertly get into Iran and get operationalized," said Tiger. "Is there any good news?"

"The good news," interjected Thomas, "is that over the years we have developed a network of hundreds of agency assets throughout the country, a benefit of a great number of the population, particularly younger generations, bristling against the authoritarian rule. In addition to that, private military contractors like Constellis have an additional set of resources in the country. The good news is that once in country, we have help."

As she often did when she was digesting information from others, Tiger ran her hand through her hair. After a few quiet seconds she asked, "So what are you suggesting as the best way to enter Iran?"

"We want to drop you into northeast Iran," said Rasmus, "in the province of North Khorasan, close to the city of Bojnurd, across the border with Turkmenistan."

"What do you mean, 'drop?'" Tiger asked.

"A high-altitude, high-opening jump, allowing you to glide undetected into Iranian air space and land in country."

"Like a parachute jump?"

"Yes, Tiger, exactly," came the reply from Rasmus. "Is there a problem there?"

"Well, it's just that I'm not jump qualified."

"What?" asked McHenry with incredulous surprise. "You've never jumped out of an airplane?"

Tiger looked at him. "Why is that so hard to believe?"

"It's just that practically everyone I know has jumped out of an airplane before," replied McHenry. "Plus, you've been doing this for like seven, eight years!"

"I prefer to exit my airplanes when they're on the ground," responded Tiger. "Besides, I'm sure there are plenty of people you know who haven't jumped out of perfectly good airplanes."

"Oh, I don't think so," said McHenry. Looking around the room at Bragg, he asked, "Who here has jumped out of airplanes?"

Both Villapiano and Hadid raised their hands.

Waving his left hand at both his teammates, McHenry added, "See, everyone here has jumped but you. It's you."

"The best thing about jumping for the first time, boss," Hadid added with a smile, "is that it's pretty much a pass/fail kinda thing. So, I mean, you have that going for you."

"Yeah," McHenry continued, conjuring his best Carl from *Caddyshack*. "Which is nice."

Less than pleased, Tiger stared both of them down.

Chapter 10

McHenry could think of no better place to learn how to parachute than at Fort Bragg, home of the US Army's XVIII Airborne Corps and its primary fighting element, the 82nd Airborne Division. Thus, while Rasmus and his group pored over mission planning at Langley, McHenry and the team put Tiger through the paces with repeated jumps into the sandy fields of the base's Sicily Drop Zone.

Tiger wasn't exactly a willing participant, at least not at first. But the team started her off easy, with her first experience a tandem jump from 10,000 feet, where her harness was strapped to McHenry's harness at connection points at the shoulders and hips. After a fifty-second freefall, McHenry pulled the chute and they drifted slowly down to the drop zone, flying in a slow, circular pattern to begin to give Tiger an understanding of how wind affects each leg of a landing pattern. Landing into the wind, McHenry could have sworn she let out an excited yelp of accomplishment.

On their first day of impromptu, yet still intensive, jump school, the teammates took three jumps, Villapiano and Hadid both solo, Tiger and McHenry in tandem. The second day, the training wheels came off for Tiger and they all jumped solo, with the first two being static line jumps, where their parachutes were automatically deployed by a static line as they exited the aircraft at 800 feet. Finally, on the afternoon of the second day, Tiger took her first solo jumps without a static line, at an exit altitude of 12,000 feet.

The third day was more of the same, only they split their four jumps with two in the afternoon and two after the sun set. All four jumps were at altitudes between 10,000 and 14,000 feet. Tiger wasn't able to get any experience at jumping from a height of 30,000 feet or more like she would experience in a high altitude, high opening jump into Iran, but she was comfortable in being a fast learner. Besides, as Hadid had said, it was very much a pass/fail thing.

With her intense three-day jump school behind her, Tiger and the team packed up from Bragg and flew to Joint Base Charleston 200 miles south in South Carolina. There they caught a ride on a Boeing C-17 Globemaster III operated by the US Airforce's 437th Airlift Wing to Ramstein Air Base in Germany.

Rasmus's mission plan was complete, and the team was now entering the final phases in its preparations to become operational.

After flying all night, the team landed early morning at Ramstein Air Base in the southwest German state of Rhineland-Palatinate, about sixty-five miles from Luxembourg and eighty miles from France. Part of the Kaiserslautern Military Community, the largest American community outside of the United States, Ramstein was home to, among others, the 86th Airlift Wing, the self-proclaimed "Global Gateway" to Europe, Africa, the Middle East, and parts of Asia.

Over 54,000 American service members worked and lived in the KMC, along with over 5,000 American civilians. More than 16,000 of those service members and civilians were stationed at Ramstein. Tiger and her team blended in with complete anonymity.

With a little sleep captured on the plane, about as reasonably as one could expect in what was essentially a cargo plane with some jump seats, the team got straight to work once they unloaded. Tiger made her way to the base's Command Headquarters in Building 201. McHenry and the rest of the team tracked down their gear supplied by the agency's Directorate of Support, the division responsible for providing equipment, logistics, and other support.

Covertly entering Iran required complete plausible deniability in case the mission plan turned sideways. Nothing the team members wore or brought into the country could be sourced from countries that have trade sanctions with Iran, and that meant the team would be outfitted with non-preferred equipment.

McHenry, Villapiano, and Hadid started with the weaponry, in this case Russian manufactured rifles, pistols, and knives. The team had four AK-12s, a gas-operated assault rifle chambered in 5.45×39mm, designed and manufactured by Kalashnikov Concern, the fifth generation of the famed Kalashnikov rifles. Villapiano took the responsibility of tearing each rifle down, inspecting and cleaning every part, and then reassembling.

For sidearms, the team was equipped with four MP-443 Grach pistols, chambered for the 9×19mm 7N21 cartridge, a different bullet than that shot by the rifles. It wasn't perfect out in the field, but the team was more than capable of adapting. Hadid tore each pistol down, oiled the moving parts, and rebuilt them.

McHenry busied himself by getting reacquainted with the Russian-made SV-98 sniper rifle, a bolt-action rifle with a free-floating barrel and an adjustable stock, chambered in 7.62x54mmR and equipped with twenty specialized 7N1 sniper rounds. Like the others, McHenry inspected every part and re-assembled the weapon.

With the weapons thoroughly inspected and cleaned, the team boxed them up and took them to Ramstein's Combat Arms Training and Maintenance (CATM) facility to put them through their paces. They first ensured each weapon was in working order and then spent the rest of the range time zeroing in the sites. Confident everything was in perfect working order, they then cleaned each weapon again.

After a quick lunch, the team went back to sorting and organizing the rest of their gear, starting with perhaps the most important bit of kit, their four parachutes. The team was provided Special Operations Vector 3 HH (SOV3-HH) Harness/Container System units, a specialized military parachute system designed primarily for high altitude jumps, either high- or low-opening, allowing an operator to carry a full complement of weapons and combat equipment. The team looked over each over-the-shoulder ripcord configured unit, then rotated them among the others, ensuring each of the four chutes was checked three times by three different operators.

Lastly, the team got to organizing their clothing. While Villapiano and Hadid preferred the Salomon Forces Quest 4D GTX boot, a holdover from their time in the US Navy Seals, and McHenry favored the Oakley Light Assault Boot 2, neither of those could be worn in Iran. After trying on the BYTEKS Kalahari, each man settled on its companion model, the lower profile Mongoose.

For outer wear, the team picked through a variety of gear from Techinkom, a Saint Petersburg company specializing in manufacturing quality military kits for the Russian military. Each selected garments in both olive and a sandy brown. Finally, they finished up by gathering a selection of headwear, including *kolah namadihā*, traditional Iranian hats associated with nomadic tribes and rural communities, as well as olive green *keffiyehs*, a traditional scarf-like headdress worn by men from parts of the Middle East and seen periodically in Iran.

Their full day complete, McHenry organized and set aside a variety of gear for Tiger to peruse later in the evening. That was for her to figure out. But before complete exhaustion set in, McHenry and the boys set out to meet her for dinner.

McHenry led Villapiano and Hadid off a Ramstein Air Base Shuttle Service microbus and into Ancho's Pub, a favorite meeting place of the team's when in the area. For McHenry, its barbeque and Tex-Mex menu brought back feelings of being back on the ranch outside of LaGrange, Texas. For the others, it was a place to get a big, homestyle meal with plenty of cold beer with which to wash it down.

Spotting Tiger posted up at a four-top table in the corner with eight bottles of cold beer, the team slid out chairs, took their seats, and helped themselves to a frosty reward for a day-long toil. McHenry took his customary place directly across from Tiger.

"Hey boss, it looks like you've had a long day," he said.

"Mac, don't you know that when you say someone looks tired, or even insinuate it, the other person takes it as you think they look like warmed over dog shit?" she replied.

"Oh hey, didn't mean anything by it," he replied. "You look like you do all the ...," he stammered as he realized he was talking himself into a deeper hole, "...uh, time."

Tiger just stared back at him while Hadid and Villapiano cut up in laughter.

"There's that southern sweet talkin' that Cal McHenry is known for," Tiger finally said. "And, to get back to the point, yes, I have had a long day with Rasmus and the group over at Langley. Long but productive. You all get sorted out over at the hangar?"

"Yeah," Hadid answered. "We got our kits all selected, organized, and ready to go. Got the weapons sorted too."

"We'll stop by after dinner to get you outfitted with clothes and boots," McHenry added. "Sami and JV have got your weapons ready and zeroed in, and the chutes are all ready to go."

"You got a final mission package for us, Tiger?" asked Villapiano.

"That I do, James, and we'll have a full briefing tomorrow after lunch," she replied. "But the crux of the matter is that we're to be wheels up at 1800 hours tomorrow."

"So that leaves our dinner conversation tonight to be pleasure, not business?" asked McHenry.

"That's most certainly the case, my friend," she responded as she passed out laminated menus like a casino card dealer. "Let's load up on some grub and get started on these first two rounds of beer."

McHenry raised his bottle, prompting the others to do the same to tap against his over the center of the table. "Team," he said.

"Team," came the reply from the other three.

Chapter 11

Liu Jun Hie sat idly outside of Zhau Xiang's well-appointed office, waiting for his unscheduled visit in an antechamber that, in addition to seating Zhau's personal secretary, could also comfortably house an entire family of four. The large, opulent surrounding, he thought, was further evidence of the ongoing hypocrisy of the hardline old guard that continued to rankle him.

Under the current General Secretary, in his office for well over a decade, hardliners like Zhau advocated for consolidating and maintaining Chinese Communist Party power and returning to greater state control. They strove to shift the economy towards domestic consumption and indigenous innovation, reducing any perceived reliance on foreign markets and technologies and strengthening state control over the economy. Worse, those policies were crafted with an authoritarian approach dressed up as "common prosperity."

However, all those public-facing declarations to address inequality and perceived excesses only created increased central control that benefited, primarily, the small band of men who were in control.

Liu and some of the younger generation knew the World Bank estimated over 15 percent of the Chinese population lived below the poverty line of a typical upper-middle-income country. Progress had been made over the decades, Liu admitted to himself, but poverty was still rooted in many urban areas. Like Beijing, for instance, where Zhau and his cronies worked and lived in a prosperity unknown to the vast majority of the populace.

Liu's thoughts were interrupted as Zhau's secretary walked over to him and softly said, "The minister will see you now." He stood and followed her the ten paces to Zhau's closed door, where she knocked twice, waited a few seconds, and then opened the door.

Silently, she led him to between the two leather upholstered chairs stationed in front of Zhau's hard-carved wooden antique desk, of which the minister sat behind, busily reading a document bound in a red leather folder. She then asked if he would like a cup of tea.

"No, thank you," Liu responded, for he knew the offer wasn't sincere. If it had been, he would have been offered tea sometime during his twenty-minute wait out in the antechamber. Besides, it was just another silly power play test of Zhau's, and he wasn't going to let the small man's games play with his mind.

It was with that stubborn perseverance that he stood at attention in front of the desk while he waited for Zhau, surely just pretending to be deep at hard work, to welcome or even recognize him. He also didn't allow himself to look at either of the chairs, for he knew he would never be invited to sit—he hadn't once in his many visits to this office. No, Liu thought to himself, he would respectfully stand there and wait. While he might not win, he would certainly not lose the Minister's trivial game of power.

Finally, after a seemingly interminable silence broken only with the sound of Zhau flipping pages of the document, Zhau, without looking up, said, "I wasn't aware of a meeting this morning with you, Liu."

"No, sir, this meeting was not on your schedule."

Still looking at his document, Zhau said, "Then to what do I owe this interruption, Liu?"

"I thought it best not to use the telephone to update you on the latest intelligence we have on the American agent, Swanson."

That got the old man's attention, Liu thought as Zhau's head snapped up and he looked directly at him.

"What is it? Did your man finally get through? Is she dead?" Zhau asked in rapid-fire succession.

"No, sir, the Triad's resource has not been heard from," Liu specified, carefully trying to distance himself the best as he could from what he considered an increasingly reckless scheme that was dangerously close to spinning out of control. "However, we have learned that the agent is currently in Germany and will be making her way tomorrow to Pakistan."

"Pakistan? Why is she going to Pakistan?" Zhau asked.

"That we do not know, Minister Zhau," Liu replied. "However, what with our 'all-weather' friendship with our Pakistani allies, I thought the information might warrant discussion of a cooperative operation."

"Yes!" Zhau exclaimed. "Getting the American outside of the United States should be an easier job for you."

"Getting to the American in Pakistan or another country should be easier," agreed Liu, "but it is not something that I, in the Foreign Affairs Office, can properly facilitate. Our relationships with the Triads still exist, but they are not heavily involved in Pakistan, mostly limited to transporting young women for arranged marriages. For an operation in Pakistan, I advise you to engage your own leaders in National Defense, or possibly include the Ministry of State Security."

"We're off the books with this; we can't include State Security!" Zhau shouted, slapping his hand on his desk for emphasis. "Working with them would mean starting over again, and that delay will cost us this opportunity!"

"As your ministry includes the Intelligence Bureau of the Joint Staff Department of the Central Military Commission, associated with the People's Liberation Army, which is directly under your control," Liu responded, "might I suggest you engage the military intelligence department, who undoubtedly has resources and assets in Pakistan."

Taken aback, Zhau stared at his subordinate for a moment, then said, "I don't need you to advise me on how to best utilize my organization, Liu. As you have failed with the Triads, I will, of course, have to look into using other more accountable professionals. But there's still opportunity for you to redeem yourself."

"Yes, sir, Minister, how may I further assist?"

"Your Triads will have connections with locals in Pakistan," Zhau continued. "Have them recommend locals to execute the job. It's better for all concerned if the American meets her demise by Pakistani hands in Pakistan, no?"

Chapter 12

Tiger and the team were in the belly of another C-17 Globe-master III, sitting with their gear among crates of airplane parts and specialized tools strapped to pallets and secured to the floor. The cargo was headed for Karachi, Pakistan. Tiger and her team, however, wouldn't be on the airplane when it landed at Jinnah International Airport.

Five hours into their flight from Ramstein, McHenry had rallied the team at their equipment, where they had gone over the plan one last time before checking parachutes and packs. For the last thirty minutes, each team member had been properly suited up and prebreathing oxygen through individual OXYJUMP oxygen supply systems. Manufactured by Collins Aerospace, the demand breathing regulators constantly adjusted the proper mix of oxygen to the altitude, conserving oxygen and optimizing system and mission performance.

Tiger found the silence and the oxygen to be meditative, alleviating a bit of the anxiety she felt going into the jump. Still, she was plenty nervous, she could admit to herself, and she kept wondering if she'd have to bolt to the head and relieve herself.

With that thought floating in her head, McHenry walked by and tapped each team member on the top of the helmet, shouting, "Three minutes to drop." Too late, she thought. Things were about to get real.

Tiger stood, along with Hadid and Villapiano, and circled around McHenry. All three of the experienced servicemen took turns patting Tiger on the side of her helmet. The gestures spoke for the men rather than words. They said, "You got this."

As the back ramp of the plane dropped, the ambient noise level inside the fuselage grew substantially and air turbulence whipped fore and aft. Surprised and shaken a bit off-balance, Tiger grabbed a hold of a cargo crate to steady herself.

Shouting to be heard through his mask and the din, McHenry gave the final instructions. "When that light goes green," he said, pointing to a light next to the ramp at the end of the aircraft, "Sami and JV go out. Five seconds later, Tiger, you go, followed by me. Ten seconds out the door, pull your cords. JV, you lead us to the LZ. Everyone else, follow his beacon, fly behind him, and keep twenty meters of space between each other. Anything goes wrong, just get to the ground safely and the others will pick you up."

Finished, he raised his right hand, palm facing outward. Once each of the others had met his hand, he shouted, "Team!" with the rest following in suit.

Villapiano and Hadid then walked to the center of the ramp and Villapiano activated small LED beacons on his helmet and on his ankle. McHenry led Tiger up behind them, stopping at the front of the ramp, three or four steps behind their teammates. Just then the light turned green and a second later both Villapiano and Hadid took a couple of big strides and dove out of the tail of the aircraft.

McHenry placed his hand on the back of Tiger's chute and guided her toward the exit, counting out with each step, "Five, four, three, two, ..."

Tiger's heart was pounding in her throat. All her instincts told her to stop walking, but still her legs moved forward. Then, without making a conscious decision, she found herself falling into the dark nighttime sky.

The first thing Tiger noticed was the change in pitch of what she was hearing. Gone was the ferocity of the wind and engine noise in the aircraft. In its place was the roar of falling through the air as she approached a terminal velocity of nearly 120 miles an hour. But as the faster she began to drop, the more it seemed like she was ... slowing down.

She knew that by jumping at such high altitudes she would reach terminal velocity after a little more than ten seconds. Oh shit, she thought. In her nervous anxiety, she had failed to count to ten to deploy her chute.

Figuring she had to be at least at eight seconds, she reached for the ripcord handle over her shoulder with her right hand. Feeling as though there was no better time than the present, she gave it a big tug.

Just like with her first jumps at Bragg, it seemed for a long second or two as if nothing had happened, that the parachute opening had not been activated. When the chute finally unfurled and the canopy opened, her descent slowed to a relative crawl. While the sky above the horizon in the distant east showed some light, Tiger, in her own space, was engulfed in darkness. If it wasn't for her rapid heartbeat and heavy breathing, she would have sworn she was in some sort of state of unconscious suspended animation.

Knowing she needed to fly in a southwest direction, Tiger oriented herself away from the lightened eastern horizon and, assuming McHenry was above and behind her, began searching for sight of either Hadid or Villapiano. As the seconds ticked by without any identification of her teammates, her anxiety increased nearly to the point of panic.

Just as she really started to properly freak out at the prospect of floating alone in Turkmenistan air space and into Iran, she made out the flashing strobe beacons Villapiano had on his right ankle and the top of his helmet. In the dark she didn't know exactly how far away she was from him, but she felt she was neither too close nor too far.

Using the toggle hands on her steering lines to fly toward Villapiano, she allowed herself to start relaxing, taking deep breaths from her oxygen system. More relaxed, she more slowly, more purposefully looked around, and spotted Hadid to her right at pretty much the same altitude. Understanding he was the vastly more experienced skydiver, she would follow Villapiano and let Hadid check his spacing to her and adjust as necessary.

Finally, looking up and over her right shoulder, she could make out the silhouette of McHenry, backlit by the high eastern sky. Tiger allowed herself a smile. She was with her team. No sense fighting it anymore. All she needed to do was guide her glided descent to follow Villapiano. Might as well enjoy the peaceful, quiet ride down, she thought.

When McHenry and the team jumped from the aircraft, it had been in Turkmenistan airspace, about ten miles from the northeast Iranian border of the Razavi Khorasan province. It was an unnecessarily close flight path to the border, but not an unusual one, for the US military enjoyed a frequent cat-and-mouse play with Iranian air defenses.

The goal was to glide over twenty-five miles to enter Iran well away from border security, and if they could get twenty-eight miles, all the better. While they didn't have the benefit of strong advantageous tailwinds, they also weren't fighting against headwinds. Villapiano believed they would hit their target easily.

Like each member of the team, Villapiano carried an AON2 X2 GPS Altimeter strapped to his wrist. Ordinarily he would've used the altimeter's measure of altitude to deploy his chute. This night, while still measuring altitude, it served a different purpose as well.

Villapiano was using the altimeter's GPS function to fly toward his landing zone target. With a long flight time and continually shifting winds, it required frequent checking and subsequent adjustments in his flight. Using the GPS function most of the way down, he came back to the altitude function as the flight neared its end.

While his beacons were relatively small, he didn't want to inadvertently alert anyone who might be looking into the nighttime sky that he was floating down. As his team expected, when Villapiano's altimeter read 2,000 feet, he turned off his two flashing beacons. At that point, he and the rest watched their altimeters to understand how close they were to touching down.

The night sky was mostly clear and had a halfmoon illuminated. While plenty dark, Villapiano and his team had plenty of time for their eyes to adjust—their flight had taken a touch more than twenty-one minutes. Still, it was nice to have the altimeters to supplement what their eyes were seeing.

As Villapiano neared the ground, he began to make out the hills and valleys that made up the Hezar Masjed Mountains and, a little further to the west, the Binalud Mountain Range. In this part of Iran, the environment was arid and harsh, and what trees dared to sprout did so in valleys and along streams. Wanting to avoid the dangers of landing in a wooded area, Villapiano began to fly along the hills, keeping a keen eye on his GPS readings.

At 500 feet, Villapiano knew he had to make a decision on the final approach to landing. He flew to the west of a ridgeline and aimed himself for a target about one-third of the way down from its high point. At the same time, he maneuvered back and forth to make a note of the prevailing wind, determining that it was a relatively mild crosswind from the west that probably shifted to the north as it hit the ridge.

About fifty feet off the ground, Villapiano made a quick half-turn to fly toward the slope of the ridge, then banked hard to the south and into the wind. Just off the ground, he smoothly yet forcibly pulled down both toggles to flare his parachute, increasing the lift and dramatically reducing his descent rate. Seconds later he hit the sloped ground in a gentle trot, his para-chute, its canopy still partially filled, softly offering resistance and arresting his progress.

Once stopped, both boots firmly planted on Iranian soil, he spun around and quickly started gathering in his chute. To his right, out of the corner of his eye, he saw one of his teammates land about fifty meters away. Who it was, he didn't know. He was just happy that he wasn't alone.

By the time he had his chute bundled up, he saw a second team member silhouetted in the dim moonlight next to the first. As they outnumbered him, he started walking in their direction. After about a half minute of walking, as he was just a couple of strides away from the two, he saw his fourth teammate ap-proaching from the other side. All four had made it down, ap-parently safely and in good health.

Tiger was the first to greet Villapiano. Visibly shaking with exhilaration from not only gently flying across the sky for over twenty minutes but also landing safely after jumping out of an airplane at 35,000 feet, she said, "Holy shit, JV, that was incred-ible. You sons of bitches get to do that all the time?"

"Well, boss," Villapiano replied, "I wouldn't say 'all the time.' But we do get to play with some neat toys and do some pretty cool stuff every now and then."

"Yeah, and while that was cool and all, Tiger," Hadid added, "you should try the opposite sometime, a HALO jump where you freefall for nearly three minutes."

"Uh, that might be a bit much for my next jump," Tiger responded. "But I'll do this again anytime. A half hour ago I would never believe I would be saying that was damn invigorating!"

Just then McHenry arrived at the group having overheard the end of the conversation. "It's a little early to get the party favors out. All we've done so far is land in the middle of Iran, where if we're caught, the only thing we'll have to show for our fun and games will be nooses around our stretched necks."

Chapter 13

While not exactly buoyed by McHenry's reality check, the team snapped out of their collective post-jump revelry and got to work. Villapiano and Tiger huddled together to agree upon not only where they were in the arid, mountainous terrain of eastern Iran, but which direction they needed to go. McHenry and Hadid got busy concealing their parachutes.

The ground on the side of the ridge was rocky and hard-packed. The slope was steep enough that what little rain fell during the year washed away any loose dirt, and that made digging a difficult chore.

McHenry had dropped with a Soviet-era MPL-6E5 small infantry shovel, a tool that had served Russian soldiers over the years in a variety of manner, from digging trenches to acting as a skillet. Plus, McHenry knew, it made for a lethal hand-to-hand combat weapon and could even be thrown like an ax.

This night, though, McHenry set about using the shovel for its primary purpose, and it was not easy going. At just 50 centimeters in length, he struggled to get any real leverage with the tool. But scooting along on his knees, he began to fashion out a shallow trench.

At the same time, Hadid hurried around the area, collecting rocks, starting with the biggest he could carry, and started putting them around the trench.

Five minutes into the chore and with a full sweat beginning to break out, McHenry was relieved by Villapiano on the shovel, and, along with Tiger, they joined Hadid in collecting stones and rocks.

After another five minutes, Hadid spelled Villapiano for the final push. With the shallow trench ten-feet-long and two-feet-wide, the team deemed it good enough. Panting with exertion, they laid out their oxygen systems in the trench first, then covered them with their parachutes, harnesses first. They then laid out their desert camouflage-colored chutes, billowing them out to cover all the equipment below.

With the equipment squared away, McHenry shoveled the previously dug dirt over it while the rest of the team started placing stones and rocks around and over, in as natural looking a manner as they could make. Finally, they took a few steps back and quickly evaluated their work. Satisfied that it would suffice from a distance, McHenry laid the shovel behind the biggest rock and the team gathered on Villapiano.

"Alright, guys," Villapiano said, "We've got some good news and some bad news."

"Let's hear the good news first, bother," replied McHenry.

"The good news is that Tiger and I both agree on exactly where we're at and where we need to go. Plus, we agree that we're within our time window."

"Okay," McHenry said hesitantly. "I sense there's a 'but' coming up and I'm wondering how big of a 'but' that's gonna be."

Villapiano smiled. "We didn't fly quite as far as we wanted, so we're two klicks and change from our target LZ. We got a little bit longer hike than we wanted."

"A touch over two klicks, you say?" asked McHenry.

"Affirmative, Mac," came the reply.

"Well, shit, JV, that ain't so bad."

"Yeah, but it's that way, Mac," Villapiano said, pointing west and uphill, over the ridge.

McHenry chuckled. "Of course it is. What's a walk in enemy territory without making it an uphill one at that to start. Sami, you're on point. Tiger, you follow and keep him pointed in the right direction. I'll be on our six."

"Copy that, Mac," Hadid said as he spun around and faced uphill. "On me, team."

With that, the team set off on the next stage of their mission.

Thanks to Villapiano's in-flight decision to land closer to the top of the ridge than the valley below, the team used the rocky and stoic mountainous landscape to their advantage, quickly ascending to the ridgeline and over to the other side. Once there and again freed of cumbersome vegetation, the team made good progress on foot.

This northeast region of Iran offered a rugged, harsh landscape of high hills, rocky outcrops, and numerous peaks and valleys. The weather could be counted on to be dry and steppe-like, and winter often proved to be cold and dry. On this summer night, the temperature was comfortably cool for a quickly paced hike, but it would certainly heat up once the sun rose. The team looked to be long out of sight by the time the sun was high in the sky.

Their objective was a small automotive junkyard on the outskirts of Amirabad, a sleepy village of about 250 people situated next to a small lake in a valley about fifty kilometers as a bird would fly northeast of Mashhad, which, with well over three million people, was the second-largest city in Iran. And while fifty kilometers seemed like a short distance, there was a world of difference between the bustling big city and the mountain villages.

In the hill country, the population was sparse, with little villages spread out very few and very far between. In many respects, it was perfect for a covert team that needed to quickly infiltrate, for the likelihood of crossing paths with other people was small. On the other hand, on the rare instance of crossing paths with others, curiosity would be piqued and alarms almost surely raised.

For those reasons, Hadid, while leading at a quick pace, was still carefully scanning the environment. It started with looking for secure footholds for the placement of his feet. A stumble on a hillside could result in an injury, and any injury at this stage of the mission would seriously jeopardize the mission's outcome. Then he would lift his eyes upward and scan for any telltale signs of potential threat. In the dark, he was looking primarily for movement of any kind, but in the moonlight, also for any shapes that looked man-made, like a hut, lean-to, or tent.

While Hadid kept his eyes peeled forward, the team took responsibility for scanning the flanks. Second in line, Tiger, while also ensuring her stable footwork, scanned from up and down the hillside from nine o'clock on the left flank to eleven o'clock. Third in line, Villapiano covered downhill from one o'clock to three. At the tail end of the single file line, McHenry double-checked both sides. All of them carried their rifles in the low carry/low ready position, with muzzles pointed downward at a safe, but ready, angle. The position allowed for unobstructed sightlines while at the same time a quick, upward motion to engage any targets.

After an hour, the team took a quick break and hydrated. Using GPS, Tiger confirmed their location and timeline. While hard on ankles, knees, and hips, they agreed to continue to traverse the side of the hillside about 100 meters up from the valley floor, where trees and other brush had sprouted. They needed to make good time, and the trees and other vegetation not only made for time-consuming obstacles, but also perfect locations for others, be they smugglers, goat farmers, or others to set up camp.

After another five kilometers and well over an hour, Tiger gave a bird-like whistle, alerting Hadid to stop. Her GPS said they were about a kilometer from the junkyard, where they were scheduled to rendezvous with in-country agency assets. It was an uncertain, high-risk stage in the mission plan and one that required caution. Time to slow things down.

Alone, Tiger walked along the edge of a dirt road barely one-and-a-half-lanes wide, the edges of both sides sprouting tall weeds, evidence of its scarce use. Along the road was a decrepit wood plank fence, but she could see no fence around the rest of the small junkyard.

The junkyard was home to about thirty abandoned vehicles, mostly small trucks. From what she could tell by the side of the road, if ever a truck died in the village of Amirabad, it came here to slowly decay into the arid landscape.

Seeing a small wooden structure, a significant lean to one side indicating both its age and general lack of upkeep, sitting at the end of the fence, Tiger stopped her progress and looked around. She was to meet a middle-aged male agency asset by the name of Massoud Shaheen, a tow truck driver from Gorgan, close to the Caspian Sea. While Langley trusted him based on a decade of past experience in providing valuable intel and in-country cooperation, Tiger had never worked with him before. Therefore, she had zero trust in him.

She knew she was well within a thirty-six-hour window for the rendezvous, so Shaheen had to be around, and as such, he probably had eyes on her. She swung her AK-12 rifle on its sling until it was under her right arm. Then she unholstered her MP-443 Grach pistol and gripped it with both hands, the muzzle pointed to the ground in front of her, but ready for her to lift and shoot if necessary.

Eight meters from where the fence met the building, Tiger heard the unmistakable sound of a semiautomatic pistol's slide being racked rearward to chamber a bullet.

In a soft but firm voice, she heard a voice command in Farsi, "*Lotfa cpehmin ja baistid ve dastenpeheitan ra bala bebrid.*" Please stop right there and raise your hands.

Tiger stopped and raised her hands. Then she turned very slowly to her left, at the direction of the voice. There she saw a man behind a rusted pickup truck, dressed in a brown *qameez*, a long-sleeved shirt that draped well below the bed of the truck behind which he was stationed.

Knowing her side of the coded greeting, she replied in Farsi, "*Man yek mosafer sargardan npastam keh bah radiator baraye yek toyotaye madel payin niaz daram.*" I am a stranded traveler in need of a radiator for a late model Toyota.

She waited anxiously for the coded return message to validate Shaheen. After a second or two, the man replied, "*Eger khili dor az inja gir niftadeh bashid, bayad asan bashod.*" If you're not stranded far from here, that should be easy.

She relaxed slightly as it was the return phrase for which she was looking. She relaxed further when Shaheen lowered his weapon.

In English, Shaheen said, "My apologies for coming at you in threat from the dark. But surely you didn't expect me to be out in the open, empty handed."

"And surely you didn't expect me to come alone," she replied as she glanced up the road in the direction she had walked just a moment before. As Shaheen turned and looked, McHenry rose up over the fence, his AK-12 trained on Shaheen.

"Ah, yes, I would of course expect you would have company. Surely you won't be surprised to know I brought company as well."

He turned and glanced over his left shoulder, where a man stood brandishing what looked to Tiger as an old AK-47 assault rifle.

"Not surprised at all, Mr. Shaheen. And please, stop calling me Shirley." With that, she stuck the thumb and index finger of her left hand into her mouth and unleashed a loud whistle, then pointed over beyond the second man. As both Shaheen and the man turned around, they saw Villapiano and Hadid twenty meters back, their AK-12 trained on each of them.

Shaheen turned toward Tiger, threw his head back, and erupted in a roar of laughter. After a few seconds, he composed himself, tucked his pistol into his waistband, and walked up to Tiger, extending his hands in greeting. "Nice to meet you, Tiger. Please, bring your men inside. I'm sure you're hungry and we've brought food."

Shaheen and his colleague, a younger man named Noor-Ali Mohammadi, brought Tiger and the team into the wooden structure, which consisted of a single room that had doubled, at one time, as both a workshop and an office. On the makeshift workbench, Shaheen and Mohammadi had placed three broad clay pots with lids next to a battery-powered lantern. One contained rolls of lavash, a thin, leavened flatbread. The other two pots contained *kotlet*, pan-fried meat patties made of ground meat, onions, and potatoes, and *dolmeh*, stuffed grape leaves filled with rice and a mixture of savory herbs.

While Hadid and McHenry stood guard at positions outside, Villapiano and Mohammadi quickly ate while Tiger and Shaheen huddled to confirm their transportation plans. After Villapiano and Mohammadi scarfed down a quick snack, they went outside to relieve Hadid and McHenry.

"Shaheen, I trust you brought two vehicles with you, as planned, yes?" asked Tiger.

"Yes, Tiger," came his reply. "I have my tow truck with a 2007 Toyota Prado. Both are not exactly easy on the eyes, but they fit in and they are mechanically sound. We should have no troubles."

"Good. When do you suggest leaving?"

"I think now, as dawn quickly comes," he responded. "We'll make our way into Mashhad and blend into the morning traffic. We'll then move west, toward Qom, south of Tehran. Eat, though, as it's 1,000 kilometers to Qom, and it will not go fast."

Tiger nodded and walked over to the workbench, nudging aside McHenry, who was working his way through a lavash-wrapped *kotlet*. Just as she picked up a rolled piece of flatbread, Mohammadi slunk in the door and said in Farsi, "*Tamas. Mardi nazdik mishod.*" Contact. A man approaches.

"Mac, get behind the door," Tiger ordered. "The rest of you against the far wall."

The group waited anxiously for over ten seconds, collectively holding their breath and being as silent as they could. Each hoped the man would pass by the building without any problem.

Finally, the door creaked open, just an inch or two at first. Then, with a sudden and violent burst, it abruptly flew open, causing McHenry to quickly raise his arms to prevent getting clocked on the head. Through the door frame, a middle-aged man burst into view and crashed onto the floor, Villapiano on top of him.

As the man had reached for the doorknob with his right hand and began to swing the door open, Villapiano, running up behind him, had grabbed the man's left wrist and twisted his arm behind his back. At the same, Villapiano had used his right foot to trip the man forward.

The result was one unconscious Iranian man in the middle of the shop floor, most likely with a significant shoulder injury.

Reaching under his *qameez*, Shaheen pulled his pistol, a Kaveh 17, the Iranian copy of the Austrian-made Glock 17, and walked toward the unconscious man. Leveling his pistol with the back of the man's head as he arrived, he was met head on by McHenry, who quickly ran his left hand down the muzzle of the pistol until the webbing between his thumb and forefinger stopped against the Kaveh's hammer. At the same time, McHenry brought his right hand across and grabbed Shaheen's wrist, using his thumb to aggressively press into Shaheen's hand, just below his right thumb.

Just like that, in about a second, McHenry had disarmed Shaheen and was now holding the Kaveh. Across the room, before Mohammadi could react, Hadid stepped in front of him and placed his hand on his chest. Unspoken, the message was clear: Stay put.

Three inches taller, McHenry looked down into the eyes of Shaheen and said, "We don't do that."

Still a little shocked at the turn of events, it took a moment for Shaheen to collect his thoughts. Finally, he said, "We can't let him go. It's too dangerous for us."

"We're not going to let him go," said Tiger as she walked up to the scene. "But we sure as hell aren't going to kill him either."

Turning to McHenry, first, then Hadid and Villapiano, she instructed, "From this point on, no spoken English within earshot of this man, understood?"

The three nodded in agreement.

Then in Farsi, Tiger filled in Shaheen and Mohammadi on what the plan would be. They would constrain the man's arms and legs with zip ties around his ankles and wrists, effectively incapacitating him. They'd then leave him blindfolded in the back of the shop where eventually, probably, he would be found. But they would not kill him now.

Shaheen protested. "It's too dangerous to leave him alive. He might be able to identify us."

"Where's your truck?" Tiger asked.

"It's parked at the far end of the yard away from the road," came his reply.

"Okay," Tiger replied, "then your vehicles are clean. And he hasn't seen any of us, at least not yet. For all he knows, he stumbled across a group of smugglers."

"Or enemies of the state," responded Shaheen. "It's a risk we don't need to take." Pointing to Mohammadi, he added, "Our lives are here, in Iran. It's our lives at stake."

Tiger swept her hand around and said, "It's all our lives at stake here. We're not here to harm noncombatants. He's just some guy looking for a water pump or something. He doesn't deserve to die just because he was in the wrong place at the wrong time. We tie him up and leave him here. That is not up for discussion, clear?"

Shaheen looked at Tiger for a long moment, then sighed. "Clear. Now I suggest we get as far away from here as quickly as we can."

Chapter 14

Using an old burlap bag they found in the shop, McHenry masked the man and then, just as he was beginning to come to, zip tied his hands behind his back, around the wooden four-by-four leg of the workbench. Still struggling to come to consciousness and likely feeling the effects of his twisted shoulder and the bump on his head from the floor, the man didn't put up any resistance to having his ankles bound with another set of zip ties.

Hoping to add another layer of subterfuge to the situation, Tiger gave directions in Russian, "*Nam pora otpravlyat'sya k granitse.*" Time to make our way to the border.

Silently, McHenry and Villapiano, the only two still in the building, made their way to the door. Tiger followed, and at the door, stopped and turned in the direction of the man. In Farsi, she said, "*Sakt bash. Vaghti bah marz residim, barayat kamak mifarestim.*" Stay quiet. When we're at the border, we will send help for you. She then closed the door and walked to the edge of the building.

Shaheen had pulled up his tow truck onto the road and already disengaged the Prado. As he was putting his equipment away, a variety of chains and straps, Mohammadi double-checked the gear in both the tow truck and the Prado. When McHenry, Villapiano, and Tiger arrived at the truck, they were met by Hadid.

"You get the party favors laid out in the junkyard, Sami?" McHenry asked.

"Affirmative, Mac," came his reply. "They're rigged and ready to go, if necessary."

"Oh, it's gonna be necessary, my friend," McHenry said with a wink. "I've no doubt about that."

"Alright, boys," Tiger said as the sky began to lighten with the rising sun in the east. "You all know the plan and ready to saddle up?"

"We're good," responded McHenry. "JV's with you in the truck with Shaheen. Sami's watching over me and Mohammadi in the SUV."

"Alright, Mac, with your job ahead of you, we'll likely lose track of you for most of the trip west. We'll catch up at Qom," Tiger said as she opened the door to the tow truck and began to slide in.

"We'll be following behind you, Tiger," McHenry said as he held the door open for Villapiano to slide in behind. Superstitious about wishing fellow operatives good luck, he simply said, "See you in Qom."

After McHenry closed the door, he walked back to the Prado. "Sami," he said with a smile, "you've got the back seat. I'm too old for that shit." With that, the last three climbed aboard their vehicle, Mohammadi behind the wheel, and began the next stage in the mission.

In the lead vehicle, Shaheen's well-used 1987 Scania P112H 6x4 slowly navigated the country roads until the outskirts of Mashhad, where it then fell into the city's chaotic morning rush hour traffic. Shaheen's tow truck, euphemistically referred to as a "recovery vehicle" in some circles, was about as conspicuous as an inconspicuous vehicle could be, thought Tiger. It was a tow truck for crying out loud, and what white paint that was left on its dented and chipped front cab hadn't been washed in God knows how long. Without a doubt, she was fairly certain it would be the only tow truck she would see for the entire 1,000-kilometer journey.

But she also knew it was like hiding in plain sight. The tow truck was noticeable, but completely unremarkable and un-memorable. In getting from point A to point B, the truck would more than suffice.

Getting there in comfort wasn't going to be part of the deal, however. The cab featured a single bench seat, and there was no way Villapiano was going to be able to fold his big frame into the middle. Thus, Tiger had taken the middle with Villapi-ano wedged in next to her, their packs crammed into the small cargo area behind the bench, their AK-12 rifles lying on the floor. Tiger sighed and shook her head. Bouncing along an Iran-ian highway all day, more than likely below the 120 kph speed limit and under a baking desert sun no less, was going to try her very last fiber of patience.

From Mashhad, Shaheen drove south on 97 until it blended into 44, the Imam Reza Highway, and headed west to Neyshabur and Sabzevar. To help kill the time, he played Persian pop music through the truck's radio, a genre that blended traditional Per-sian music with Western influences like rock, hip-hop, and elec-tronica music. While not exactly her preferred musical accompaniment, Tiger was thankful that it was at least upbeat and that the lyrics were in Farsi, which she could understand.

She nudged Villapiano with her right elbow, jarring him out of a quiet stare out the side window. "I guess the price you pay for getting the comfortable seat is that you have to listen to mu-sic you can't understand," she said.

"What comfortable seat you talkin' about, boss? That gonna be in our next ride?"

The two shared a relatively humorless laugh. It was going to be a long, hot day.

"Mac's going to have all the fun today," Tiger said as she scrunched lower into the seat, laid her head on the back window, and closed her eyes.

"How the hell does JV keep pulling the easy jobs with Tiger?" grunted Hadid as he walked up next to McHenry and Muhammadi in the small parking lot of an automobile repair shop just off the Imam Reza Highway in Mayamey, a small, roadside hamlet in Iran's Khar-Turan National Park. Khar-Turan was the largest wildlife park in the country and known for its rich, diverse flora and fauna. Hadid and McHenry both knew that in two or three days, attention would be focused on something other than the park's plant and animal life.

Or at least that was their intention.

Since the three of them had left the auto salvage yard in Amirabad, they had been on a distinctly different agenda than Tiger, Villapiano, and Shaheen, who were rather simply trying to get from point A, Amirabad, to point B, the safehouse outside Qom, in the shortest amount of time without breaking the speed limit and drawing undo attention to themselves. While the three in the Prado SUV were in effect following the lead car and would eventually get to the same rendezvous destination, their path was slightly more circuitous and much, much slower.

While Mohammadi focused on driving, McHenry and Hadid had been looking for appropriate places to leave figurative breadcrumbs for their escape out of the country. Not for them to follow, but for their seemingly inevitable pursuers to follow.

If a snatch and grab mission went to plan, a person would, by definition, go missing. If the team was successful in their snatch of Bo, they knew that he would be missed, much more likely sooner than later. And when his absence was noted, it would spark an extensive manhunt, first by Iranian forces, and then followed quickly by a Chinese contingent as well.

Hadid and McHenry were tasked with distracting future pursuers by leaving a false trail on which to expend attention and energy. Whatever resources they might be able to later deflect might be the difference between mission success and mission failure.

The first breadcrumb left would eventually be the last one revealed, an IED with a mobile phone activator planted under an abandoned truck at the Amirabad salvage yard. From there, the team had followed the path of the tow truck to Neyshabur, where they had spent the better part of an hour scouting for a location to plant another diversion.

Scouting was time-intensive and required utmost patience. Being broad daylight, the three needed to ensure they didn't draw attention to themselves. Yet, at the same time, they needed a spot where the diversion, when activated, would be readily noticed and reported. So, they needed a location that was well-trafficked but not too well trafficked, and one that was logically placed in close proximity to the highway.

After scouting areas in the Farhangian Town district in Neyshabur, they ended up planting another device under a dumpster outside of the Simorgh Cultural Center on the other side of the highway. The incendiary explosive charge was contained in a double-lined plastic bag, along with about a dozen 5.45×39mm shell casings. The hope was that a preliminary investigation of an explosion and resulting fire would draw attention to the spent shell casings, the size of rounds for both AK-12 and AK-74 rifles. In time, of course, investigators would understand that an IED had been used. The ruse laid, however, in presenting the possibility of a small shootout having taken place, and thus being a logical sequence in an escape with a kidnapped victim.

After Neyshabur, the trio had resumed their journey and driven past Sabzevar, eventually arriving at the small town of Davarzan, the capital of both the county and the district, as well as the administrative center for the Mazinan Rural District. A town with a population of less than 3,000, the town marked a perfect spot along the map to plant another device.

After loitering around under the guise of eating lunch, waiting for the precise moment Hadid could plant a device without being noticed, they had finally succeeded in securing another charge to the alcove of a seemingly abandoned adobe-like structure constructed from mud, clay, and straw.

The fourth and final of Hadid's little surprise packages had now just been secured to the inside of the repair shop's air compressor. The team was now freed to make their way directly to the Qom safehouse.

"Good work so far today, Sami," said McHenry as they got back into the SUV. "You too, Mohammadi. But we're only halfway through our mission tasks of the day. We still have a long ride to get to where we need to be, so stay alert and vigilant."

"Understood," said the soft-spoken Mohammadi as he started the engine. "We still have 600 kilometers, so we'll be stopping for fuel again. Past Shahrud, I know a place we will stop and eat. Until then, I'll blend into traffic."

Looking at their driver, McHenry nodded and patted him on his right shoulder. "Thank you. We'll be even more hungry by then I'm sure," he said with a grin. Pulling his *keffiyeh* tight around his face, McHenry turned to Hadid in the back. "If you want to, Sami, catch some shuteye. I got us covered up here."

"Thanks, Mac," came the tired reply from Hadid as he laid down on the backseat. "I'm gonna take you up on that kind offer."

"Yes, Liu, what do you have for me?" Zhau Xiang asked coldly to his subordinate. While Liu Jun Hie didn't work for him in the Ministry of National Defense, he also was not the rank of a minister as was Zhau. To him, that made Liu much more of a subordinate than a colleague.

"I have an update from Pakistan that you should be made aware of," Liu responded. "According to two different sources on the ground, our person of interest, the American agent, Swanson, did not disembark in Karachi from the plane that traveled from Germany."

"What? You mean she travelled all the way there just to continue to another destination?"

"No, sir, let me explain," continued Liu. "While it had been confirmed that she and three others were on the plane at take-off, neither she nor the other three were on the plane when it landed in Karachi."

Angry, Zhau slapped his right hand down on his desk. "One set of your sources are buffoons!" he shouted. "They didn't just disappear into thin air!"

Already composed, Liu took a deep, calming breath. "Sir, I think due consideration must be given that they did indeed, in a matter of speaking, disappear into thin air."

"What do you mean, Liu?" Zhau responded with a steely glare.

"A distinct possibility that should be examined is that Swanson and the others parachuted out of the airplane as it was enroute to Pakistan."

"Of course," said Zhau as he nodded and clasped his hands together in his lap. "Do we know the route of the plane?"

"We do," answered Liu. "Based on intelligence from your Ministry of National Defense, it appears the aircraft went through the airspace of several central and eastern European countries before routing over Türkiye, Azerbaijan, Turkmenistan, and Afghanistan."

"That's a lot of area, of course," said Zhau. "She could be anywhere."

"Possible, sir, but not likely," replied Liu. "With the diplomatic relations enjoyed by the Americans, Swanson could have flown directly into any of the countries they flew over, no questions asked and with no difficulties at customs, with the exception of Afghanistan."

"So, you think she's there?"

"It's possible, sir, as she has a record of operational activity in Afghanistan, but there is another possibility too."

"Where's that?" asked Zhau impatiently.

"Sir, the final five countries the aircraft flew over border Iran."

In the silent pause that followed, a grin slowly formed across Zhau's face. "Yes, Liu, that is quite interesting. This is good data to share with our comrades in the Ministry of State Security."

Chapter 15

Animated conversation in the safehouse broke Tiger out of her concentrated focus on mission planning. One of the first to have awoken in the morning, she had sequestered herself into a fig tree-shaded corner of the *hayat*, the central courtyard in the safehouse, situated in a quiet neighborhood south of Navab Safavi Boulevard and a short walk from Bonyadi Park in the Shi'a Islam holy city of Qom.

Situated 140 kilometers south of Tehran, Qom, with a population of nearly 1.5 million people, was the seventh-largest city in Iran, and served as the capital of the province, county, and district. While Qom had developed into a commercial center with foundations in the petroleum industry, it was perhaps best known internationally as the largest center for Shi'a scholarship in the world.

The site of the shrine of Fatima bint Musa, sister of Imam Ali ibn Musa Rida, Qom was an important destination of pilgrimage for the Islamic faithful, with estimates of over twenty million pilgrims visiting annually. While most of the pilgrims were from Iran, Shi'a Muslims from around the world also visited.

Tiger and her team, of course, were an entirely different group of pilgrims.

The safehouse played perfectly into the needs of the team. Traditional homes in culturally conservative enclaves like Qom had long been designed with an inward focus on a central courtyard, surrounded by high exterior walls to deliver not only a high level of privacy, but also a sense of social equity, as outsiders were unable to judge a resident's wealth.

Like the entire neighborhood, the safehouse was constructed in the culturally traditional style and featured plain, unadorned fired clay walls three meters high. Any visitors, expected or un-expected, entered through an enclosed transitional vestibule called a *hashti*, which prevented a direct line of sight into the courtyard.

All the rooms of the safehouse opened to the courtyard, and like many traditional homes, it featured a large, central hall in the *biruni*, a public reception area kept distinctly apart from the *andaruni*, or private family areas.

Walking into the safehouse, Tiger saw that McHenry and Ha-did had joined Villapiano in the dining area immediately off the kitchen. They were seated on the floor around a *korsi*, a low wooden table about eighteen inches tall, covered with a deco-rative cloth called a *sofreh*. On the tabletop were earthen plates and bowls with fresh lavash, feta cheese, butter, honey, and sliced tomatoes and cucumbers. At one end of the table was a glass pitcher filled with sweetened black tea.

As Tiger walked up to the table, Mohammadi came through the opened kitchen door carrying two bowls, one filled with fig jam, the other with shelled walnuts. In his soft-spoken manner, he bowed his head to Tiger and said in English, "Sorry for late *sobhāné*."

Tiger stopped and turned to him. She had awoken from a very light sleep when Mohammadi had arrived at the safehouse with McHenry and Hadid in the middle of the night, just over five hours ago. By all accounts, she thought, he should justifi-ably be asleep. The fact that he was up and had prepared break-fast for the team was both unexpected and highly appreciated.

In accordance with Islamic principles regarding interactions between genders, Tiger lowered her gaze to avoid sustained eye contact and said in Farsi, "*Ma az tamam zahmat shma, bah khsus baraye in ghzayi keh ba npam bah eshtarak migozarim, sepasgazarim. Moteshkaram.*" We are grateful for all your work, especially for this food we share. Thank you.

Raising her head, she saw a smile of pride etch itself on Mohammadi's face. He bowed slightly one more time, then placed the two bowls on the table in front of the hungry Americans. Before he spun and returned to the kitchen, he paused and said, "*Nooshe jan.*" May it nourish your soul.

As Tiger sat cross-legged on the floor next to Villapiano, McHenry asked, "Get any sleep last night, boss?"

"Quite a bit more than you," she replied, "as I was awoken from a pretty decent sleep by you three stumbling around in the middle of the night. That wasn't long ago. How're you two gettin' on?"

"Yeah, it was a long day, but we're good. Sami and I both got some shuteye in the car," McHenry responded. "The one who didn't, Mohammadi," he said nodding toward the kitchen, "will probably be feeling the long drive later this afternoon."

"At least he's got youth on his side," remarked Hadid, invoking a chuckle from the rest of the group.

As the four tucked into the prepared breakfast, McHenry asked, "So what's on the agenda for us, Tiger?"

"Today and tomorrow," she said, "we're all about mission planning. The pattern of life constructed on Bo Jianguo by Shaheen and other intel assets doesn't exactly paint a picture of an abundant number of good snatch-and-grab opportunities."

"So, what do we got there, Tiger?" asked Villapiano.

"Yeah, boss," added McHenry, "we got anything to work with here?"

"A little, guys, but very little. Bo is pretty much a prisoner at the Fordow facility. He lives in a double-wide trailer on the premises, one of a small compound of four that houses him, his translator, and two Russian nationals, one of them a fellow nuclear scientist who works alongside Bo. Every morning—five, sometimes six times a week—a minibus picks up the four and takes them into the mountain to work. Outside of work and time in his trailer doing whatever a foreigner in the middle of freakin' Iran does, Bo takes a walk every evening before sunset.

"While that regular schedule might appear to offer up opportunity, it would be a fool's errand. Being a nuclear facility, and a recently attacked one at that, security is extensive. No way we could reasonably expect to both break in and break out without being detected."

"So where does that leave us, boss?" asked McHenry.

"Well, for a pure-blood Texan like yourself, Mac, you'll be keen to hear that leaves us with football."

"Football? What do you mean?"

"Ah, my friend," Tiger replied with a wink, "I'm afraid I got my wires crossed and perhaps misled you a bit. I meant to say, '*futbol*.'"

"Soccer?"

"Precisely, my pigskin obsessed friend. The local team, Vahdat Qom, provides a welcomed distraction for Bo and his mates from Fordow. As either luck or brilliant mission planning would have it, Vahdat Qom is hosting Foolad Novin in their season finale, an Iran 2nd Division match in two nights at Shahid Heydarian Stadium."

"And we're, and when I say 'we're' I very much mean 'you're,' certain Bo's attending the game?" asked McHenry.

"As sure as we can be, Mac," Tiger replied with a sigh. "Bo's been attending all the club's home games for the past couple of months. We'd better hope that streak continues, 'cause we really don't have any other options. If it's not Friday, I don't know what choice we have but to wait Bo out."

"So, you're thinking the stadium then?" asked Hadid.

"Maybe, Sami, that's to be determined over the next couple of days," said Tiger. "The stadium is a small venue, with a capacity of just 3,000, of which the club would be pretty lucky to draw half of that on Friday. Still, that's a lot of people to get in the way. On the other hand, they could also act as cover."

"Of course, all those fans would still be cover on the way in, where we could perform a vehicle interdiction on their way to the stadium," added McHenry.

"You're reading my mind, Mac," Tiger replied with a smile. "We'll plan a stadium caper, but that'll be plan B to a vehicle interdiction. One way or the other, we'll get our guy."

Colonel Rostam Jahan uncomfortably paced across the earthen tile floor of his office on the ground floor of the Iranian Revolutionary Guard Corps' Samen-al-Aeme Headquarters in Mashhad. A twenty-three-year veteran of the Iranian military, he was much more comfortable leading forces either on a base or in the field. Even after nearly a year in his position commanding the IRGC Intelligence Organization for the eastern and northeastern regions of the country, he bristled at the thought of being a cake-eater administrative bureaucrat.

Jahan longed to have dirt under the soles of his boots, not tiles.

Based on his excellence in the field, he had been plucked from the ranks and promoted into his current position. A loyal public servant to the regime, he had accepted the new position, but he certainly didn't consider it a promotion.

Throughout his career as a soldier, Jahan had been all too painfully reminded that the intelligence apparatus in Iran was as complex and dysfunctional as it could possibly get. Now he felt he was just another cog in the system.

Iran's Ministry of Intelligence, or the MOIS, was chartered as the primary civilian intelligence agency focused on gathering intelligence, both domestically and internationally, to protect the country and its power in the Middle East. The minister was appointed by the president but had to be approved by the supreme leader. Importantly, the minister overseeing the agency had to be a cleric and a *mujtahid*, or a cleric who could interpret Islamic sources and was accepted as an authority in Islamic law. Not quite a politician, knew Jahan, and not nearly an intelligence professional.

From there, the problems only got worse. While the lead organization, the MOIS was just one of over fifteen agencies that made up the Intelligence Coordination Council, an organizational structure deliberately convoluted with overlapping mandates between agencies to ostensibly prevent any single entity from gaining and holding a monopoly on information.

Jahan's IRGC-IO agency was perceived to be the primary rival of the MOIS, and it operated independently within the military's chain of command, reporting directly to the supreme leader. The IRGC-IO had a domestic focus, and as a result, slanted toward the Islamic ideology.

Where Jahan really wanted to be was within the IRGC Quds Force. The Quds Force was the IRGC's external intelligence and covert operations arm, and oversaw extraterritorial operations, including supporting proxy militias across the Middle East. It was Iran's elite external operations unit, responsible for unconventional warfare, intelligence, and supporting, training, and directing proxy groups like Hezbollah, Hamas, and the Houthis to advance Iran's influence and, of course, destabilize the infidels in Israel and the United States.

Jahan knew his talent and passion were being wasted behind a desk, essentially shuffling papers while others operated. What he needed was an opportunity to show his superiors that the more action-oriented Quds Force was where he should serve.

A knock on his open door startled Jahan out of his introspective musings. In walked Major Mitra Afsoon, one of Jahan's trusted allies in his chain of command.

"Colonel, in following up on the intel we received earlier today," Afsoon said, "we had one incident that we wanted to present to you. A possible corroboration of the intel."

"What do you have for me, Major?" Jahan asked as we walked behind his desk and took a seat.

Afsoon opened a folder and spun it on Jahan's desk so that it faced the colonel.

"Not too far from here, outside of the little village of Amirabad, a local stumbled across a band of smugglers."

"And how are you thinking it confirms the Chinese intel?"

"Sir, the villager, who was injured in the incident, said that the group spoke both Farsi and another language, but one that was not Turkmen, a language this man knows from his proximity to our Turkmen friends across the border."

"Did he know what language it was?" asked Jahan.

"He can't be for certain, but he thought it might have been Russian," Afsoon answered.

"Russian, you think?" mused Jahan as he stroked his chin in thought. "That is interesting. Did the witness say where they went?"

"He assumed they were smugglers and maybe headed into Turkmenistan."

"But you, perhaps, think maybe differently," responded Jahan with a raised eyebrow.

"As you say, sir, 'perhaps,'" the junior officer replied. "With no other accounts of any other suspicious activity in the last twenty-four hours in any of our border provinces, what if this band of so-called smugglers were coming into the country, not heading out?"

"Yes, Major," Jahan said thoughtfully. "It's thin, but it's all we have to work on. Monitor all the police and security channels, and raise all anomalies to me."

"Yes sir, Colonel," Afsoon answered before he spun on his heels and exited the office.

Jahan lowered his head and quickly reviewed the open file. First the call from the Chinese and now this, but nothing else. What are the odds they could be related, he asked himself. Right now, pretty long, he thought. But if something else comes in, maybe this will present an opportunity to take action and show his superiors exactly what he could do.

Chapter 16

During the morning hours, Tiger and the team reviewed the pattern of life previously established by the agency. Over the past ten weeks, Bo had established a routine of making the approximately one-hour commute to attend home games of the Vahdat Qom club. On all his previous visits to the stadium, seven in total, he had attended the game and then returned directly to the Fordow facility afterwards. No stops, either at restaurants, cafes, or fuel stations, on either leg of the trip.

While he made a habit of regularly attending home games, his commute to the games had differed. On five of the seven most recent occasions, he and his translator were driven in a four-door sedan, the two Chinese being the only passengers. On the two other occasions, they were driven to Qom in a minibus, Bo's Russian colleague and his interpreter riding along as well.

As the transportation vehicles never stopped, the team unanimously agreed its options for affecting a vehicular interdiction were limited. It would have to be either en route, either to the stadium or in return to the facility, or it would have to be at the point of drop off and pick up, in front of the Baran Cafe on the traffic circle formed where 5th Golestan intersected with Shahid Mofatteh Boulevard West.

The team decided that attempting an interdiction near the Fordow facility would be too dangerous, for as soon as the inevitable alarm was sounded, the immediate response from the authorities, especially the Iranian military, would be both swift in timing and daunting in size and scope.

One attractive option was in the desert between Fordow and Qom. But the trip into Qom would be conducted in the bright afternoon sunshine, compromising the team's ability to act covertly. However, regarding a return trip to the facility, the team didn't like the idea of operating in the desert in the dark with no margin for error, knowing that if anything went wrong in their lone opportunity, the chance to snatch Bo would evaporate. There would be no second chance, at least not for a considerable time, as the soccer match was the season finale.

Therefore, it was agreed to attempt the interdiction on the trip to the stadium, knowing that if the initial plan went south, there could be a second attempt made on the return trip. They decided that the busy urban area, if used correctly, would provide cover for their escape. While there would be witnesses, by the time they were vetted by authorities, the team and Bo would be a far distance away.

A complication in the already tight confluence of mission parameters was the need to greatly limit the use of mobile phones. The Iranian government possessed extensive and sophisticated capabilities to track mobile phone usage through a combination of mandatory direct access to mobile carrier systems, specialized surveillance software, and an extensive web of spyware. All those capabilities were utilized in real-time for mass surveillance, censorship, and suppressing dissent.

For the team, the worst of the countermeasures was the government's direct access to mobile carrier data, a legal constraint imposed by Iran's Communications Regulatory Authority (CRA) that required all telecom operators to provide direct, real-time access to their systems. This access allowed intelligence agencies and law enforcement authorities to track location and monitor users' movements by identifying to which cell towers phones connected. More importantly, those agencies actively intercepted voice calls, text messages, and data usage records, and used enormous computing resources to analyze metadata, producing detailed summaries of who contacted whom, when, and where.

It would be critical for the team to greatly limit the use of mobile phones.

With a rough framework in place that included several options, the team left the safehouse in the afternoon to scout the roads of the expected route into the city and the areas around the stadium. Shaheen took Tiger and Villapiano in another SUV, a late-model Hyundai Santa Fe. McHenry and Hadid piled into their familiar Prado with Mohammadi. With mission tasks in hand, the two cars left the safehouse thirty minutes apart, with a schedule to rendezvous back at the house in eight hours for a coordinated debrief.

Joonas Rasmus walked into Devin Thomas's office on the seventh floor and, as offered by Thomas, sat down in one of the two leather-upholstered chairs in front of the desk. Using his computer mouse, Thomas removed the file he was reviewing from his monitor and turned his attention toward Rasmus.

"What can I do for you, Joonas?" he asked.

"Sir, per your request, we've followed up with analysis on the signals intelligence we collected from Beijing. It's clear they're getting intelligence from a variety of sources, one of which appears to be from our side," Rasmus replied.

"Much as we suspected, I'm afraid," responded Thomas. "Do you have any directional analysis that begins to pinpoint a source? Is there anything to take to the Office of the Inspector General?"

"Yes, sir, we do. By analyzing the information known and being acted upon by Beijing, we're able to narrow it down to a couple of different sections based on who in the agency would have access to the compromised data."

"Well, Joonas, don't keep me waiting. What do you have?"

"One section that has had knowledge is Jeanie Clayton Slater's group in the Directorate of Support. As such, I'd recommend the OIG handle the internal investigation exclusively because, as you know, the Office of Security is part of that same directorate—there's an inherent conflict of interest brewing there," Rasmus said.

"Yes, understood," Thomas replied, clearing his throat. It was never easy acknowledging an internal leak at the agency. "You did say one section, Joonas. Do you have others to investigate?"

"Yes, sir. Collett and the China Mission Center are out, as is Tayebeh and the Iran Mission Center. That leaves me and my group, sir," answered Rasmus.

An uneasy silence fell before the two men. After a handful of seconds, Thomas broke the stillness and asked, "You suspect someone from your group?"

Rasmus smiled a humorless smile. "No sir, I don't. But members of my team, me included, had the data that is being acted upon by the Chinese. We wouldn't be thorough and authentic if we didn't include me and my team."

"Yes, Joonas, I respect your professionalism, but you weren't aware of the information that seems to be previously leaked," Thomas countered.

"Doesn't matter, sir. Our team needs to be included in the investigation."

"You do know that once the OIG gets sicced on the case, they're going to latch on like a pit bull to a bone from Sunday's roast, right?" Thomas asked.

"Yes, sir," came the quick reply. "I've nothing to hide, and I'm confident no one on my team does either."

"Alright, but before I add you to the list, Joonas, I need you to be sure. The OIG is one beast, but it doesn't take a stretch of the imagination to see the pending involvement of the NSA and the FBI. Everything—and I mean everything—will be on the table. Nothing will remain hidden; they'll be up your asses with an electron microscope," Thomas warned.

"Understood, sir. I go into this with eyes wide open. The investigation targets should be Clayton Slater and her group; me and my group. Now, before I let you get on with your day, let me give you a quick five-minute debrief on what we know so far about the status of Tiger's mission."

Mid-morning on Friday, Shaheen dropped Tiger off in front of the market on Resalat two blocks south of Amin Boulevard. Dressed in a long, loose fitting black skirt and modest gray blouse, and covered with a lightweight beige long coat, called a *manteau*, and a red, blue, and yellow scarf wrapped around her head and covering her face from below her brown eyes, Tiger fit in among the many Qom residents running errands around town.

She walked into the market and browsed the aisles, doubling back and looking for any signs of a surveillance tail. Confident that she wasn't being followed, at least in the store, she exited and made her way south on Resalat.

Tiger walked along at a casual pace, gazing at the reflections from the windows and mirrors of parked cars to make a mental note of the pedestrians behind her. After two blocks, she turned right, giving a furtive glance over her shoulder to see if anyone from Resalat had also made the right turn.

She continued for a couple of more blocks, passing the Imam Khomeini Education and Research Institute where the pedestrian traffic intensified. Picking up her pace, Tiger knifed through the crowd and made another right turn. Off to her left, she could make out the outlines of the stadium bleachers and its light stanchions.

Cutting left, she walked along 5th Golestan toward the traffic circle, then took another left to 10th Saduqi, where she began to backtrack toward the direction she had begun.

Surveillance detection routes, or SDRs, were time-consuming, Tiger knew, but they were essential tradecraft for covert operatives, and they were taken both going to and returning from any local destination. If Tiger was being followed, it was absolutely critical that she first identify the tail and then, secondly, lose the tail.

Confident she was not being followed, Tiger took a left on Dey 9 Bridge and finally started making her way to her target, a four-story apartment building on the far side of the towering Computer Research Center of Islamic Sciences.

Still conscious of moving casually and blending in, Tiger passed the Center and took a right, walking past the Civil Servants Pension Fund Building to the apartment building next door.

She walked through the open front doors and into the modestly adorned lobby, eschewing the wrought iron "birdcage" elevator for the spiral staircase that circled it. Walking to the top floor, she walked back to the front of the building, to apartment number 401. She bowed her head, tightened the scarf around her head and face, took a deep breath, and knocked on the door.

Hearing a mumble and footsteps behind the door, Tiger braced herself. As the door opened, she took a quick step forward and raised her arms in exasperation, shouting, *"Zahara, bavar nemikony an sheytan cheh kard*!" Zahara, you won't believe what that devil did!

She glanced around quickly, making a note of as much of the apartment as she could see, swiftly looked at the surprised elderly man who had opened the door, then jumped back out of the open doorway.

Tiger bowed her head. Sheepishly, she said, "*Bebakhshid aga, montazar zahara vida bodam.*" My apologies, sir, I was expecting Zahara Vida.

The old man chuckled. "*O yek tabagheh payintar, dar apartaman 301 est.*" She is one floor down, in apartment 301.

Continuing to avoid direct eye contact, Tiger muttered, "*Ozrkhaehi forotenanekye man. Khili motesfam.*" My humble apologies. I am so sorry. No sooner had the words left her mouth, than she turned and scampered back to the stairs.

The man chuckled again, saying "*Eslan dardasari nist,*" and closing his door. No trouble at all.

On the stairs, she keyed her radio and said, "*O dar apartamanesh taneyast.*" He's alone in his apartment.

Ten minutes later, McHenry closed the tailgate of the Prado and helped Hadid lift a rolled carpet onto their shoulders. They followed Mohammadi, who was carrying a large woven bag by two handles in his right hand, into the apartment building and to the staircase.

Mohammadi softly chanted out a song as the men climbed their way to the fourth floor. Once there, they turned left and walked to the corner apartment, number 401, and Mohammadi knocked three times on the wooden door.

After a short time, the door swung open and the old man said, "*Beleh*?" Yes?

Mohammadi leapt forward and pressed his left hand on the man's mouth, at the same time tripping him backwards toward the laminate floor with his left foot. As the two fell to the floor, Hadid and McHenry quickly slipped into the apartment, McHenry closing the door behind him.

With Mohammadi muffling the struggling old man underneath him, McHenry and Hadid placed the rolled carpet on the floor and Hadid moved toward the resident's head. There, Hadid knelt with the man's head cradled between his knees. As Mohammadi slipped his hands off the man's mouth, Hadid instantly stuffed a small rag into it, and used another cloth to fold over it and tied it behind the man's head.

Mohammadi whispered, "*Nah yek kolmeh, hati yek sada, ve to asibi nakhaehi did.*" Not a word, a single sound, and you won't get hurt.

The man's eyes were wide with terror. But he didn't utter a single sound.

Hadid lifted the man's back off the floor and secured his hands behind him with two zip ties. Then, together with McHenry, they lifted him and placed him on a wooden chair, binding each ankle with zip ties to the chair's legs. With the man secured, Mohammadi extracted a pair of headphones from the bag and placed them over the man's ears. Finally, he placed a black cloth bag over his head and helped the other two slide the man into a far corner of the kitchen.

Having secured the apartment and incapacitated its resident, Hadid turned to McHenry and asked, "You good to go, Mac?"

McHenry walked to the windows on the far side of the apartment's living room and closed the curtains. After a quick look around, he replied in a quiet voice, "I've got it from here, Sami. You two can head out."

"Copy that, Mac," Hadid responded as he and Mohammadi moved to the door. "Keep your powder dry and I'll meet you tonight at the pickup point."

"Roger that, Sami," McHenry answered. Until then he would be on his own.

Chapter 17

With the entire day ahead of him, McHenry took his time to set up his sniper's lair. While he didn't anticipate any unexpected visitors, he took one of the chairs from the dining room table and wedged it under the door handle of the front door. It wasn't a completely foolproof lock, but it would give him ample time to respond if someone tried to force themselves into the apartment.

As for the dining room table itself, he adjusted its position slightly relative to one of the windows and cleared it of a couple of piles of papers and correspondence. Then he unrolled the carpet over the table, freeing the SV-98 sniper rifle that had been concealed inside.

Outfitted with an optical sight and a suppressor, the weapon weighed in at slightly over seventeen pounds. McHenry rested the rifle on its center bipod and its heel stock and tended to the suppressor.

The suppressor was rated at twenty-three decibels, but to be optimally effective it required subsonic rounds. McHenry knew his 7N1 sniper rounds would travel over 2,700 feet per second, over twice the speed of sound. As a result, the bullet's supersonic speed would create a powerful sonic boom, a very loud cracking sound, as it traveled down range toward its target. No suppressor could affect that.

The suppressor, however, would reduce the sound of the rifle shot in the apartment, but it would be far from silent. Without the suppressor, the rifle would fire at a sound level of between

165–170 decibels. With the suppressor, it would be about 145 decibels.

While not a drastic difference, McHenry knew that decibel ranges were not a linear scale, and that every ten-decibel increase represented a tenfold increase in sound pressure level. Reducing his rifle's report by twenty-three decibels would represent a very significant decrease in acoustic energy.

Still, the rifle would be loud. Ear damaging loud. There was nothing McHenry could do about that now.

He climbed up on the table to test not only if it would hold the weight of his 220-pound frame, but that the perch, with him laying prone on the tabletop, would afford the proper sight lines out the window to the target zone three blocks away.

With the table and rifle staged in just the right spots to address the cover zone, McHenry tended to the last of his pre-mission chores. He carefully loaded ten rounds into two different box magazines, and after inserting one into the bottom of the rifle, he placed the second on the table to the left of the rifle, where it would be easily in reach should he need it.

He hoped he wouldn't need it. However, plans tended to go a bit sideways in the field, McHenry thought to himself. As a precaution, he put a box of rounds out on the table too, as one could never be too prepared.

His set up complete, McHenry moved a chair to the end of the table and sat. Now, all he could do was wait.

Hadid knelt beside the right rear tire of the Prado, which was jacked up to be about two inches off the ground. Mohammadi walked behind him, rolling the spare tire toward the back of the SUV, which had been parked on the right-side shoulder of southbound Highway 7, the Persian Gulf Freeway.

Tipped by one of his sources at the nuclear enrichment facility, Mohammadi was expecting a black IKCO Soren sedan to come into his view. Based on the Peugeot 405 platform, the Soren was manufactured domestically, and with its relatively inexpensive procurement and maintenance costs, it was a prominent vehicle in the motor pools of both the military and the police.

A popular car in Iran, it was possible for many Soren sedans to be on the highway. However, Mohammadi was on the lookout for a military-registered car, featuring black characters on a plate with a brown background, distinctly different from civilian plates with their black on white lettering.

Mohammadi spotted the target vehicle as it closed on their location at speed, 100 meters away. As he swung the tire into the open back of the SUV, he shouted back to Hadid, "Here they come!"

Hadid dropped the jack and slid it from under the car, leaving it and the tire iron by the side of the road. He then jumped into the passenger seat as Mohammadi jumped behind the steering wheel. As the truck accelerated and moved onto the highway, Hadid pulled out a mobile phone, powered it up, and called Tiger.

When the call connected, it was silent on Tiger's end. Knowing the cue, Hadid said simply, "We're Oscar Mike southbound. Atom's in our sight."

"That's a hard copy," Tiger responded.

Hadid disconnected the call, powered off the phone, and slid it into a jacket pocket. He then picked up his AK-12 from between his feet and laid the rifle on his thighs. Turning to Mohammadi, he said, "I've got eyes on the target. Stay about 150 meters back. We know where they're going."

Mohammadi nodded. He would stay a comfortable distance behind the sedan for the approximately thirty-minute drive into

Qom. He wouldn't close the distance until they approached the target zone.

With the confirmation that Bo was inbound to what she could only assume was the soccer game, Tiger walked into the dining room where Shaheen and Villapiano were whiling away the time playing chess. "Alright, guys," she said, "Three's following the target. We'll get an update on timing in a little bit, but right now, it looks like about thirty minutes. Let's saddle up."

Getting up but still looking at the chessboard, Villapiano moved his knight and took a pawn from Shaheen. "When this is all over, Massoud, it's your move."

"Yes, it will be," Shaheen answered with a grin as he, too, rose from his chair, "and I have you just where I want you." He then started following Tiger out of the house as Villapiano stayed at the table looking at the board and its pieces.

Tiger shouted over her shoulder, "There's nothing you can do about that now, JV."

Before she stepped out of the house, she checked the ammunition magazine of her MP-443 Grach pistol, slid it back into the gun, chambered a round, ensured the safety was on, and slipped it into the right waist pocket of her long, beige skirt. Then she fixed her concealing head scarf tight around her head and neck and walked to Shaheen's choice of vehicles for the mission, a white Hyundai Santa Fe.

Among SUVs in Iran, the Santa Fe was the most popular import model, and white was the most prevalent color. The domestically produced Saipa Atlas and Saipa Shahin models had slightly higher shares of the Iranian market, but the Santa Fe would easily blend in as the team made their escape.

Tiger slid into the back seat on the right side of the SUV. Stopping at the driver's door, Villapiano handed his AK-12 to Shaheen before taking his spot behind the wheel. Shaheen took the front passenger seat, where he positioned Villapiano's AK-12 between his left leg and the truck's center console, within easy reach for Villapiano. He positioned his own gun, an AK-74, between his right leg and his door. He would need easy access to the weapon the moment he exited the SUV at the target zone.

As Villapiano fired up the Santa Fe, Tiger tried her Thales RT-2129 CNR combat net radio in an effort to reach McHenry. The CNR was a secure, software-defined tactical radio developed for the US Army to replace older SINCGARS radios. As new technology, it had a great many advantages. One disadvantage, however, that was shared with the older radios it was replacing was its line-of-sight limitations. The high-end of its range was ten kilometers, but its effective range was limited by obstacles like mountains and, in an urban environment like Qom, buildings.

Having tried in the house without success for the entire day, Tiger hadn't expected to reach McHenry so easily. She had no choice but to sit back and anxiously wait until they got closer to contact him. Luckily, they still had time on their side.

Fifteen minutes later, Hadid called Tiger. Upon the connection being made, he said simply, "Atom is inbound, now southbound on Zaer Boulevard. Ten minutes out."

"Copy that, Three," replied Tiger. "We're on site at staging. Keep visual on Atom."

After disconnecting with Hadid, she keyed her radio, addressing McHenry. "Two, Atom is inbound, ETA ten mikes."

She heard McHenry's prompt reply. "Copy that, One. In position."

Tiger then reached forward into the front seat and placed her two hands on the shoulders of both Villapiano and Shaheen. "Okay, fellas, Bo is on Zaer and inbound. This is where I get out."

Villapiano turned his head, looking over his shoulder, and said, "Okay, boss. Be careful out there. We'll see you on the other side of all the excitement."

Tiger smiled and pulled her head scarf tight. She then opened the door on the passenger side and stepped out into the warm Qom evening and onto the sidewalk of Saheli Street. Leaving the car behind, she walked to the intersection of Dey 9 Bridge and took a right, leisurely walking toward the target zone. Halfway down the block toward Amin Boulevard, she took a seat on a bus stop bench for the Qom Municipality Urban Bus Organization. Sitting on the bench, she kept her gaze toward the north, where she expected to see the target vehicle in just a few minutes. Inconspicuously, she slipped her right hand into her pocket, gripped the handle of her pistol, and disengaged the safety selector with her thumb.

After hearing Tiger's radio call, McHenry had climbed on the table in the fourth-floor apartment and was now peering through the rifle's scope. He spotted Tiger rounding the corner and watched as she took a seat on the bus stop bench.

With Tiger now in position, he tilted the rifle up ever so slightly to look for signs of Villapiano and Shaheen in the Hyundai Santa Fe. Right on cue, he saw the SUV inch up and stop at the end of Saheli Street.

In his earpiece, McHenry heard Hadid, now in radio range, report, "On the ramp. All units go."

Villapiano responded, saying, "Confirm. All units execute."

Through his scope, McHenry saw Villapiano pause at the corner of Dey 9 Bridge, then abruptly turn in front of their target car, the black IKCO Soren. The driver of the Soren hit the brakes hard to avoid contact, and just as he was about at a standstill, Villapiano accelerated forward three car lengths.

With a clear target, McHenry exhaled fully to steady himself and pulled the trigger, sending a round through the apartment's open window and downrange, hitting the Soren's radiator. Quickly he grabbed the bolt handle, moved it backward to eject the spent shell casing, then slid it forward, loading a new cartridge. He fired again and repeated the process one more time.

Three shots downrange, all on target, in two seconds. But they were loud. He knew he was now on the clock. While his specific location was unknown, his general vicinity was clear. He had just a few minutes to make his retreat.

Still looking through his scope, he saw the Soren lurch forward a car length and angle toward the curb before it died. As it did, Villapiano backed the Sante Fe to stop right in front of it, Shaheen stepping out of the passenger's side with his rifle raised.

At the same time, Mohammadi came screeching to a stop in the Prado, stopping in a lane of traffic at the back and just to the left of the Soren. Hadid jumped out of the passenger seat and strode across the front of the stricken vehicle, his AK-74 aimed toward the back seat. Mohammadi leapt from the driver's seat and aimed his rifle at the driver.

McHenry scanned the area through his scope as Hadid made his way to the back door next to the curb and tried to open it. Discovering it was locked, Hadid swung his rifle violently at the window, shattering it with its polymer shoulder stock. He then reached in and opened the door.

Just at that moment, McHenry saw another black Soren arrive at the scene, accelerating as it approached and slamming into the back of the Prado, the SUV lurching forward and to its right, knocking Mohammadi off balance and sending him stumbling backward.

Almost instantly, the bearded man driving the second Soren opened his door and stood halfway out of the car, his left foot on the ground and his left hand holding a semiautomatic pistol. As Mohammadi scrambled to regain balance, he leveled his rifle toward the second car. But it was too late. The driver fired twice and Mohammadi went down.

"Shit," mumbled Henry as he exhaled fully and pulled the trigger of the SV-98 once again, pumping a round into the chest of the driver of the second car and eliminating the threat. As he worked the bolt action of the rifle, he knew that this op had just gone irreversibly off script.

Chapter 18

When the target vehicle had been disabled, Tiger had gotten up off the bus stop bench and started walking slowly to the scene, covertly covering the team's six, its rear, for the duration of the snatch and grab. She had help with McHenry as overwatch in the sniper's lair, but she kept a keen eye to make sure no bystanders could get in the way.

Jesus, those shots had been loud, she thought as she registered the second Soren speeding onto the scene and crashing into the Prado. As she pulled her pistol out of the pocket of her skirt, she saw the driver of the second car get part of the way out of the car and shoot at Mohammadi. Just as she was about to target the driver, she heard McHenry's shot that put the target down.

At that moment, one of the two passengers in the back seat got out on the right side of the car, semiautomatic pistol drawn, and started exchanging shots with Shaheen. Still walking, Tiger raised her right hand, sighted her target, and from no more than ten meters away, shot the man twice in the back.

The man dropped his pistol and fell into his open door, twisting as he bounced off it and landed in the street on his back. As Tiger walked up, she could see that he was a white man, and she pumped a third shot into his head to ensure he wasn't getting back into the fight.

Looking into the back seat, she saw another white man cowering in fear, his hands lifted in surrender. It was Bo Jianguo's

Russian colleague, the man working alongside him at the Fordow facility.

The man she had just downed must have been the Russian's translator. But he was armed, she thought. More like a bodyguard than a translator.

Knowing she didn't have time to get to the bottom of the situation, she pointed her pistol at the Russian and fired twice, shooting him in both thighs. As the man screamed in pain, she closed the passenger side door, bent down to pick up the dead man's pistol, and started to make her way to the target car of Bo's.

It was then that she saw Shaheen writhing on the ground, clutching at an abdominal wound on his right side.

"Well, this has turned into a real shit show," she mumbled as she made her way forward.

McHenry scanned the entire target zone and the areas surrounding it, both to the sides and to either end. Southbound on Dey 9 Bridge was blocked due to their handiwork. A delivery truck had stopped on the right lane northbound when the shooting started. To keep the driver out of sight and out of the fight, McHenry had sent a round into the window of his driver's side door.

Surveying the scene, he saw that both Mohammadi and Shaheen were down. Villapiano was tending to Shaheen. No amount of aid, McHenry saw through his scope, was going to benefit Mohammadi, who was lying in the street, a crimson pool of blood swelling around his head. The young man was surely dead.

Having shot the driver of the target vehicle, Hadid was now training his rifle back toward the highway, taking over covering the rear for Tiger, who was now leaning into the backseat of the first Soren. At the back of the scene, McHenry saw the second, unexpected car, with two men down, one on each side.

Accessing the situation, McHenry recognized that the only two targets that remained were being handled by Tiger in the target vehicle. It was about time for him to exit the apartment.

Finding the back door of the Soren unlocked, Tiger opened the door and leaned it. Recognizing Bo as the man closest to her, she confirmed, asking, "Are you Bo Jianguo?"

The man, holding his empty hands up as high as he could, nervously nodded his head.

Tiger looked over to the second man, who was also holding his hands up. "I'm sorry about this," she said. She then leveled her pistol and shot him in both thighs. She took care to ensure she missed the femoral artery of the first leg she shot, the far leg. He had, of course, jumped in pain after the first shot, but she was fairly certain she had missed the artery on the second leg as well.

"He won't be happy," she said to Bo as she grabbed his shirt collar behind his neck with her left hand and started to pull him out of the car, "but he'll be okay."

Dragging Bo alongside her, she glanced toward Hadid on the other side of the car to her left and said, "After we're in motion, go get Mac."

Taking a moment to look Tiger directly in the eye, Hadid nodded in both agreement and acceptance. Then, directing his vision northbound to their rear, he began to slide back around the stricken Soren and make his way to the Prado.

As Tiger approached the Santa Fe, Villapiano, with his rifle slung over his shoulder and on his back, picked up Shaheen from under his armpits and dragged him to the SUV. Shaheen, applying pressure with both hands to his wound, grimaced in pain as he was shoved into the front seat. Villapiano shut the door, then turned his attention to Tiger and Bo.

"Hands behind your back, Bo," he ordered.

Still in shock over the events that had happened in well less than a minute, Bo did as he was told. Villapiano then zip tied his wrists and, holding his hand over Bo's head to prevent it hitting the roof, slid him into the backseat of the Santa Fe.

As Villapiano moved to get to the driver's seat, Tiger pushed her way into the back seat, pressing the barrel of her pistol into Bo's ribs to gain his full attention and cooperation. As she grabbed the door to close it, she shouted to Villapiano, "Get us out of here, JV!"

McHenry continued to surveil the target zone through the scope mounted on the SV-98. After Tiger closed her door, he watched as Villapiano got into the Santa Fe and began to drive off, southbound on Dey 9 Bridge.

His final part of business was covering Hadid, who had made a quick assessment of his now damaged Prado. Just before Hadid climbed behind the steering wheel, he stood straight and looked directly toward McHenry's sniper nest, knowing his teammate would be covering his escape.

Hadid very deliberately raised the index finger of his left hand and held it steady for a two count. Then, he used the thumb of the same hand to slowly draw a line across his neck, from right to left, signifying a slit throat. Then, he held up two fingers and held them steady for another two counts.

His message sent, Hadid hopped into the damaged Prado and limped away from the scene, like Tiger, initially heading southbound.

McHenry slid off the table, recognizing that Hadid had just scrubbed the first rendezvous spot and would meet up with him at the agreed upon second site.

McHenry then worked swiftly. He raced into the kitchen and took the hood and headphones off the old man's head, then spun him around in his chair, where he could now see the rest of his apartment. He saw the old man's eyes wide in terror.

Those eyes grew even wider as McHenry pulled a large chef's knife off the kitchen counter and held it in front of the man's face. He reached behind the old man and cut the zip tie around his left wrist, freeing that single hand. McHenry then silently held a raised index finger directly in front of the man's face, about three inches from the bridge of his nose.

Having fully captured the man's attention, McHenry walked across the room and stuck the chef's knife into a windowsill. Leaving the SV-98 where it lay on the table, McHenry picked up his prepared kilim bag, a woolen satchel woven with a variety of colored fabrics, nodded at the old man, and walked to the apartment's door.

Opening the door a crack, McHenry saw the hallway was empty. He knew his shots had made a tremendous racket, but no one was here yet. Good news. He also knew the old man was thirty minutes to an hour from freeing himself. Also good news.

Using his free hand to drape his *keffiyeh* over his head and around his mouth and neck, McHenry walked into the hallway and closed the door behind him. Now the hard part came, he knew. Time to get the team—and Bo—out of Iran.

Chapter 19

Tiger turned to Bo and said, "Stay put. You're going to be alright. We're not here to hurt you. Understand?"

Bo nodded, then asked hesitantly, "Why are you doing this?"

"We'll get to that later," she answered. "Right now, I've got to tend to other matters."

With that she glanced toward the front seat, catching Villapiano's eyes in the rear-view mirror. "JV, what's the situation up there?"

Villapiano glanced to his right, accessing the condition of Shaheen, who was slouched in his seat, gritting his teeth and maintaining compression to his wound. "Single gunshot to the upper right abdomen. No exit wound."

"Shit," replied Tiger. "Think it hit the liver?"

"It's sure bleeding like it did."

Tiger knew the liver was a highly vascular organ, and that even a superficial wound could result in significant hemorrhage. However, as an abdominal wound, it was considered a non-compressible body area where the wound shouldn't be packed but rather required an external pressure dressing. Working quickly, she turned around and reached into the SUV's cargo area and pulled a pack toward her. Flipping it over, she released an IFAK, an individual first aid kit, that each of the team had readily accessible on their packs.

With Villapiano driving a diagonal path southeast across the city, Tiger rifled through the kit to withdraw a package of Quik-Clot Combat Gauze. Having pulled one of the two available packages out of the kit, Tiger leaned over the front seat and put her right hand on Shaheen's right shoulder.

"Massoud, I need you to lift your shirt," Tiger directed. "Can you do that for me?"

Groaning, Shaheen moved his bloodied hands from his wound and lifted his shirt above it. Tiger saw that blood was still flowing freely.

Using her teeth, she ripped open the olive drab packaging and passed the wad of gauze to Shaheen. "Listen up, Massoud," she said. "This is QuikClot, which will help stop the bleeding. Importantly, though, you can't pack it into this wound. Just apply pressure. The QuikClot won't sting, but the pressure on the wound is gonna hurt like hell. Think you can do that?"

Shaheen nodded his head as he grabbed the gauze. Placing it over the wound, he then bit his lip and firmly pressed down with both hands. He moaned as pain racked his entire body.

Through gritted teeth, he asked, "What about the boy?"

"I'm sorry, Massoud," Tiger answered. "He didn't make it."

Shaheen accepted the news stoically, dipping his head and trying to focus on his breathing while he continued to tend to his wound.

An operator with extensive experience behind enemy lines, McHenry was as anxious as a first timer as he stepped out of the apartment building and took a right, walking away from the building traffic on Dey 9 Bridge.

The original plan had been for Hadid to pick him up at the end of the block and they would then cover the rear for Tiger's escape from the city with Bo. That initial plan had been scuttled due to the damage suffered by the Prado when the second Soren crashed onto the scene.

Now McHenry would meet up with Hadid at the alternate pick-up spot. That is if both he and Hadid made it there without incident.

Throughout a career in the US Army and his time as an operative with Tiger, McHenry knew he had a well-practiced history of knowing when to react and when to respond. It was more than just semantics.

Many times in his career, he had been put into tense situations, like firefights with enemy combatants, that required immediate action. You put your trust in your training and you reacted.

Far more often though, he had depended on measured responses, thinking through situations and contingencies, then choosing the best course of action. Responding effectively meant rational, considered thought.

When missions went sideways, like this one had, it was a time for purposeful, intentional response. That, above all, required a clear head.

Walking away from the commotion, McHenry used his left hand to adjust his *keffiyeh*, trying to cover as much of his lower face as he could. Parts of his beard were visible over the top of the head scarf, which was a bit of a plus in his effort to blend into the city's population. He also wasn't worried too much about his blue-gray eyes, as while brown eyes were predominant in Iran, a significant portion of the population had lighter eyes due to the country's diverse ethnic groups, which included Persians, Azeris, and Kurds.

What worried McHenry most was his frame. The average Iranian male was about five-foot-nine-inches tall. He stood a good five inches taller, and on top of that, probably thirty or forty pounds heavier than the typical man in the country. So, as he carried his kilim bag that contained his AK-12 and other supplies, he allowed himself to slouch a little.

Taking a right onto Resalat, he slid his left hand into the pocket of his baggy trousers, finding comfort in the grip of his MP-443 Grach pistol. He didn't want to have to use it, but he felt a whole lot better knowing it was there. The evening sun was still in the sky, but it was low enough to cast long shadows throughout the city. As he had frequently during his career, McHenry eagerly anticipated the additional cover of full darkness.

Samir Hadid drove the battered Prado southbound on Dey 9 Bridge, distancing himself from the scene further up the road as quickly as he could without drawing undue attention. He knew the vehicle was undoubtedly identified at the scene and the car, with him included, would soon be the subject of an intense search. He knew he had minutes to ditch the car and create some distance between him and it.

To make matters worse, the SUV was damaged. The rear end was buckled, as was the hood, and the radiator seemed to have been damaged as steam was beginning to rise from the front of the vehicle.

Hadid navigated the traffic circle that surrounded Sepah Square and took a right onto Shahid Akhlaghi. A half mile later, just six blocks away from the stadium, he took advantage of a break in traffic and turned left onto Shahid Sadooqi Boulevard. Nervously glancing in his mirrors as he heard the wail of emergency response sirens converging on the scene behind him, he looked to get off onto lesser traveled streets.

In four blocks, he found his opportunity, just one block north of the busy Attaran Boulevard. With the engine warning light on his dash now illuminated due to the overheating engine, Hadid turned into a mixed-use neighborhood of street corner markets and residential housing. He crept his way deep into the neighborhood, taking a circuitous route while looking for a quiet place to abandon his vehicle.

Finally, in a shady area on 17th Mofatteh, he pulled to the curb and turned off the sputtering engine. Accessing the cargo area, he grabbed his kilim bag, walked to the front passenger door, and, while looking around to ensure there were no onlookers, discreetly slid his AK-12 into the satchel. He zipped the bag shut and started walking east.

One task completed, Hadid set off on his next, rendezvousing with McHenry. He figured he would need to make the trek to the prearranged spot on foot, as he didn't want to risk stealing a car before dark. But he kept his eyes open in case an opportunity too good to pass up presented itself.

"What do you want from me?" demanded Bo as he leaned to look out the windshield as Villapiano continued to serpentine his way through Qom, all the while retreating away from the interdiction scene south, toward Jamkarān. "I'm not a soldier. I'm not a spy."

"Oh, I know you're not a spy, Bo Jianguo" answered Tiger. "I don't know much about you, other than you were born and raised in Guangzhou and studied nuclear engineering first at Tsinghua University, then at the University of Michigan. But I do know what you aren't, and that's a spy."

"You're American. Are you a spy?"

"I'm much more of an agent than a spy, wouldn't you agree JV?"

Villapiano shook his head as he fought off a grin. "Whatever you say, boss."

"Agent, spy, they feel the same from my seat," said Bo. "What do you want from me?"

Twisting in her seat to face him, Tiger said, "Look at me, Bo."

When Bo turned his head to look at her rather than the road, she continued. "My boss wants to speak with you."

"He could have just called!" he said, his voice rising. "You shot my friend!"

"I'm sorry about that, I really am," she said. "I had to make sure he didn't interfere like that second car did. But I let him off easy. I had to kill one of those other guys."

"You killed the Russians?" Bo asked in alarm.

"I wasn't certain of them being Russians," Tiger explained, "But I did put down the guy who popped out of the backseat shooting at my friends."

"That must have been Lavrenty, the translator for my colleague, Dariy Veniamin," Bo replied. "What did you do to Veniamin?"

"Well, first of all," Tiger responded, "That shooter seemed more like a bodyguard than a translator, at least from what I saw. The second guy got shot in the legs for his trouble. I made sure he wasn't going to get out of the car and become a further pain in my ass."

"I don't understand any of this!" he said in a raised voice.

"I don't expect you to right now," Tiger replied. "And while it might not feel that way at the moment, you're safe. We're not going to harm you. I'll explain more in a bit, but right now I have to tend to something."

Tiger leaned between the front seats to check on Shaheen, offering another wad of QuikClot gauze to replace the soaked bundle in his hands. "Massoud, you want us to get you to a hospital? Get you patched up?"

Slouched in his seat, Shaheen turned to his left and took the gauze from Tiger. After tossing the first application to the floor between his feet, he pressed the fresh gauze to his wound. He then turned back to Tiger.

"Ah, my friend, it's kind of you to ask, but we both know that's not an option. First, too dangerous for you. Secondly, I wouldn't make it through the night at the hospital. It wouldn't be thirty minutes until Quds Force or MOIS was there to torture me for information. No, Tiger, for me to live, I need to get all of us out of Iran as quickly as possible."

"Okay, Massoud, you'll resume your tour guide duties for us," Tiger said. "Give me a minute and I'll get you something for the pain." As she leaned back to rummage through the first aid kit to find a syringe of ketamine to apply intermuscularly, she thought to herself that she and the team had gotten themselves into another fine mess. Tonight and tomorrow would most assuredly not go by quickly and, most probably, uneventfully.

Chapter 20

Colonel Jahan had just sat down at the table in the small, well-appointed house he shared with his wife, Azadeh, when his mobile phone rang. Glancing at the screen, he was tempted to ignore it, as Azadeh had set the table with one of his favorite dishes, *ghormeh sabzi*, a slow-simmered stew of herbs, beans, and meat that she served with an aromatic, fluffy rice called *chelow*. Seeing it was Major Afsoon, he reluctantly picked up.

"*Alo*? *Salam*," Jahan said as the call connected.

"Colonel, my apologies for interrupting your evening," Afsoon reported, "but we have a developing situation in Qom that you should know about."

"Qom?" asked Jahan curiously. "What do you have, Afsoon?"

"There was a shooting downtown. Four dead at the scene, and two injured."

"How does that impact us here in the east?" asked Jahan.

"The incident involved two cars carrying personnel from the Shahid Ali Mohammadi Nuclear Facility in Fordow. One of the dead is a Russian national working at the facility. Most importantly, there appears to have also been an abduction of a Chinese engineer, a man by the name of Bo."

Jahan's attention immediately perked with interest. "Chinese? This can't be a coincidence considering the intel we received earlier, right Major?"

"No, sir," replied the subordinate officer. "We've been in this profession too long to believe in coincidences. What do you want to do?"

Jahan quickly thought through multiple scenarios in his mind. Qom was certainly well out of his geographic jurisdiction. But he had received intel that was now actionable, and it was an opportunity to take the lead in an investigation and any resulting mission that could eventually pave his way into the Quds Force. It was perhaps a bit risky, a step outside of his command, but he knew what he wanted.

"Get a helo ready at the airport, Major, departing immediately," he ordered. "We're going to Qom and we're going to be the first to get to the bottom of this."

It was never easy being behind enemy lines, McHenry knew, but it was even more unsettling to do so alone. A long-time member of the US military, he had spent the bulk of his adult life ensconced in a culture of camaraderie where his primary purpose was to protect the well-being of the man, woman, brother, sister to either side of him. With that obligation, of course, came the trust and reassurance that those next to him had his well-being top of mind as well.

Now, however, he was alone in a foreign land whose people spoke a language he did not understand. Moreover, he had committed what surely would be seen as crimes against the state. But while being on his own produced more than a bit of anxiety, it was, McHenry thought, perhaps the best way to make his way from the snatch and grab location.

Aside from the initial early responders to the scene, sharpened investigators wouldn't descend on the site and begin their tasks for another thirty minutes, at the earliest. They would quickly ascertain that this was a highly organized job that had enlisted a team of operatives. Their initial scope would entail looking for multiple suspects, most likely together.

That plays into my advantage, McHenry thought to himself.

He continued his walk at a casual pace, using the reflective surfaces of car and storefront windows to catch a glimpse behind him, on the lookout for anyone who might be tailing him. As bad as a tail would be for him, it would be worse if he brought one to his rendezvous with Hadid.

To make detection of any surveillance easier, McHenry made frequent turns, never backtracking his route completely, but causing enough of an inefficient variation of course to make anyone who was following the twisting route an identifiable threat.

Walking south on Jomhoori Eslami Boulevard, he turned left once again at the Talkh Cafe and walked in an easterly direction toward Resalat. He didn't have a map, but from the detailed mission planning he did have a general understanding of the layout of the city, rooted in a familiarity with major thoroughfares. However, he didn't want to spend more time on those big, heavily trafficked streets than necessary. With that in mind, he meandered in the general direction he needed to go, bouncing along in between the main thoroughfares he had painstakingly memorized at the safehouse.

Speed was important, as he couldn't leave Hadid out in the cold forever. However, McHenry knew, speed came secondary to not raising any unnecessary attention. Sticking to the long shadows of the late evening, he continued his prolonged walk.

Hadid whistled as he walked in the relatively crisp air, his bag looped over his right shoulder and laying across his back, his hands stuffed in the pockets of his light jacket, his right clasping the grip of his MP-443 Grach pistol.

He felt comfortable fitting in with the citizenry of Qom, what with his Lebanese heritage making him appear, visually at least, to be native. Unfortunately, he thought, his understanding of Arabic wasn't much help in a country that primarily spoke Farsi.

Still, he felt comfortable blending in, but worry began to grow as the pedestrians on the sidewalks grew fewer in number as the sky drew darker. He knew he didn't stick out in a crowd. But, without a crowd, he was considerably more noticeable.

Hadid's real worry was the lack of confirmation that McHenry had received communication that the backup exfiltration rendezvous site was now in play. He had given a signal to Mac, but being blocks away meant he couldn't see if McHenry was in location and had sighted the signal. All he could do was assume the message had been received. But he also knew the well-versed saying often attributed to Oscar Wilde about what happens when you assume: you "make an ass out of you and me."

Eager to collect his teammate, Hadid continued walking purposefully down Ferdowsi Boulevard, aiming to skirt south of Koodak Park and then turn north toward the Imamzadeh Ali Ebne Jafar Shrine. In this mission suddenly fraught with unwelcomed danger, his destination, ironically enough, he thought, was the second national cemetery of Iran.

Zhau Xiang was roused out of a deep slumber by the incessant ring of his mobile phone. As had been his routine for several years now, he had enjoyed a couple of nightcaps before going to bed, draining three goblets of *baijiu*, a strong, colorless, sorghum-based spirit with a deep, time-honored history in Chinese culture.

Fumbling with his eye shade, he missed answering the call before it went to voicemail, all the more lifting his level of frustration and anger. Then, with his phone in his hand, it rang again. Zhau raged internally as he saw Liu's name on the caller identification.

"Liu, what's the meaning of this interruption at this hour?" Zhau huffed.

"Sir, my apologies for the late hour of this call," Liu replied calmly, "but circumstances require that I notify you of a situation developing in Iran."

The mention of Iran grabbed Zhau's immediate and full attention. "What is it, Liu?"

"Information has come in simultaneously to both the Ministry of State Security and the Ministry of Foreign Affairs, and with our open inquiries over the past weeks, it has escalated to my attention. A short while ago, one of our citizens, a nuclear engineer called Bo Jianguo, was abducted in Qom. Based on our recent programs together, it necessitated I notify you as soon as possible."

"What's being done so far?" asked Zhau.

"The MSS has two units of personnel in Tehran on the move to Qom. One unit is official and will be liaising with the Iranian authorities. The other unit will be working covertly to remedy this situation as quickly as possible."

"Previous intel signals the kidnapping of foreign nationals for ransom is a significant risk in Iran," Zhau added. "Any data that suggests that's the case here?"

"No, sir," Liu responded, "there's no evidence that this is a K and R, although it perhaps might be a bit too early to tell. My working theory is that this abduction is the work of the American agent, Swanson."

Gritting his teeth in anger, Zhau grunted, "I think your theory is correct. Meet me in my office first thing in the morning."

Tiger Swanson stood at the digital keypad that provided access to a small warehouse behind a boot repair shop in a commercial district in the far south of Qom, near Baghiatolah Mosque. With the mission taking an unexpected turn, she had guided Villapiano to a safehouse that not even Shaheen had known about.

While Tiger knew many languages, she had far from an eidetic memory. So, to help with number sequences, she used jersey numbers from her most favorite ice hockey players. "Leetch, Ovechkin, Orr, Howe, Leetch, MacInnis," she recited under her breath as she pushed 2-8-4-9-2-3 on the keypad.

As the garage door groaned into motion, she stepped to the side and allowed Villapiano to drive Santa Fe into the shelter, parking it directly behind a relatively new Khodro H30 Cross, the Iranian-assembled version of the Chinese Dongfeng H30 Cross crossover SUV. When the Santa Fe came to a stop, Tiger repeated the number sequence to close the door.

With a single bulb from the garage door opener providing the only light, Tiger opened the door next to Bo while Villapiano exited and walked around the front of the car to get to Shaheen. Just then, the back door swung open, revealing a middle-aged man holding a Zastava M70 pistol, a small, compact semiautomatic pistol generally chambered for the 7.65mm Browning centerfire cartridge.

With the entire team frozen in place, Tiger raised her hands, palms facing forward, and said calmly, "Hassan, *ma mosafrani az langli npastim keh bah kamak shma niaz darim.*" Hassan, we are travelers from Langley who need your assistance.

The man raised his pistol higher and sighted Tiger. As Villapiano slowly moved his right hand behind his back to get to his MP-443 Grach, Tiger said firmly, "Relax, JV." Then, directed to the man, she said the code phrase, "*Gham ghabrestannpehei zyadi dard.*" Qom has many cemeteries.

Upon hearing the phrase, the man engaged the safety lever on the Zastava and slid it into the waistband of his pants, completing the phrase with the confirming portion, "*In shehar sheedaye zyadi ra bah khod dideh est.*" The city has seen a great many martyrs.

Tiger reached into the Santa Fe and grabbed Bo by the collar, lifting him out of the SUV. Then, reverting to English, she said, "Hassan, it wasn't the plan to get you involved and I know we're a surprise to you, but we need your help real quick then we'll get out of here. First things first, do you have a first aid kit?"

"Of course," he replied as he waved his unexpected visitors toward the door in a sign of welcome. "Unfortunately, as you obviously know my name, I'm afraid I'm at a disadvantage in not knowing yours."

"Call me Tiger, and my friend over there is James. Our friend who needs help is Massoud."

Hassan Ghorbani was a long-time agency asset established in Iran, the second generation of his family to assist in clandestine intelligence gathering and covert operations in Iran. And while he hadn't known of the operation, it wasn't a surprise to him. Certainly, he thought and knew, *I don't know everything that happens in Qom.*

He did, however, know that he could help. That's the reason he and his extended family were so well rewarded. Dutifully, he led Tiger and the team into the back of his boot repair shop and then directly through a door to a staircase that rose to his upstairs apartment. Through another door into the apartment,

Ghorbani motioned with his head to a sofa and said, "Tiger, lay out that blanket on the sofa and I'll get my kit."

Once Tiger stretched the multicolored, striped throw blanket over the cloth upholstery of the sofa, JV gently laid down Shaheen, positioning his wounded right side next to the sofa's edge. By the time Shaheen was placed, Ghorbani was back carrying a medium-sized sports satchel.

Kneeling next to Shaheen, Tiger took the bag, unzipped the dual zippers that secured the bag's top panel, and quickly surveyed the kit's contents. "Perfect," she said more to herself than anyone else. Then, turning to Bo, she said, "Sit your ass on the floor, next to the wall. And unless you have advice on trauma care, I don't want to hear a squeak from you." She lowered her chin, raised her eyebrows, and glared out the top of her eyes at Bo. "Understood."

Silently, Bo slid his back down the wall and seated himself on the floor.

"Okay, JV," Tiger resumed. "Get an IV line started on Massoud and properly dress that wound. I need to speak with Hassan here about a car swap."

Chapter 21

McHenry strode purposefully toward the Qom Martyrs Cemetery, officially known as Golzar Shahada Ali Ibn Jafar. The largest cemetery in Qom province, it was the final resting place of over 3,000 martyrs belonging to the Iran-Iraq war, as well as martyrs of the Iranian revolution and victims of the 2015 stampede that occurred during the annual Hajj pilgrimage in Mina, Mecca, Saudi Arabia.

With the late evening hour, the cemetery was closed, but McHenry wasn't there to pay his respects at graves and mausoleums. Outside of the well-lit gates, he walked quietly on the reflective marble tiles, keeping to the edge of the courtyard-like entrance. As he walked, he noticed Hadid sitting alone on a blue metal bench across the open space.

The two men made quick eye contact, then resumed their activities, McHenry on a seemingly solemn trek of remembrance and respect, Hadid a visitor reading a pamphlet about the cemetery. For over an hour the two had been working diligently to make sure they themselves weren't being surveilled. Now, they would check to see if their teammate had missed or been unable to shake a tail.

McHenry made his way around the right side and closed end of the U-shaped courtyard, pausing occasionally and bowing his head in apparent prayer. All the while, he kept his eyes moving, looking for anyone lurking in the shadows or otherwise suspicious. With the exception of two clerics leaving the cemetery, he saw no one.

While McHenry performed his tasks, Hadid positioned his eyes to cover the path McHenry had taken and ensure no one was following. Moments later, as McHenry walked along the wall just behind the bench where he was seated, he heard a soft bird-alike whistle. He then heard McHenry's footsteps trail off to his right.

After a deliberate quiet count to thirty, Hadid stood up, grabbed his bag, and walked to the entrance of the courtyard. There he saw McHenry standing, looking at traffic passing by on Enqelab Street. Stopping next to McHenry, he said softly, "You're clean, Mac, no tails. Oh, and nice to see you."

Still looking straight ahead, McHenry replied, "Nice to see you too, Sami. Now, how 'bout we get the hell out of Iran?"

Colonel Jahan sat in the backmost bench seat of the Russian-built Mil Mi-17 helicopter as it bounced through the air on the fast track to Qom. Needing to cover the nearly 750 kilometer as-the-crow-flies distance as quickly as possible, Jahan had ordered the two pilots to push the aircraft to its maximum-level flight speed of 250 kilometers an hour. He was now paying for that decision as the helo buffeted against the winds in an exaggerated manner because of its speed.

Knowing the flight would be turbulent—after all, what helo flight wasn't?—Jahan had positioned Major Afsoon across from him. If one was going to suffer more by moving backwards through the air, it wasn't going to be him.

Both men wore headsets, as the interior of a Mil Mi-17 at full song produced in-cabin noise levels of over 100 decibels. The headsets were needed for hearing protection, and they were absolutely necessary to facilitate any conversation inside the cabin.

Afsoon had spent nearly the entire flight thus far in conversation with ground personnel, gaining as much information as he could and feverishly jotting down notes in a hardbound journal resting on his thighs. After disconnecting to one of his ground sources, he toggled over to the intracabin line and provided an update.

"Colonel, the situation in Qom has advanced considerably in the last hour. What started as an investigation of the police has now gained the very active participation of the IRGC, including our group at Thar-Allah."

Jahan inhaled deeply through pursed lips and stroked his chin in thought. The news wasn't a surprise. The Police Command of the Islamic Republic of Iran, known as both FARAJA and NAJA, was led by a Chief Commander, but ultimately fell under the direct control of the supreme leader. Likewise, the IRGC also answered to the supreme leader, and it handled broader internal security issues. Involving the elite forces from the Thar-Allah Headquarters in Tehran signaled that the investigation was a top priority, not only with respect to national security, but politically as well.

He had jumped into this course of action primarily to eventually play a political card relative to his own career advancement. Now, his hand was being forced.

If he held onto actionable intelligence without sharing and the mission failed, if he was discovered, it would be the end of his career. It wouldn't be a far stretch for his actions to be considered a treasonous crime against the state and lead to his execution.

However, handing over the data to his IRGC colleagues already on the ground would likely push him out of the investigation entirely. Just another interminable delay in directing his career to where he wanted.

What to do?

This far into it, he decided there was only one possible course of action. He would try to straddle the line and play the middle against both ends, all the while pushing a good amount of accountability up the chain of command.

"Major Afsoon, I believe we are best positioned to leverage our intel and drive to a successful conclusion. However, as the intel is actionable across all current operations, we need to make sure command is updated. Notify command that we are currently en route and give them a broad overview of the Chinese belief that the covert insertion came from the east."

"Yes sir, Colonel," Afsoon snapped in reply.

"And one more thing, Major. You're telling them, not asking. Understood?"

Tiger sat across from Ghorbani at a small table in the corner kitchen overlooking the street. Thin curtains covered the window, but the powerful streetlamp still provided a lot of light. Feeling secure, at least for the moment, Tiger took a deep, relaxed breath.

The adrenaline-fueled past hour had temporarily waned, and she felt the foggy edge of exhaustion looking to settle in. She knew, however, that now was not the time. Whether Shaheen got stabilized or not, they needed to move, and they needed to do so much sooner than later.

Tiger took another long, deep breath, clearing her mind to focus on her task at hand. Prioritizing, she said, "Hassan, we need a clean vehicle. Can you help?"

"My car is clean," he replied, "but presents a bigger problem, at least for me. You take my car and it likely burns me."

"What if we take your car, but switch it out for different transpo later?"

"What, you're going to take the train? An airplane?" he asked sarcastically. "Wherever you dump my car, it's going to get tracked back here, and the questions coming my way will be … intensive."

"What ideas do you have to make some distance from Qom and keep your cover secure?" Tiger asked.

"Surely you had an exfil plan other than this?" Ghorbani asked as he swept his arms, palms up, to his sides, offering his home as consideration.

"We lost a young man in the op," Tiger countered, "and if he's traceable back to Massoud, the man bleeding out on your sofa over there, which he very likely could be, then everything associated with the two of them is now burned. I don't like the odds. Not interested in playing them."

Ghorbani looked down at the table and thought for a moment. After a short pause, he looked up at Tiger and said, "I must drive you. Once we're on the move, we either bring in some of my, uh, associates in employment with your organization, or we take advantage of any opportunities to procure you alternative means of transportation."

"When can we leave?"

"As soon as your man is ready," he responded, nodding his head in the direction of the living room. "You tend to him and I'll get your gear sorted in my car. Hurry. We want to beat any roadblocks that might get put up."

Devin Thomas exited the elevator as it opened on the seventh floor, the executive level at the agency's Langley, Virginia headquarters. Usually a man who brought food with him to the office, today he had felt the need to get away from his desk for a moment, something he hadn't been able to do the entire day.

So, despite having brought a selection of meats, cheeses, bread, and fruit from home, he had taken advantage of a rare opening in his schedule to go to the on-campus Starbucks, known as "Store Number 1." It was a unique cafe among the tens of thousands of Starbucks locations around the world, one where baristas went through extensive background checks, and where they didn't ask for names to go with orders out of discretion. The percentage of the store's clientele that were covert agents was high.

As Thomas walked down the hall toward his office, he saw Rasmus waiting outside of his door, engaged in small talk with Thomas's assistant. As he walked up to him, he extended his free hand and gestured for Rasmus to enter the office first, saying, "What have you got, Joonas."

Rasmus stopped in the middle of the room and paused while Thomas gently shut his door. Once it was closed, he began his report.

"Sir, the Iranian op is live, having gone off as scheduled. However, it's not going completely to plan."

"Shit," Thomas growled. "When does it ever, Joonas? Cut to the quick. How bad is it?"

"Don't really know at this time, sir. We're gathering intel from the tremendous uptick in communications between Iranian authorities. What we know was there was an incident, a brief firefight. Multiple casualties, including fatalities."

"Any of them ours?"

"It doesn't appear so, sir. Our team, the entire team, appears to be in the wind, along with, apparently, the Chinese asset. Of the two Chinese nationals, one is being actively looked for by the Iranians."

"And Tiger is comms silent?"

"As expected, yes sir."

Thomas thought for a moment and then shook his head as he sat behind his desk. "Well, certainly not ideal, but then again, we're sort of used to that. I've got a lot of trust in that group, but right now our options for support are limited. We've got to let this play out a bit, right?"

"I believe so, sir," Rasmus said. "We're prepared at the primary and secondary exfil points at the border. When they get close, we can help."

"Excellent, Joonas. As we discussed, keep those exfil options top secret; you and me only. But fly up a flag in the Directorate of Support for a bogus exfil at the spot of insertion a few days ago. Park a couple of trucks on the safe side of the border and warn our guys on the ground there might be some unwanted attention coming their way."

"Copy that, sir. I'm on it."

Chapter 22

McHenry and Hadid lurked in the shadows of one of the secondary outbuildings on the sprawling Nekuei Hedayati Forqani Hospital campus. Located off Shaid Rouhani Boulevard where Taleqani Street turned into Del Azadr Boulevard, the hospital was a teaching hospital associated with Qom University of Medical Sciences. Significantly for the two men, it was a major medical center comprising multiple interconnected structures to house its various departments. Even more importantly, the hospital had people coming and going at all hours of the day and night.

While they had walked through the Iranian night, McHenry and Hadid had a long conversation about resolving their most immediate problem, that being remedying their current lack of transportation.

They knew they had to steal a vehicle. Importantly, though, their discussion led to the determination it would need to be a theft that wasn't discovered and reported for hours, preferably a day or two. That criteria seemed completely founded on chance for any car or truck they would take off the street, and neither man was eager to continue their game, along with its potentially lethal consequences, with the outcome dependent on nothing but chance.

What they needed was a theft that would go unnoticed, and thereby unreported, until they were safely out of the country. Together, they had decided they would need to conduct an old-fashioned carjacking, taking the driver with them, not so much as a hostage, but rather as insurance against the theft being reported.

It was decided that it had to be a young man whom they would victimize. In Iran's patriarchal social system, a missing woman would be noticed almost immediately, triggering the very alerts McHenry and Hadid wanted to avoid. Thus, they were hunting lone men returning to their vehicles from one of the hospital buildings.

They were at the hospital purely out of happenstance, as it was the first best place they had come across since leaving the cemetery. In ten minutes of waiting, they had passed on both a single woman and two men walking together. With each elapsing second, their tension ramped inexorably upward.

The men faced each other, visually covering doors on each end of a multistory building they had chosen simply because it had more windows illuminated than other buildings. Looking over McHenry's shoulder, Hadid saw a door open and a man wearing green scrubs and a white lab coat exit. Hadid lifted his head in a nod and said softly, "I got a promising target behind you, Mac."

"Wanna follow him, Sami? Your call."

"Been slim pickings so far, Mac, so let's see where he's going."

With that, Hadid picked up his bag and took a step forward, with McHenry picking up his bag and pivoting alongside. McHenry then put his arm around Hadid's shoulders and leaned his head in as if in quiet conversation.

Following a comfortable distance behind the man, Hadid mumbled a variety of phrases in muted Arabic, figuring if anyone could make out what he was saying, it would be way better than if the words were in English. For his part, McHenry softly chuckled, as if they were sharing a joke.

The man entered the parking garage and immediately went to the stairwell in the corner, climbing the steps upward. Wordlessly, McHenry pointed to the far end of the garage forty meters away where another stairwell was positioned at the corner. On cue, Hadid ran toward the far stairwell.

McHenry followed the man into the near stairwell and listened for either footsteps or a door opening or closing. Hearing footsteps, he ascertained that the man had walked past the second floor and was ascending higher in the structure. Using this time, McHenry glanced both upwards and backwards to ensure there were no other passersby.

Moments later, McHenry heard the squeak of metal door hinges, indicating the man had entered the third floor. When he got there, the door was still an inch or two from completely closing, confirming his assumptions.

McHenry slipped his hand in the space, swung the door open, and walked into the well-lit garage floor. The man was ten meters ahead of him, walking close to the parked cars on his left, alongside the edge of the parking structure.

Glancing around the floor, McHenry noticed the structure was mostly empty, with the two center aisles about half full, and the far-right wall only one-quarter full. Luckily, he thought, it didn't appear as if anyone else was on the floor.

By the time he turned his head back toward the man, McHenry noticed there were a handful of empty spaces and then just one more car along the wall. "Shit," he mumbled to himself as he rolled his eyes in frustration. "Maybe this guy ...."

Aware that he was being followed to no car other than his own, the man suddenly stopped and turned toward McHenry. In a voice loud enough to echo off the cement walls, he said, "*Inja chizi baraye to nist.*" There's nothing here for you.

When the man had turned around, McHenry had been looking directly at him. Facing him now, he realized for the first time that he was a big man. I might have a few pounds on him, McHenry thought, but we look at each other eye to eye.

Slowly closing the distance, McHenry kept his left hand, his empty hand, open as nonthreatening as he could, and he veered his path slightly to the right and not directly at the man. Knowing he was being addressed, he fell back to what he knew: high school Spanish from Ms. Goncalves's class. "*Disculpe.*" Excuse me.

The man's eyebrows furrowed in confusion as McHenry continued his walk. Suddenly, McHenry looked into the distance over the man's left shoulder and raised his left arm up in greeting, shouting, "Ah, Samir!"

Startled, the man swiveled his head and shoulders to look behind him, and it was the only opening McHenry needed. Tossing his bag forward and to the right, he took two lunging steps toward his prey.

The man turned back to face McHenry, and knowing something was wrong, took a half step back with his right foot to get into a defensive stance. *This man has got some skills,* thought McHenry, *but not mine.*

Moving quickly with trained precision, McHenry drove his right elbow into the man's face, jolting his head backwards and sending his key fob spiraling under the car. As the man stumbled a couple of small steps, McHenry reached both hands behind the man's head, interlacing his fingers in a Thai plum clinch.

Pulling his arms down on the man's neck to break his posture, McHenry drove his right knee into his unprotected groin and followed it up with a left knee into the same spot.

Feeling the fight leave the man in a sharp moan, McHenry pivoted to his left, around the man's right shoulder, and took his back, sliding his left arm under the man's chin and locking it in place with the crook of his right arm. His choke completely compressed the man's right carotid artery and most of the left one too for good measure, cutting the blood flow to his brain. In seconds, the man's limp, dead weight told McHenry he was unconscious.

Taking his time to roll the man off him gently, McHenry looked up and noticed Hadid standing at the rear of the car, twirling the man's key fob around his right index finger. "Well, I guess that's one way of doin' it, boss. Now that you're done winnin' friends and influencin' people, can I offer you a lift?"

Ghorbani led Bo down the stairs, into the back of the shop, then into the garage, where he had previously swapped around the cars, placing his IKCO H30 Cross at the back, next to the rollup garage door. Following behind was Villapiano, who had his hands under the back of Shaheen's knees, and Tiger, who carried him from under his armpits.

Villapiano had staunched the external bleeding from Shaheen's abdomen and had started an initial intravenous fluid resuscitation using the lactated Ringer's solution Ghorbani had stored in his first aid kit. It was the perfect solution for the task at hand, and a common supply for trauma kits in the field. A fresh 1,000mL bag laid on top of Shaheen's chest.

Training had taught Villapiano that for trauma with blood loss, IV fluid resuscitation should use isotonic crystalloids like normal saline or lactated Ringer's to rapidly expand blood volume. Because of its better buffering, the ability to help maintain or restore the body's normal blood pH levels, lactated Ringer's was preferred for non-brain trauma. As for brain trauma in the field, the prognosis was never good.

The sedatives Villapiano administered had Shaheen in a semiconscious state which helped with his pain but hampered patient transport. With Ghorbani and Bo looking on, he and Tiger struggled to situate Shaheen in the back of the SUV, where

Ghorbani had folded down the driver's side half of the back seat. After a few minutes, the two had Shaheen laying down, head toward the front and feet adequately cleared to allow the hatchback to close, with the majority of their gear piled snugly alongside.

Standing up straight and breathing deeply from the physical exertions, Villapiano addressed Tiger. "He's stable for the moment, boss, but still critical. External bleeding is looking good, but dollars to donuts he's bleeding internally. We need to get him care, and we're talking minutes more than hours."

"Understood, JV," Tiger responded with a dour look. "But if we drop him at a hospital here, the worst case would be that he survived to then face enhanced interrogation. He goes with us and we try our best to get him out of here still breathing."

Villapiano frowned, knowing the seriousness of Shaheen's wound, but nodded his head in agreement. "Copy that boss. Ready to load out when you are."

Tiger turned to Bo and said, "Bo, you're going to be with me in the backseat. I'll scoot in next to Shaheen, and JV here will position you beside me."

Bo turned a quarter turn, revealing to Tiger his wrists bound with zip ties, and said, "Just free my hands and I can take care of myself."

"Can't do that, Bo," Tiger replied as she slid into the back of the SUV. "As much as I want to, I don't trust you. I can't have you opening the door and making all this bloodshed for naught."

"Look, I'm not going anywhere," Bo began to protest.

"Oh yes you are," said Villapiano as he grabbed the man by the elbows and forcibly walked him to the car. "You're joining my friends on a trip to a CIA interrogation site. If you obey our commands given to you, I'll make sure you go to one of the good rooms, with padded chairs and food and drink. If you act up even once, I'll personally ensure you go to the waterboarding room. Got it, Bo?"

Resigned to his fate, Bo looked down and complied as Villapiano guided him into the seat, bent his head down to prevent hitting the door frame, and buckled his seat belt. Done tending to Bo, Villapiano positioned himself in the front passenger seat, nestling his rifle between his legs, muzzle down.

"Okay, Hassan, we're as ready as we're gonna get." shouted Tiger through the open driver's door. "Open the garage and let's get on the road."

Chapter 23

Hadid carefully drove down Del Azar Boulevard to 71, but instead of getting on the highway, he used the cloverleaf to go southwesterly on Qaem, still a major thoroughfare but smaller and less trafficked than the highway.

He had used the name badge and key card of their hostage, Yaser Jahangir, to exit the garage. Along with the card, Jahangir had also attached a small, thin wallet carrying his driver's license and two bank cards on his lanyard. Hadid had carefully pocketed those cards, as they would certainly come in handy when it was time to refuel.

The car they were using was a no-frills, late-model Saipa Tiba, an inexpensive, fuel efficient four-door sedan popular for its reliability and affordability. By the time Hadid and McHenry had positioned Jahangir across the backseat, he had regained consciousness. Gagged and with wrists and ankles bound, terror emanated from his eyes.

Hadid had tried to speak to him in Arabic, but Jahangir had shaken his head, apparently signaling he hadn't understood. McHenry then tried in English, explaining that he wasn't going to be hurt, but that if he caused any problems, they wouldn't hesitate to fold him into the tiny trunk.

Jahangir seemed to understand those directions. That or the pistol McHenry held in his hand conveyed a similar message. Either way, he was curled up in the fetal position in the back seat and had been silent since they had driven off.

Left hand on the steering wheel, Hadid used his right hand to slip into his jacket pocket and retrieve his mobile phone. He powered up the phone, and once the home screen loaded, he handed the phone to McHenry.

"Mac, I figure it's time to light the fuse on that small diversion in Mayamey. Just go to the phone keypad and press and hold the number nine. Speed dial will do the rest, and the package should pop."

McHenry followed the instructions, saw that the call connected, and then saw that it almost immediately disconnected. "The call connected then disconnected, Sami. Seems you successfully made a big noise on an otherwise quiet night." McHenry then immediately powered down the phone and returned it to Hadid.

"When do we need to trigger the next one, Sami?" he asked.

"An hour fifteen to an hour thirty," Hadid replied. "Hopefully that second one establishes a trail too hot not to follow."

Leaving Qom, Ghorbani followed Tiger's directions and swept west part way across the city, then turned south on Jomhoori Eslam Boulevard. In no time there were in the desert, east of both the Iman Khomeini Town and Zeinoddin enclaves. Once past the turnoff for Zaer Mountain Park, they crossed a swath of dark desert.

Turning around from the front seat, Ghorbani addressed Tiger. "So far, so good. We've avoided any roadblock that may have been put up. But I don't want to turn north and get to 56 yet. To get there, we will have to return close to Qom and might find ourselves at a roadblock."

"Knowing where we gotta be, Hassan, what do you suggest?" Tiger asked.

"Two choices. One, we can sweep around Pardisan and go towards Tayeqan and beyond until we get to 65 at Neyzar. Second, we make our way to Verjan, then cross a stretch of desert to eventually get to Tayeqan. Option two requires us to backtrack and adds an hour. It's longer, but safer."

"Understood, Hassan," she replied. Tapping Villapiano on the shoulder, she asked, "You got any particular druthers, JV?"

"I trust Mac and Sami to be at our rendezvous ahead of us. They'll be waiting on us, and Shaheen needs every minute we can give him," as he nodded beyond Tiger and into the back. "Besides," he said with a grin, "don't you find choosing safety kinda contradictory to our accepted line of work?"

Tiger returned his grin and patted him on the shoulder. "You heard the man, Hassan. Option one it is. Get us on that road to Pardisan!"

Zhau Xiang's attention was drawn away from his paperwork by the buzzing of the intercom on his desktop phone. Pressing the speaker button, he inquired of his assistant, "Yes."

"Liu Jun Hie is here for you, Minister," came the prompt reply.

Zhau pressed the speaker button once more to disconnect, then carefully moved his paperwork out of the way. In its place, he moved a notebook and a pen. Then, he casually picked up an ornate porcelain teacup from its saucer and took a couple of sips, all the while making Liu wait just a moment longer.

Satisfied that he had further reinforced his position as the younger man's superior, he put down the teacup and pressed the intercom to connect with his assistant, directing "You may send in Liu now."

Moments later the hand-carved wooden door swung open and Liu entered, closing the door before turning around quickly taking position between the two chairs facing the desk. In his numerous visits to the office, Liu had never sat in one of the chairs, and he wasn't expecting an invitation now.

Always looking to remind subordinates of his hard-earned official status, Zhau certainly wasn't going to change his pattern of behavior now. "Yes, Liu, what is it?"

"We have an update about the Iranian situation, Minister," responded Liu. "While our sources can't confirm there is an active US operation in the country, they can confirm that the Americans are amassing a small exfiltration force in southern Turkmenistan. Whether the engineer Bo will be transported out, we don't know. But it appears the American operatives, including the Swanson woman, will be exiting from the east."

Thinking for a moment, Zhau stroked his chin. "There still has been no ransom demand received?" he asked.

"Nothing, Minister," came the prompt reply from Liu. "While this situation is still developing, there's been no indication that the Bo abduction is part of some kidnap for ransom plot by any number of the groups that are in play in the region. With what we can ascertain by the information on the American movements, the situation would appear to be an intelligence-gathering mission on Iran's nuclear capabilities."

"Yes, Liu, I believe you are correct. I want you to keep the intel lines open on both ends. Find out more about the American movements. But before you share any intel with our Iranian friends, come to me first. For now, let them know that the Americans appear to be headed east toward Turkmenistan."

"Yes, Minister, of course," responded Liu. "What should I share with the Ministry of State Security?"

"I'll connect with the minister myself, Liu," Zhau firmly stated. "I'll convince him to have the official embassy team work closely with the Iranian authorities. But I'll also convince him to have his covert team one step ahead. I want that Swanson woman. She has a debt to pay, and I want to collect!"

Major Afsoon keyed the intercom and softly interrupted Colonel Jahan, who had been lost in thought on this sleepless night, looking out the window at the dark desert sky. "Colonel, new intel has arrived, nearly simultaneously from two different sources."

"What is it, Mitra?" Jahan asked.

"First, there's been reports of a skirmish in Mayamey. Details are light at the moment, but local authorities are at the scene. But of particular note, reports of gunfire and explosions are very rare in the village. It's a small town of about 4,000 people."

"Where's it located?"

"It's located off of Route 44, sixty kilometers east of Shahrud."

"If it's related to Qom, it's going the direction we just came from," said Jahan.

"Exactly, sir."

"You mentioned a second piece of intel. Does it corroborate that this skirmish in Mayamey might be related to the incident in Qom?"

"Yes, sir, Colonel," came Afsoon's prompt reply. "Intel through the Chinese channel tells us that the Americans are in the process of putting a small extraction team across the border in Turkmenistan."

"Hmm," muttered Jahan. "Again, the direction we just came from and consistent with what we think was the insertion into our country. Where are we now in relation to Mayamey?"

"We passed south of it maybe ten minutes ago," Afsoon reported.

"Okay, Major, tell the flight crew to divert to Mayamey and put us on the ground," Jahan ordered. "Also, get us ground transportation from the local authorities from where we put down to where the fight happened."

"Roger that, Colonel," snapped Afsoon. "We'll be on the ground as quickly as we can get there."

The quiet ride experienced by Hadid and McHenry was still tense. Both men knew that unnecessary chatter wasn't going to help much, so they kept quiet and kept alert. Traffic on Route 56 was moderate, with generous spacing between cars in both eastbound and westbound directions.

Still, Hadid kept his eyes on his rearview mirrors. His vigilance paid off as he noticed a pair of headlights quickly approach, then abruptly slow down and fall in behind their car.

"Mac, I think we have some unwanted company," he said, breaking the long silence. "A sedan just dropped on our bumper."

Not wanting to turn and look toward the back, McHenry glanced into the passenger side rearview mirror. Bright headlights prevented him from seeing any details, but he saw the car was close.

Just then, the night sky was illuminated with red and blue lights from the light bar on top of the trailing car.

"Shit just got real," Hadid mumbled, "or at least more real."

"You weren't speeding, Sami," groaned McHenry. "Cars have been passing us!"

"I don't know, Mac, maybe the car has been reported as stolen?"

"Can you tell how many officers are in the car?" McHenry asked.

Glancing in the rearview mirror on the windshield, Hadid reported back, "Two officers."

"We sure as hell can't have them come up on the car with that jabroni tied up in the back," McHenry replied. "Comply and pull over slowly. When they get out, I'll get out first. They'll react to me. That's when you get out."

"What's the rules of engagement, Mac?"

"The only thing it can be, brother," McHenry replied with a deep sigh as he moved the slide back on his MP-443 Grach to ensure it held a 9x19mm Parabellum/NATO round in the chamber and then put the semiautomatic pistol in waistband at the small of his back. "We've no choice but to move first and put them down hard."

"Copy that, Mac."

Hadid pulled to a full stop on the far side of the highway shoulder at a slight angle facing back onto the road, his right wheels in the desert sand, allowing plenty of room for he and McHenry to operate. Both men sat looking in their mirrors, hands on their door handles.

"Driver's door is opening, Mac," reported Hadid, just as McHenry noticed the passenger door was opening.

"Alright, Sami, here we go," McHenry replied as he took a deep centering breath. He opened the door and stepped out of the car.

He was immediately met with a shout from one officer at the passenger side of the door. "*Dar jayi keh npastid toghof konid*!" Stop where you are!

McHenry had no idea what the command meant, but prudence combined with experience led him to believe it wasn't a casual greeting. He immediately raised both hands in the air and knelt down to both knees. In doing so, he partially concealed himself by the rear end of the sedan.

Hearing the crunch of the patrolman's boots advancing in the sand and seeing that he had drawn his sidearm, McHenry quickly grabbed his pistol with his right hand and fired two shots at the officer's chest. Both shots landed on target, spinning the man around and causing his return shot to fall harmlessly in the desert. Rising and pivoting to his right, McHenry fired two more shots into the chest of the other patrolman, felling him before he could lift his own weapon.

McHenry had acted so fast that Hadid was just now standing beside the car, his own weapon drawn.

"Damn, Sami, I didn't want to do that," McHenry said with a frown as he ran over to the officer lying on the desert sand. There he saw the man moving, still alive because of the bullet-proof vest he was wearing. McHenry fired two shots into his skull to finish the job, and Hadid did the same as he dragged the wounded driver over to the side and out of sight of any passing traffic.

"What now, Mac?"

Shaking his head in disgust, McHenry thought for a quick moment while looking over the patrol car, a white IKCO Samand with a broad green stripe denoting the Traffic Police of FARAJA, known locally as the RAHVAR, painted down each side. "We stay on mission, Sami, nothing's changed that much for us. But we can't leave this vehicle and these bodies here. Help me put these boys in the trunk. I'll grab the rifle out of my bag and follow you in the cruiser. That will be a pretty good blocker car to take suspicion off you in case that ride has been reported as stolen."

"Copy that, Mac. Let's get a movin'."

"One last thing, Sami."

"What's that, Mac?" Hadid asked.

"Pop that second diversion. We just might need it."

Chapter 24

Colonel Jahan knelt at the perimeter of the police scene in Mayamey, a large area cordoned off with barricade tape. Four police cars sat on the outskirts, including the patrol car that had transported him and Afsoon from where their helicopter had touched down in a field, their lights illuminating the scene.

Something just didn't feel right to him about the site.

The first officers on the scene had responded to calls of a loud explosion at an automobile repair shop but had arrived at a smokey scene devoid of any activity. Once on site, they had taped off the surrounding area and called in for lead investigators. Word had spread quickly, and within thirty minutes, Jahan was on the scene.

The majority of the evidence consisted of 5.45×39mm shell casings scattered about, the rounds used in both the AK-12 and AK-74 rifles so prevalent in the area. However, it was difficult to visualize how the skirmish had played out.

Where had the shots come from? What were the combatants aiming at? More importantly, who were the combatants? All were questions going through Jahan's mind.

His thoughts were interrupted with a couple of indiscernible shouts and one officer walking briskly to his patrol car and leaving the scene quickly enough to squeal his tires. Afsoon jogged over and stopped by his superior officer.

"Colonel, a call just came in about a similar type of fight in Davarzan, a little over 100 kilometers east of here on Route 44.

Based on the intel we've shared with Tehran, units from IRGC-IO and MOIS are in transit to both here and there. Command is also mustering selected troops from our base for patrols."

"Come, Major, kneel beside me. Tell me what you see."

"Colonel, I see the rather superficial damage of a small blast site and the evidence of a small, relatively contained gunfight."

"Yes, Major, I see the same things. But look at the shell casings and tell me this: In what direction were the shots being fired?"

Afsoon thought silently for a moment, then said, "If the casings haven't been moved, it would appear that someone or some ones were firing single shots almost randomly at different target locations."

"Exactly, Major," responded Jahan. "The shells came from a rifle that has semi-automatic, three-round burst, and full-automatic selections, yet there are no groupings of multiple casings. What does that indicate to you?"

After another minute of contemplative thought, Afsoon broke the silence, stating, "Perhaps it was a singular gunman, moving about and firing single rounds into the night in different directions. Or, maybe, perhaps multiple gunmen in close quarters, within this marked perimeter, maybe firing at each other. But there are no bodies or even blood trails."

"My thought exactly, Major," confessed Jahan. "And who would be firing upon whom?"

"If this is related to what happened in Qom, it would be unlikely that this scenario here would be the result of any infighting within that team of perpetrators," replied Afsoon. "And we know that it didn't involve law enforcement. There are plenty of armed groups out here, but they are supported, even sanctioned, by the government. There would be no incentive for them to hide their involvement in this incident, Colonel."

Jahan stood and patted his Major on the back, leaving his hand on his shoulder. "I concur with your observation and reasoning, Afsoon," he said. "Put together, this looks more like an orchestrated scene to me than the site of a spontaneous battle. Nonsense."

"And another scene that appears to be similar down the road," added Afsoon.

"It's like someone wants us to look east, right?" inquired Jahan.

Jahan collected his thoughts for a moment. He had lost the initiative in the investigation as elements outside of his control were already being deployed at Qom and locations eastward. But he had shared his intelligence data, and he knew his backside was covered. He also knew he could follow the investigation east, but regardless of the outcome, it wouldn't change the course of his career as he wished.

No, there was but a single play.

"Tell me, Major," he said, "if you were to deploy subterfuge to indicate you were going east, where would you likely be headed?"

"Any place but east, Colonel," he replied, "and probably west at that."

Jahan chuckled. "Yes, Major. South would be a tough exfiltration, what with the Persian Gulf and the Gulf of Oman, both heavily patrolled and surveilled. But west into Iraq is no easy way out either. That leaves north and northwest."

"Türkiye, Armenia, or Azerbaijan," agreed Afsoon with a slow nod of his head.

"Our colleagues have the east covered," Jahan said. "Will you join me in investigating the other direction?"

Afsoon snapped off a polished salute. "Yes, sir."

McHenry sighed as dawn began to rise across the desert. Driving the FARAJA cruiser, he closely followed Hadid in the Saipa Tiba, about one second behind on the freeway.

He had followed closely all night, not allowing room for another vehicle to get between them, and not allowing easily visible access to the Tiba's license plate.

Dawn brought a new risk though. McHenry was not wearing the dark blue FARAJA uniform.

McHenry had contemplated the roadside shooting for the entire trip. Remorseful guilt racked his emotions.

McHenry had long ago made moral, ethical, and spiritual amends to taking lives, something he had done in far too many instances in his forty-year career in service of his country. It was never, ever easy taking a life, and each and every instance left a mark on his soul.

It was easier to rationalize, of course, if the victims were active enemy combatants, or members of criminal or terror organizations. Those would be cases of self-defense or a proactive strike against bad actors that would benefit society as a whole. That whole "greater good" bullshit one told themselves.

The bodies of the two men in the trunk, McHenry thought, didn't fit in those categories though. They were in all likelihood two officers out doing their jobs on what turned out to be a fateful night. He could tell himself they were bad officers, but that would just be a mind game.

McHenry never subscribed to the "you can't make an omelet without breaking a few eggs" school of thought when it came to matters of life and death. It was the primary reason he steadfastly turned down repeated opportunities to be promoted into the officer ranks during his time in the US Army.

McHenry was never comfortable with the idea of sacrificing one or more of his charges for a strategic or tactical gain. Rather, he lived by the code of the grunt whose boots were on the ground. You fought for the brother and sister beside, and you did absolutely everything in your power to ensure everyone came home. If someone wasn't going to come home, it would be better to be you.

While he was far from happy about it or even reasonably satisfied, he also knew he took the only action he could on the roadside that night, not only for his own sense of self-preservation, but that of the well-being of his teammate, Hadid, as well. Any other course of action would have endangered the lives of himself and his teammate, and maybe even the lives of Tiger and Villapiano. It was them or us, that was the bottom line, he thought to himself.

Still, that knowledge didn't make him feel better.

"C'mon, Sami," McHenry muttered under his breath as he pounded a fist on the steering wheel and reflexively scanned the countryside as the morning lightened, "let's speed it up a bit and get to the safehouse."

Tiger's head snapped up suddenly, bringing her to her senses. She shook her head side to side in an effort to heighten her alertness. It had been a long night. Their circuitous route in fleeing the drama in Qom had added hundreds of kilometers to their trip. A numbing fatigue, precipitated by the incessant drone of tires rolling across tarmac, had crept in on everyone.

"How are you doing up there, Hassan?" asked Tiger as she reached up and placed a hand on Ghorbani's shoulder.

"Other than being tired, I'm doing alright," he said.

"Do you need relief from driving?" she asked.

"Not necessary, friend, for we're in Qeydar and only five minutes from our stop."

Qeydar was a town of fewer than 40,000 people about 250 kilometers west of Tehran, situated in the Central District of Khodabandeh County, Zanjan Province, Iran, where it served as capital of both the county and the district. More than being the capital, the town carried significance for its very name.

Through her religious studies at Yale, Tiger knew Qeydar was named after the biblical figure, Qedar, who was the second son of Ishmael, and therefore a grandson of Abraham. He became the progenitor of the Qedarite tribal confederation, one of the most historically significant tribes of North Arabia. Today, the Shi'ite sect of Islam, the predominant sect in Iran, believed Qedar was a prophet.

Ghorbani navigated the light early morning traffic south of the city on Route 47, exiting at Azar 2 Street and driving east. Four blocks later, Tiger's stomach growled as she spied a supermarket on the right-hand side of the road.

After a traffic circle and another couple of blocks, Ghorbani slowed his SUV and pulled into a short driveway that led into a gravel parking lot along the side of a bookstore. At the back of the bookstore, separated by five meters, stood an aged warehouse with brick walls set on a concrete foundation. Along the side of the warehouse was a rust-colored kerosene tank, and past it a large sliding door opened at its far end.

Ghorbani put his SUV in park but left the engine running. He turned to Villapiano in the front seat and said, "Wait here. I'll be right back."

As Ghorbani exited the vehicle, Villapiano gave a furtive look back at Tiger. Both gripped their pistols and held their breath in heightened anxiety.

A few seconds later, Ghorbani returned and opened his driver door. "You sir," he said to Villapiano, "back the car into the building so we can offload your wounded. We've got a clean vehicle for you to get across the border." Before he turned around to go back inside the warehouse, he said, "We're safe here."

"Yeah, I'll be the judge of that," Tiger mumbled as she eased down the hammer of her pistol.

After Villapiano had backed the SUV into the space, Ghorbani slid the warehouse door shut. In a few seconds, Tiger's eyes adjusted to the dimly lit interior.

She reached over Bo and opened the door. "Alright, Bo, time to get out again and stretch our legs."

"It would help with these restraints loosened a little bit," he said with low spirits as he swiveled his hips in the seat and placed his feet outside the cabin.

"Let me go one step better for you, Bo," Tiger responded as she gently assisted by pushing on the small of his back. "You're in this as deep or even deeper than we are now. I'm not letting you free, but I will free your hands."

"I have no idea where we even are," Bo said. "So, I'm with you and your guys, whether I like it or not."

"That's the spirit, Bo," Tiger said with a tight smile.

As Villapiano took Bo aside and cut off the zip ties binding his wrists, Tiger stepped to the tailgate to tend to Shaheen. There she was met by Ghorbani, who stood alongside a woman.

"My friend, this is Shadi Tayebi," he said, extending his open palm toward the woman. "She is a trusted colleague of mine in Tehran, a person who has served our collective interests well in the past."

Tiger nodded and extended her hand in greeting, a gesture not uncommon among women in the Middle East, and more conservative and less familiar in nature than a hug or a kiss on each cheek. As Ghorbani spoke in English, she assumed she understood. "Thank you for your assistance, *khanoom*."

"My pleasure, *dost man*," Tayebi returned. "I understand you're in a hurry, so let me show you what I've prepared."

"Yes, please," Tiger replied. "A 'hurry' doesn't begin to describe our urgency."

Chapter 25

Hadid activated the turn signal on the Saipa Tiba to indicate he was going to pull over onto the road's shoulder. Traffic was very light, and as they were approaching an *esterāhatgāh*, a typically well-equipped highway rest stop that often featured gas stations, restaurants, coffee shops, and even *musola*, or prayer rooms, he figured now was as good a time as any.

Following, McHenry turned on the red and blue lights of the lightbar and followed Hadid off to the side of the road. Looking in his rearview mirror, he let a distant motorist approach and pass before he hustled out of the patrol car and ran up to the passenger side door.

"What's up, Sami?" he asked.

"We're a few clicks out from a rest stop, and we need fuel."

"Yeah, copy that, Sami," replied McHenry. "I'm getting low on fuel as well. Anyway, I figure it's about time we ditch the patrol car. We've pushed our luck far enough. Those boys in the trunk are surely at the end of their shift, and when they don't report back, the GPS tracker on the car will get a careful look."

"You wanna scuttle the car?" Hadid asked.

McHenry looked back at the patrol car. After a moment of thought, he said, "I don't see what good that would do. It would only make it discovered sooner, I think, rather than later. Plus, I'm not worried about any evidence, be it DNA or other. Here, let me get my rifle."

Hadid sat with the car idling, waiting for McHenry to return. Just seconds later, McHenry was back at the door, sliding his rifle next to the center console. "Pop the trunk real quick, Sami."

Returning from the trunk with both of their kilim bags, McHenry opened the rear door on the passenger side. "Yaser Jahangir, I don't know if you can understand me or not," he told the man lying across the back seat, "but here's what we're going to do. I'm gonna slide you into the footwell and place these bags over you for about fifteen minutes. I expect you to be silent that entire time. If you make any noise, even just a little, I'll shoot you."

McHenry set down a bag and made a pistol gesture with his right hand, pointing it directly at Jahangir's head.

The man, still bound and gagged, nodded fearfully.

"Okay, so we have an understanding," McHenry said. He then gently pushed Jahangir's torso toward the front of the car and into the footwell of the back seat as Hadid reached back and pulled on his legs. To accommodate the drive train running down the center of the car, they rolled him onto his front side, pivoting him at the waist. McHenry then placed both of the kilim bags on top of him.

Getting into the car, he tossed the patrol car's keys into the desert. He then turned to Hadid and said, "Let's get a-movin', and let's tighten up our *keffiyehs* before we stop for fuel."

"Copy, boss," replied Hadid. "Here's to our last day in Iran."

"From your lips to God's ears," responded McHenry with a smile. "From your lips to God's ears."

"How's your man doing," Bo asked softly as their car, a green Saipa Atlas crossover SUV, moved in sync with the light traffic around it. The Atlas had been provided by Tayebi, and if it was as clean as she vouched for it, it was as inauspicious a vehicle as possible for the final leg of their trip.

It was an affordable SUV in a country with limited options due to international trade embargoes. The car, produced by Iranian automaker SAIPA, was based on older Kia Pride underpinnings, and featured rugged looks with options like roof rails.

Unfortunately for the team, it wasn't as rugged as its external appearance, with an undersized 1.5L engine paired with a 5-speed manual transmission and limited to only front-wheel drive. So, while the car blended into the general environment well, it was less than ideally suited for the tasks that would be at hand in getting across the border.

Tiger leaned back from the reclined passenger seat where Shaheen laid and turned to Bo. "He's not good. That swollen abdomen, combined with blood in the vomit he spit out a little while ago, pretty much confirms internal bleeding. We've got him sedated, but with his low blood pressure, we can't give him much more. We need to get him to a hospital as soon as we can."

"Is there anything I can do?" he asked solemnly.

Tiger looked at him for a moment and saw the sincere concern in his eyes. "I don't think so, Bo, but thank you for asking. JV, here, and I are both trained as field medics, and we're doing all we can with what we have at our disposal."

"I still don't know why I'm here," he said. "I'm not worth your man dying for, or those who died back in Qom."

"Bo, all I know is that Iran keeps creeping forward with its nuclear technology, and it's readily apparent they're intent on weaponizing their material. Considering the ideology of its leaders, any information engineers like you know of progress and the like is extraordinarily valuable to my government and its allies."

"I don't know if I know that much," he protested.

"Well, aside from that Russian back in Qom with bullet wounds in both legs, I'd say you know about as much as anyone."

"You know I can never go back, right?"

"Shit, Bo, go back to your prison-like double-wide trailer in the desert?" Tiger replied with a smirk. "That can't be your aspirational goal. Help us get through this, Bo, and I'll make damn sure it's worth your while."

"Okay, Major, let's review what we think we know," Jahan directed to his associate as they were being driven back to the airport in the back of an IRGC sedan. They had just spent a few minutes at the scene of the incident in Qom yesterday afternoon. Even though it had been cleaned up and the wreckage of two cars removed to open the street once again to traffic, it had been useful to see the site and understand what occurred. Additionally, they had met and been briefed by a uniformed IRGC captain about the progress made in the investigation.

"We know the lead car was disabled by a sniper shooting out of a fourth-floor apartment building three blocks away," reported Afsoon. "It was then surrounded by two vehicles, one fore, another aft, both of which are currently unaccounted for. Then a fourth car, the second coming from Fordow, crashed into the scene, damaging the second suspect vehicle. Soon after the shooting started."

"The sniper shots into the car were effective, but nothing extraordinary," Jahan offered. "But the shot that killed the driver of the fourth car showed exceptional skill."

"Yes, Colonel, without a doubt the work of a highly trained shooter, most likely a soldier," agreed Afsoon.

"Of the four dead, three came from targeted cars, one came from the kidnappers," stated Jahan. "What do we know of the dead assailant?"

"He has been identified as one Noor-Ali Mohammadi, last known to reside in Karaj, just west of Tehran. He had no criminal record, although MOIS has a small file on him as a possible conspirator in activities that have occasionally spawned from the old Green Movement."

As he was finishing his thought, Afsoon's mobile phone rang, interrupting the conversation. "It's the base, Colonel, I should get this."

Jahan inhaled deeply, pursed his lips, and nodded. Everyone in Iran's intelligence network remembered the Green Movement, an Iranian protest movement sometimes referred to as the "Persian Spring," that demanded electoral reform after the 2009 presidential election. It had started as a government planted and nurtured seed that quickly grew into something unruly.

The government of Iran, including both reformists and conservatives, generally supported the Arab Spring uprisings in Tunisia and Egypt, as they viewed them as legitimate challenges to corrupt Arab monarchies. They quickly changed their tune, however, when that same anti-authoritarian spirit became the driving force of the Green Movement in their own country.

The government responded with a brutal crackdown on demonstrations and protesters, enlisting not only Jahan's IRGC, but the large, paramilitary volunteer militia under its command, the Basij. In some cities, the hardline vigilante group Ansar-e Hezbollah went to work ruthlessly patrolling streets to enforce what it determined to be law and order.

It was a bad time, thought Jahan, and one that the regime continued to work tirelessly to prevent from happening again.

There's no way that sniper is part of an internal protest group, thought Jahan, and because there has been no ransom demand, it can't be a kidnap and ransom plot. No, this was the work of a professional team, and surely one state sponsored.

His train of thought was broken by Afsoon, who had disconnected his call. "Colonel, there's been two other disturbances reported: one in Neyshabur, another in Amirabad. Similar as before: a lot of noise, but no reported casualties."

"Yes, I continue to believe those are nonsense. Intended diversions."

"I couldn't agree more, Colonel," nodded Afsoon in agreement, "because we have another piece of intel that further supports your theory of the assailants escaping in another direction. Two Rahvar never returned from their patrol shift last night. GPS coordinates have their cruiser way out of jurisdiction, south of Hamedan. If this is related to Qom, they're escaping west, northwest."

"Call our pilot, Major, and have him prepared to fly when we get there," Jahan ordered. "Then connect me with headquarters. We need to redirect our efforts away from the ruse in the east."

It was late and Devin Thomas was tired. Another marathon day at Langley, starting before dawn and ending after dusk. This grind never gets easier, he thought as he slumped back into his chair. He also knew he wouldn't have it any other way.

Despite his passion for his work, he needed to get home to his other passion, his wife, Denise. Or, at least, what was once his passion.

Years in the Langley office had steered his relationship with Denise to be more like roommates who shared a house rather than that of husband and wife. He needed to work on that. But first, before he could go, he needed an update on his agent.

He picked up his office phone and dialed Rasmus's mobile line, and the call connected before the third ring.

"You still here in the office, Joonas?" Thomas asked.

"Yes sir, Director, ensuring the final touches are in place for extracting Tiger and her team."

"Any resources I can direct your way to help?"

"No, sir," Rasmus replied. "From SIGINT shared by Zeynab and her Iran Mission Center group, we know the team has been successful in steering eyes toward the east, to Turkmenistan. However, that ruse is about played out."

Both men knew Turkmenistan wasn't a formal US ally, but rather a country that was guided by its constitutionally mandated foreign policy of "permanent neutrality." Despite its ongoing concerns about human rights, the US supported Turkmenistan's neutrality with security programs, educational exchanges, and trade, recognizing the importance of its sovereign stability in a strategically vital region near both Afghanistan and Iran. The relationship between the countries was good, but that didn't mean it was a place to push one's luck.

"Joonas, have our people on the Turkmenistan side of the border pull back and ensure they're out of any harm's way. Oh, and one more thing."

"What's that, Director?"

"Bring my agent home."

Chapter 26

Cal McHenry walked over to the front office of the defunct motorcycle repair shop two long blocks east of the highway in Shabestar, a town of nearly 25,000 residents located about fifty kilometers northwest of Tabriz in Iran's East Azerbaijan province. Angling his walk to reach the far side of the windows facing the parking lot, he tapped on Hadid's shoulder and said, "I've got watch, Sami. Get a little something more to eat and some rest. You're gonna need it."

"How much longer you figure, Mac?" Hadid asked, nodding his head in the direction of the window and the dilapidated soccer field across the street.

"To be honest with you, Sami," answered McHenry, "I thought they'd be here when we arrived. Certainly be here by now. All we can do, brother, is wait."

Hadid nodded in agreement and then moved back into the mostly empty shop. The building was a combination of corrugated steel and brick, and aside from workbenches forming two U-shaped workspaces along the back wall, the place was empty. Nestled at the back of one of the workspaces was their captive, Jahangir.

Through this terrifying ordeal, Jahangir had soiled himself at least once, urinating in his clothing. With no other clothing on hand, they had no choice but to have him sit in his damp medical scrubs. They had, however, given him plenty of water and a little food. For now, he sat, blindfolded and gagged, with wrists and ankles bound.

At one of the workbenches, Hadid helped himself to a few more mouthfuls of food, sampling from the collection of fresh bread, cheese, and pickles he had picked up from the small family-owned restaurant on the way in. In agreement with McHenry, he was saving the *qutab*, thin flatbreads stuffed with lamb and greens, for when his teammates showed.

If they showed.

The motorcycle shop was the team's rendezvous point, and it was the final staging area for their last push out of the country. Shabestar, the capital of both its country and district, sat perched at an altitude of 1,400 meters in the southern foothills of Mishudagh, a prominent mountain in the rugged province. From there, the final leg of their Iranian journey would start relatively benign. Before long, however, it would test both their nerves and their capabilities.

The plan was to skirt north of Lake Urmia, traveling under the cover of darkness on Road 14 to Salmas, where they would divert south on Road 11. A little over eight kilometers later, they would veer off onto a back country road and make a dash for the Turkish border.

The 520-kilometer-long border between Türkiye and Iran was a predominantly rugged, mountainous frontier, extending from the Aras River in the north to Iraq, and was largely populated by Kurds. Complicating illicit border crossings, long an issue with Turkish authorities who sought to curb smuggling and illegal migration, a three-meter-high concrete wall topped with barbed-wire was being constructed along the entire border. Thus far, a 170-kilometer section had been completed in Türkiye's Van province.

With the wall being a significant deterrent, the team was going to travel to the literal end of the road in Kuran and then make a sprint across the border, aiming to go between the current end of the border wall and the long-established and well-monitored border crossing between Sero, Iran and Esendere, Türkiye. Given the terrain, the final ten off-road kilometers into Türkiye would be perilous.

Hadid stretched himself out on the floor of the U next to the one that held Jahangir, using his kilim bag as a makeshift pillow. An experienced operator, both as a former Navy SEAL and as a member of Tiger's team, he knew the value of rest and how to almost meditatively gather it when rare opportunities presented themselves. He closed his eyes and calmly started visualizing the last leg of their escape from Iran.

As had been routine for the past several weeks, Liu Jun Hie had spent most of his spare time during the day thinking of ways to extricate himself from Zhau Xiang's misguided mission to exact revenge on the American agent Swanson. The entire escapade was far outside his purview at the Ministry of Foreign Affairs, but he had over a relatively short period of time let himself become a complicit aide to Zhau.

Initially seeking to establish a preferential relationship with a powerful minister, Liu had let one or two favors grow into something unrecognizable in the scope and breadth of his everyday responsibilities. Not only that, but he also felt Zhau's mission, his singular focus, was a circular trap. They were seemingly mice spinning on a wheel, going to exactly where they had started.

He sighed deeply. Now's as good a time as any, he thought.

He dialed Zhau's office. Due to the late hour and the minister's staff having been dismissed for the day, Zhau answered the line directly. "Minister Zhau."

"Good evening, Minister, Liu here from the Ministry of Foreign Affairs," he replied, emphasizing his executive department in another most likely futile attempt to claw back from under Zhau.

"Yes, what is it, Liu?"

"I wanted to update you, Minister, on the activities in Iran before you went home for the day," he responded.

"Yes, Liu, you're wasting my time. Don't tell me you're going to brief me; brief me already," Zhau demanded.

Seething internally with anger, Liu took a quick, calming centering breath before he continued. "Yes, of course, Minister. The Iranian authorities have tracked who we can only assume are the Americans east to the border with Turkmenistan. However, neither they nor our teams from the Ministry of State Security have been able to make contact. There was some massing of personnel and vehicles on the Turkmenistan side of the border, but that seems to have dispersed."

"What does all this mean, Liu?" interrupted Zhau.

"One scenario is that the suspects successfully navigated through and across the border, although that seems unlikely as the activities on the Turkmenistan side were heavily monitored, including by satellite surveillance. The second scenario, Minister, is the entire string of evidence directing focus to the east was a diversionary ruse. The Iranians are now redirecting their investigation."

In the silence that followed, Liu could sense the anger building on the other side of the line. After what seemed an interminable pause, shouts caused Liu to move the phone from his ear.

"Liu, you incompetent fool, you're no better than those Iranian dogs sniffing around in the sand. I'll handle this from within the Ministry of National Defense from now on. Consider yourself dismissed!" Zhau screamed before slamming down his phone to end the call.

Liu paused for a moment, a bit puzzled by the abrupt turn of events. He then shrugged slightly as he put down the phone. No telling what the little man might do, he thought, but for now I'm free from his half-witted demands, giving a little time to destroy any paper trail of this entire thing.

Villapiano pulled the green Saipa Atlas crossover SUV into the small parking lot of the motorcycle repair shop, dimly illuminated by a solitary streetlamp on the side street. Not knowing if they were going to be long, he turned off the ignition. Alongside the Saipa, Ghorbani pulled his vehicle, the Khodro H30 Cross, to a halt.

As Villapiano exited his vehicle, the front door of the shop opened a crack, just enough to reveal the stern face of McHenry. "Who's next to you, JV?" he grumbled.

"Relax, Mac," replied Villapiano, his hands raised to his chest, empty palms facing outwards in a mock gesture of surrender. "They're friends."

McHenry smiled and opened the door more fully, revealing the MP-443 Grach he held in his right hand. He turned slightly, making a show of him putting the weapon into the waistline of his trousers to the two unexpected occupants of the car parked next to Villapiano. JV might call them friends, he thought, but I don't know them.

Over Villapiano's shoulder, he saw Tiger step out of the backseat. "Easy, Mac," she said, nodding in the direction of the Khodro. "I brought them into the fold. We needed the help."

"Copy, boss," he replied. "What's the SITREP and how can Sami and I help?"

"We're late, obviously," said Tiger, "but we still have a handful of dark hours to make tonight's window work. If we don't get moving within sixty minutes or so, we can't try again for another twenty-four hours, and we have Shaheen laid out with a gut wound."

"Sami and I have been waitin' for y'all to show. We're ready to go now," McHenry replied. "That the best truck you got?" he added, nodding in the direction of the green Saipa.

"I was hoping you might have a beefier truck," Tiger responded.

"That's a negative, boss. We have that sedan you passed parked on the street," he said, pointing to the car. "Why don't y'all come in and grab some food, and then you'll be able to meet the car's owner."

Tiger tilted her chin down, looking at McHenry through the tops of her eyes, her eyebrows raised and her forehead furrowed. "Owner? Well, doesn't this freakin' day continue to surprise."

The team took less than fifteen minutes to gear up at the shop and prepare to move, all of it spent in hushed whispers whenever around Jahangir. One person stayed with Shaheen, who was still only semiconscious, at all times, and everyone managed at least a little something to eat. There wasn't nearly enough food to fully appease everyone's appetite since the group was bigger than expected by Hadid and McHenry, but all had a modicum of fuel to power through the night.

After everyone else had filed out of the shop, Tiger took the blindfold off Jahangir's eyes and placed a water bottle at his lips. After he had drunk fully, she said to him, "*Bah mahz inkeh bah azarbayejan residim, baraye kamak ba shma tamas khaehim garaft.*" Once we're in Azerbaijan, we'll call in to get you help.

Every little bit or subterfuge helps, she thought.

Tired of sitting in the back of a cramped vehicle and wanting to give Villapiano a rest, Tiger took to the wheel of the Saipa Atlas and signaled to the drivers of the other cars that they were to move out. She took the lead out of the parking lot, followed by Ghorbani and Tayebi in the Khodro. Ghorbani then slowed to allow Hadid, driving the Saipa Tiba sedan, to fall in place between. This formation would be how they would convoy until they got close to the Turkish border.

Quickly moving south, Tiger led the convoy to Road 14, where they took the westbound ramp, headed toward Shendabad. Twenty minutes later, they were at the north end of Lake Urmia. Too bad it's dark, thought Tiger, for she would have enjoyed seeing the desert lake. As it was, the partially moonlit night wasn't nearly bright enough to allow her a view from the passing car.

Lake Urmia was an endorheic salt lake, and at one time was the largest lake in the Middle East. Persistent drought and the damming of local rivers that flowed into it conspired to reduce the lake to just 10 percent of its size in 2017. A couple of years later, rain and water diversion from the Zab River combined to breathe fresh life into the lake. That, however, was short-lived. Tiger knew that the lake, all 2,300 square miles of it, was nearly dry now.

A little less than an hour later, Tiger steered the group onto the southbound lanes of Road 11 just outside of Salmas, and, knowing Ghorbani needed fuel, almost immediately pulled off the highway and into the Moradkhani CNG Station.

Iran had a national effort to utilize abundant domestic gas for vehicles, and Ghorbani's Khodro H30 Cross had been delivered from the factory as bi-fuel vehicle, fully equipped to run on both gasoline and natural gas. In fact, Iran historically held the world's largest fleet of bi-fuel vehicles.

Deciding to top off, Tiger pulled up to the gasoline pumps, followed by Hadid and McHenry in their car. "JV, work with Sami to top up both of our vehicles," she directed as she stepped out of the car. "I'm going to procure some water."

Strolling over to Hadid's Saipa Tiba, she was met by Tayebi, who had walked over from the CNG pumps. "*Khanam*, I will walk over to the market to get your team some water," she said while pointing to a building secluded on the far side of the parking lot. "You'll need it."

"You read my mind, *dost*. I'll go with you," Tiger replied. Then, turning to Hadid, she said, "Sami, fill up both Saipas. We'll be back in no time."

With that, she stepped next to Tayebi, and they both started walking through the dimly lit parking lot to the market.

McHenry sat in the Tiba sedan, slouching down and keeping as low a profile as he could. He watched Tiger and Tayebi walk into the night, passing a lifted pickup truck sitting on all-terrain tires. A few seconds after they passed, three men got out of the vehicle. McHenry wouldn't have given a second glance if he hadn't noticed one of the men from the backseat slip a handgun into the waistband at the small of his back.

Chapter 27

Walking beside Tayebi, Tiger heard the doors close from what she assumed was one of the cars they had passed, but nothing alerted her that anything was amiss. That changed slightly when she heard the clap of multiple pairs of boots striking pavement in a slow jog. When she heard them being addressed, however, her level of alert peaked at maximum.

"Bebakhshid, shma do ta ba in ajaleh koja raftid?" Excuse me, where are you two off in such a hurry?

Along with Tayebi, Tiger abruptly turned around to face the speaker and saw three bearded men, each in their twenties or thirties. She didn't need the lack of weight in either of her front pockets to realize she had left her MP-443 Grach in the seat of the Atlas.

"Faghat daram baraye khanavadehmon ab madani miyaram, aghayon moteorbon," responded Tayebi as the three men positioned themselves around them. Just getting waters for our family, kind sirs.

Careful not to look him in the eye, Tiger nonetheless eyeballed the man on her far right as he began to move behind them, encircling her and Tayebi. As she did, she turned around, keeping him in her sight, her back to the other two men. She brushed her right hand against the hand of Tayebi, letting both know their proximity to one another.

"Cheh no sagnpanayi zannpanayeshan ra shabeya taneya biron mifarestand?" shouted one of the men behind her. What kind of dogs send their women alone out at night?

Tiger felt Tayebi tap her hand twice, causing her to turn around again to face the two men. When she did, she saw that they each held small, black pistols, what appeared to be the PC-9 ZOAF, an unlicensed copy of the SIG Sauer P226 that was the standard-issue handgun for the Iranian Army. These men, however, weren't soldiers, thought Tiger.

"*Befarmayid, shma ba ma biaeed*," demanded the man on Tiger's right, the one she presumed was the trio's leader, as he motioned with his gun back in the direction from which they had walked. Here, you come with us.

Tiger slowly turned around again to glimpse at the lone man behind him, and found him smiling creepily, he himself holding a sidearm now. Outnumbered and outarmed, she thought. Trapped. Raising her hands in surrender, she turned around slowly and addressed the leader. "*Biaeed shma ra pish shvearane- man bebrim.*" Let us take you to our husbands.

Not liking what he had seen, McHenry had stepped out of the Tiba, tucking his MP-443 into his front right pocket. He made a sharp whistle, catching the eye of Hadid at the fuel pump, and nodded in the direction of the market, receiving a silent nod of understanding from Hadid in return.

Following the three men who were following Tiger and Tayebi, he passed the black pickup truck, a four-wheel-drive Zx-auto Grandlion, standing tall on a lift kit and big tires, and noticed the shape of at least one more passenger behind the cab's tinted windows.

He noticed the two groups stopped fifteen meters in front of them, with the three men in a circle around Tiger and Tayebi. Shit, this ain't good, he thought. That was a split second before he noticed the raised sidearms. *And ... that's worse,* he silently added.

McHenry slanted his path toward the left, aiming to give the two groups a wide berth, but he had only taken a couple steps when he heard a shout. "*Az anja dor bozan ve bah jayi keh az anja amodegyi bargard.*"

He had no idea what the words meant, but they sure sounded to him like a command. So, he acted like a scared man would, raising both his hands in surrender and backing up. It seemed to be the right move, for as he did, the men shifted their attention back to the two women.

McHenry sold his retreat by turning around, and as he did so, he lowered his hands, slipping his right hand into his pocket and around the grip of his MP-443. Using his thumb, he flicked the safety lever off and, shifting his body to his left to shield his movements, pulled out his weapon.

Spinning, he dropped to one knee and sighted the man to his right, to the left side of Tiger, and he pulled the trigger, sending two shots into the back of the assailant and sending him falling face first to the ground.

Facing McHenry as she was, Tiger had seen the entire situation unfold. At the crack of the pistol shots, the man to her left had fallen and the man to her right had turned around to face the shots. Instinctively, she took a half step back with her right leg, balled her fists, and spun toward the third attacker on the ball of her right foot.

Using a backhanded technique but throwing blindly, her right fist just grazed the bearded cheek of the man. It did, however, squarely connect with the bridge of his nose, moving it a good inch to the far side. As his head spun to his left, he pulled the trigger of his semiautomatic pistol, sending a round into the night.

Tiger followed her spinning back fist with a left hook, using her momentum to land a hard blow behind the man's right ear. Although probably unconscious before he hit the ground, Tiger jumped on his back, grabbed the man's head by both ears, and slammed it twice into the pavement for good measure.

While she had been involved with the man, she had heard four shots, three in addition to the one her target had fired. Not knowing who had shot where, she remained low, rolled onto her left side, and looked back toward McHenry. She saw him kneeling on one knee, smoke drifting up from the barrel of his pistol. Behind him, she saw a man with a rifle jump from the pickup truck.

"Mac, behind you!"

McHenry didn't need Tiger's warning to know that one or more persons had jumped out of the raised pickup to get into the fight. Having set the second of his targets down with two well-placed rounds to the chest, he twisted his shoulders to his right. Landing on his left shoulder, he tilted his head upward so he could sight the truck.

As McHenry continued his roll, he brought his right hand up and over his head to point toward the single man who had leapt from the truck. Completing his roll and now laying on his stomach, McHenry fired two shots that narrowly missed his target and thudded into the side of the truck bed.

The man was holding a rifle and while he seemed not to know where the shots came from, he knew well enough to seek cover. As he crouched by the front left tire of the truck, he brought up the rifle and fired a series of shots in the general direction of the market.

McHenry could barely see part of the boot and lower leg of the man, and nowhere near enough of either to target with a shot. He didn't want to send a wayward round when Hadid and Villapiano were downrange. He did, however, want to provide cover to Tiger and Tayebi until they got to cover.

Quickly turning his head back to them, he started to shout for them to move, but he saw it wasn't necessary as Tiger was pulling Tayebi up by her coat and hustling her over toward a series of dumpsters on the side of the market. Satisfied they were getting to safety, he returned his attention to the truck and fired two rounds into its side to remind the lone gunman that he posed a dangerous threat.

McHenry then used a two-beat gait to leopard crawl, diagonally weighting an elbow with a knee, to get a better shooting angle, all the while keeping his MP-443 Grach on target in case the man should pop out of cover.

He moved purposefully, but considering shots had been fired, not urgently. Time was on his side, he knew, not the gunman's. He fired another two shots into the side of the truck, wanting to keep the man's attention forward focused. He trusted completely that Hadid and Villapiano were coming from behind.

Soon after his own two shots, McHenry heard two additional shots from a weapon other than the man's rifle. A quick moment later, he heard Villapiano shout, "Friendly."

McHenry lowered his gun and scrambled to his feet, just in time to see Villapiano and Hadid round the front of the truck. "You all alright?" Villapiano asked.

Turning around, McHenry saw Tiger and Tayebi emerge from the shadows by the side of the market, looking from side to side for any additional threats, but seemingly uninjured from the gunfight. He turned back to Villapiano and gave a thumbs up, nodding his head.

Running over to Tiger, McHenry said, "I think it's time we got the hell outta here, Tiger."

"Not so fast, Mac," Tiger replied with purpose burning through her eyes. "I still have to get my water bottles."

McHenry knew better than to argue with Tiger, and besides, he was thirsty too. Instead, he took a different tact, asking, "Any idea who these guys were?"

Tayebi interjected, "This region is rife with multiple organized criminal networks, all directly involved with trafficking crimes. Some, like the coercion of Afghan and Iranian migrants and children to fight in militias in Syria and Iraq, are rumored to be state sponsored. Other criminal networks focus on sexual exploitation in cities like Tabriz, not too far from here, and all through the Kurdish region and into Türkiye, where women and children are then sold off. My guess is that they viewed us as an easy opportunity to add two fresh pieces of inventory."

Hearing that, Tiger extended her hand toward McHenry and said, "Hey, let me see your weapon for a minute."

Confused, he rotated the pistol in his hand until he held the barrel and then flipped his hand over, extending the grip to Tiger while ensuring the muzzle pointed away from him and Tayebi.

Tiger grabbed the weapon, walked over to the man she had knocked unconscious, straddled his prostrated form, and placed the barrel to his back, aimed at his heart. "Your time trafficking women is over," she said before pulling the trigger twice.

Tiger flipped the safety lever on the pistol and handed it back to McHenry, then turned to walk to the market. Villapiano ran over and said hurriedly, "Mac, we need to get out of here, but I think we might have solved our four-wheel drive transport issue. How 'bout we take the tangos' truck."

McHenry looked over Villapiano's shoulder to the truck and said, "Shit, JV, I pumped a handful or more of slugs into that thing."

"Yeah, Mac, you might've, but all four tires are up and nothing's leakin' from the engine compartment."

"Okay, good change of plans. Run back and get the Atlas with Shaheen and put him in the backseat of the truck, with you and Tiger up front. Sami and I will take the Atlas and have Ghorbani and Tayebi cover our six until we turn off the road. We'll ditch the Tiba here."

"Copy that, Mac," Villapiano replied. "We'll be Oscar Mike in five."

"Nothin' takes five minutes," McHenry responded with a green. "Make it three. We gotta get out of here."

<h1 style="text-align:center">Chapter 28</h1>

Major Mitra Afsoon walked over to Jahan as he was in consultation with a senior officer of the Traffic Police. Both men were sipping tea to ward off the night chill as well as keep them awake. They had spent most of the last hour expanding the dragnet to bring the killers of the two FARAJA to justice. In his mind, Jahan thought it would also bring a close to the Qom kidnapping case.

"Colonel, we have an intel update on the case," barked Afsoon as he approached the two. "Forty-five minutes ago, there was a confrontation at a CNG station just east of Salmas, on Road 11. Eyewitness accounts claim multiple men and two women, as well as one sick or injured man who needed assistance, descriptions matching accounts from Qom. Last seen heading south in two vehicles."

Jahan pointed to Afsoon's connected tablet and asked, "Where is this?"

"It's west of Lake Urmia, Colonel," he replied as he brought up a map of the province, "and not too far from here."

"And they headed southbound, correct?" Jahan asked in confirmation.

"Affirmative, Colonel, at least initially according to the reports."

"That rules out north and Armenia and Azerbaijan," Jahan said with focused intensity. "That leaves just Türkiye."

"It would appear so, sir," replied Afsoon.

Eyeing the map, Afsoon pointed to the tablet and addressed the FARAJA officer, saying, "Colonel, I suggest you set up checkpoints on Road 11 South and Road 16 West."

The Traffic Police commander nodded, then spun off to make his way to a radio.

Turning to Afsoon, Jahan added, "Major, call into headquarters and place additional security at the Sero crossing in the south. While unlikely, also suggest increased security north at the Razi crossing in case the suspects change course."

"Yes, Colonel," came Afsoon's acknowledgment, but before he could turn away, Jahan grabbed his shoulder.

"As for you and me, Major," said Jahan conspiratorially, "we need to think like them, the assailants. If it was you, would you try your hand at getting through an official border crossing?"

Thinking for a moment, he replied, "That would require extensive documentation, and with the heightened tensions from both Qom and this most recent incident, it would mean passing through increased scrutiny at the border. No, I would look for an easier way."

"And it doesn't get very easy considering the border wall Türkiye is building, now does it, Major."

"No sir, Colonel, it doesn't. So that means south of the wall, in the wilderness north of the crossing in Sero, the mountains south of Sero, or even into Iraq."

"Ah, yes, Major, but if intending to leave via Iraq or southern Türkiye, why venture north of Lake Urmia from Qom?" he asked. "To me, it's *moshakhas ast*," he added as he pointed at the map. It's clear.

"They will cross between the end of the Turkish wall and the Sero border crossing. Have our chopper get us here," he said as he pointed to Barduk on the map. "Make sure it's fully fueled for we might be circling. Also get us as many patrols as you can from local authorities and alert our IRGC border garrisons to expand their patrols in the area as soon as possible. Let's end this hunt, Afsoon!"

Tiger had taken the wheel of the gang's pickup truck, a Zxauto Grandlion, painted flat black and customized for off-road use. When they got closer to the border and needed to go off road, she planned to swap seats with Villapiano. For now, she wanted him to ride shotgun in case his shooting skills were required.

Shaheen was spread out on the backseat, sedated and unconscious. They had exhausted the last of the intravenous fluids hours ago, and the only hydration they could muster for him was to occasionally trickle small amounts of water into his mouth.

McHenry and Hadid had taken over the Saipa Atlas, with Bo along for the ride. Before leaving the CNG station, McHenry had scuttled the Tiba, lighting it afire in the hopes that it would at least slow down the authorities who were no doubt in pursuit.

Together, the two vehicles had left the station nose to tail, continuing south down Road 11, with Ghorbani and Tayebi another few seconds behind in his Khodro. Tiger led the convoy as fast as the truck would go.

Twenty minutes after leaving the station, and several clicks north of Khan Takhti, Tiger slowed and took a right turn onto Ahar, a small country road and a significant departure from the divided highways they had been on all day. She pulled over and stopped, with the two trailing cars following suit.

Walking back to Ghorbani, the third car in line, she approached his rolled down window. "Alright, Hassan, this is where we bid you farewell," she said. "Thank you, and you too, Shadi, for all you've done. I appreciate your help."

"We can continue on your journey," Ghorbani protested.

"No, you can't," Tiger replied. "Things are only going to get hotter from here on out, and if you're in close proximity to us, you're burned. Both of you."

Ghorbani stared straight ahead, into the taillights of McHenry's Atlas, and thought. He broke the dead air and said, "Okay. What can I do?"

"Well, how about you get out and change your flat tire?" she asked with a smile.

"What flat tire?" he responded.

"The one you can pretend to have. If anyone follows us back here and sees you, it might slow them down a minute or two, and where we're going, every second might count."

Ghorbani chuckled, then unbuckled his seat belt and opened his car door. "These blasted country roads," he sighed. Extending his hands, he clasped Tiger's hand and said, *"Khodavand safartan ra parbarkat gardand."* May God bless your journey.

"Ve mal shma npam cpehmintor," she replied with a slight bow of the head. And yours as well.

She turned to walk back to the Grandlion, and as she passed the open window of McHenry, she patted the roof and said, "Get your radios on, boys. We're westbound and down."

"Watch that Bandit run," McHenry replied as an affirmative.

Tiger couldn't help but laugh as she continued to the truck, picking up on McHenry's *Smokey and the Bandit* reference and their Taiwan op. This time, she thought with steely resolve, I'm bringing all my boys home.

Tiger led the team further down the road, blasting past the hamlet of Tamar with McHenry on her tail. The road was barely two lanes wide and more gravel than pavement, but traffic was nearly nonexistent and it allowed for the team to make relatively good time. Tiger was putting that to good use, as she wanted to get off the road and into the cover of wilderness as quickly as possible.

The shootout at the station had been unexpected, unwelcome, and, in the end, unavoidable. No sense second-guessing their actions, including stopping there in the first place. What was done was done, and what mattered now wasn't the action they had taken, but the actions they would be taking.

She figured they had two options. One, they could try to lay low. Doing so would likely mean sacrificing Shaheen, however, for he would undoubtedly succumb to his internal wounds. Plus, Tiger thought, stopping their egress to lay low would only allow the Iranian dragnet to close tighter.

The second option was the one they were currently taking, and that was to make a mad dash for the Turkish border. They had the cover of darkness and a head start. Plus, beginning tonight, they had exfil windows previously established with Langley for the next three nights, counting down after the interdiction of Bo, with personnel and other resources available at the border.

For her, the decision was easy. She and the team would stay on offense and press proactively until the point circumstances dictated otherwise.

Tiger turned to Villapiano and asked, "How's our guy back there?"

Villapiano turned around and saw Shaheen's chest move shallowly with breath. Leaning into the backseat, he placed two fingers on Shaheen's neck and felt for his pulse.

"Labored respiration, boss, and still shallow; pulse is weak," he reported. "At this rate, he won't see sunrise."

"We still got sedatives to keep him comfortable?" she asked.

"We do," came the reply, "but he'll crash if we give him any more right now. There just ain't anything good to fill you in on."

"Alright, you're more the medic than I am, so it's gonna be your call on if or when meds," Tiger replied, "but I'm of the opinion of making him as comfortable as possible when we drag him through the woods."

"I hear you, boss," he nodded. "If we're gonna lose him, I'll make it as painless as possible for him."

Turning her full attention to the road, she keyed her radio and called out, "Two, this is One, you copy?"

"You're five by five," replied McHenry, affirming that her signal was excellent in both strength and clarity.

"Back off a bit from my bumper. The road is gonna get curvy with switchbacks as we get close to the Bazhergah Waterfall.

"That's a hard copy," came McHenry's response as he breathed the throttle to create some space. "We'll cover your six from a lil' further back. Bandit Two out."

The Mil Mi-17 helicopter made a sketchy landing in the village of Barduk, roughly planting itself on the only remotely flat surface in the town of less than 500, across the dirt road from the central mosque. Its rotor still spinning, Jahan and Afsoon slid out of the open side door and walked hurriedly to their IRGC comrades waiting alongside two weapon-mounted Toyota pickup trucks widely known as technicals.

The trucks had started out life as the Hilux model, a nearly ubiquitous four-wheel drive vehicle found throughout the Middle East, revered for its reliability, versatility, speed, and maneuverability. Each had been outfitted with a mounted DShK M1938 heavy machine gun, a stinger in the tail that posed serious consequences for opposing targets.

Nicknamed the "Dushka," the weapon was a belt-fed machine gun firing a 12.7x108mm cartridge at up to 600 rounds per minute at an effective range of over two kilometers. The gun posed such a threat that whenever it appeared on the battlefield, it immediately became the priority target for the opposition to eliminate.

Upon reaching the trucks, Jahan was met by a uniformed *Razmavar yekom pasdar*, a mid-level, senior non-commissioned officer of the IRGC, who snapped off a hasty salute. Returning the salute, Jahan looked at each of the vehicles, noticing they were staffed by three soldiers each.

"What are your deployments, Sergeant, between here and the border?" Jahan asked.

"We have doubled our patrols, Colonel," he answered. "Based on your orders, we have deployed all available personnel at our border garrisons. In addition to these two trucks, we have three others deployed in the mountains. However, it's a long border between the Sero crossing and the wall, twenty-five or more kilometers."

"We have the helo at our disposal," Jahan replied, flicking his head in its direction. "How are you in the air?

"What do you mean, sir?"

"I'm taking your seat in that technical," the colonel responded, pointing to the truck immediately behind the sergeant. "Major Afsoon will be in the other. You and another from the second truck will be in the helo patrolling from the sky. Understood, Sergeant?"

"Uh, yes sir, Colonel," came the hesitant reply.

"I'll be in command down here, organizing the search and coordinating with you in the helo. With your eyes in the sky, you'll fill me in on how we're deployed on the ground. We've been chasing these dogs all day, and we think they're going to cross through these mountains here. We pinpoint them, either from the ground or from the air, then we converge and squeeze the life out of them. Do you copy, Sergeant?"

"Yes, Colonel," he responded with another salute. "I'll get my man from the other truck and load into the helicopter. I'll prepare the pilot to take off on your command."

Chapter 29

Going from rote memory used during the mission planning stages back in Qom, Tiger led her now two-vehicle convoy on the thin country road. After Tamar, the road had twisted through a barren patch of desert and modest foothills, in many cases twisting back on itself with hairpin turns.

Traffic was non-existent, so there had been no cars to follow. A hazy overcast had limited the moonlight, so visibility was low along the unfamiliar road, made all the more hazardous by the tight turns.

Still the team made relatively good progress and soon came upon the village of Mamakan. Using it as a waypoint on their southwesterly journey, Tiger called back to McHenry. "Two, this is One," she called, "We're twenty-five mikes from our turnoff. Status?"

Trailing Tiger's lead vehicle by fifty meters, McHenry keyed his radio and answered, "We're green, covering your six. Over."

"Copy that, Two," Tiger responded. "One more stretch like the last."

Tiger navigated the left bend that marked the halfway point through the small village. While the village was long, from front to back, Tiger thought, along with almost ten side streets, there weren't a lot of buildings and very little light. The large central mosque was illuminated, but not much else.

Once out of the village, the road curved back again to the southwest, and the team continued toward its destination. It was quiet, both in the cars and between the cars. Those who weren't driving tried to get some rest. Tiger and McHenry, the drivers, were silently counting down the kilometers at the rate of about one a minute over the dangerous road.

A nervous energy burned through Tiger. It had been just over thirty-three hours since the abduction of Bo, and from nearly the get go, it had been an op where the team had to adjust and respond, improvise and adapt. Not unlike most ops, Tiger thought, but this one had felt different from the first shot. The escapades back at the CNG station hadn't helped in the slightest.

She could only assume the police and the military were hot on their heels. Now there might be a heavily armed gang added to the chase. She did have a multiple-night window of opportunity to skate across the border, but deep down she knew it had to be tonight or never. They had made too much noise in getting this far. For this exfil point, it was tonight, come hell or high water. And if it wasn't this exfil point, it was whatever the team could make of it. A Yahtzee of a mess.

Tiger shuddered at the thought.

While it seemed interminably long to Tiger, in just twenty-five minutes the cars cruised by the hamlets of Mingul, Surman Abad, and Ghasrik, and finally reached their next checkpoint at the town of Hashtiyan.

Tiger called back to McHenry, advising him of the coming turnoff, then maneuvered off the main road, glancing back to see if he had made the turn. Confirming they were still in lockstep with one another, she pressed forward through the dark night.

"Shit," she mumbled as she looked out the windshield. "And here I thought the last road was bad."

The road into town was narrow and unpaved, more of a path marked by two tire ruts with frequent bumps and holes. Bouncing over one at too high a rate of speed, she heard Shaheen moan. As they got into town proper, all couple hundred meters of it, Tiger thought, the road improved, for only for a short stretch. Then it deteriorated even further.

Afraid to turn to Villapiano in the passenger seat for wanting to keep her eyes on the road, she said, "Hang on, JV. Looks like the good road is behind us."

"Hate to break it to you, Tiger," he replied with a knowing smile, "but the bad road is still in front of us. Our last stretch is gonna be goat paths until we go completely off-road for the border."

"Yeah, I'm afraid you're right in that respect."

"When we get to Barduk or even Kuran, we should switch seats," Villapiano suggested. "As part of my tactical mobility curriculum, I've had extensive training in driving off-road, and over the years I've had to put it to test in some pretty demanding environments."

"I know it, JV," Tiger replied. "But I like knowing your gun is right next to me."

"C'mon, Tiger," he chuckled. "You know you're every bit the shot I am. We're a push behind the sights of an AK-12 and I'm the more experienced off-road driver. Whaddya say we switch?"

"Yeah, copy that," she grunted in acquiescence. "Do me a favor and radio back to Mac advising that we'll shortly come to a stop."

It had been a long night for Jahan, but fatigue had been stymied by the fiery excitement that coursed through his body with every staccato beat of his heart. It was good to be back in the field, boots on the ground. This is where he belonged. *Elhamdola*, he thought. Praise Allah.

With his intel, the IRGC had reinforced security at all the country's official border crossings and ports, usurping control from the Border Control Command. For his part Jahan had commandeered the local garrison with his rank and now plotted the tactics.

At his disposal were five ground assets, four-wheel drive technicals with three soldiers each, and a helicopter with four hours of flying time before needing refueling. Jahan would have loved to have had a battalion at his disposal, but he had enough resources to get his job done.

Knowing that refueling the helo would take it off the board for forty-five minutes, he made the decision to temporarily ground it. His logic was straightforward, if not completely confidence-building.

If his prey were behind him, toward the Turkish border, then he was too late to the hunt and this entire chase was hopelessly *akhar-e kat*, end of the line. It would be blind luck for one of the three patrols behind him to stumble across the prey in over 400 square kilometers of space.

His only real play was to assume that he had beaten them west, that he was between them and the Turkish border. So, he did the only logical thing: he pulled back to lessen the amount of terrain he needed to cover.

On his orders, he pulled the two technicals in which he and Afsoon sat to Kuran, the last Iranian settlement east of the border. From there, he drew a jagged line parallel to the border, five kilometers out. That would be his search grid. Helping narrow the search area was Sardasht Dam Lake, a major reservoir constructed on the Little Zab River.

He'd have to play the northern edge of the reservoir with one technical for a handful of kilometers, but the rest of the border coverage in that direction would be handed off to the Sero patrols. That left four trucks on the ground for a search grid of approximately 140 square kilometers, with a border of twenty kilometers.

Using the sergeant, he had one technical reposition itself to the easternmost tip of the reservoir and initiated a search pattern along the border. The other two technicals were drawn closer to the border and tasked with patrols.

Pulling the radio handset microphone to his mouth, Jahan radioed to Afsoon. "Major, you stay here in the village, primarily posted where the road branches toward the mosque. Patrol north and south as you see fit, extending a kilometer or two, but stay local. If they are coming this way, I expect them to take the road until it ends, and that's here."

"Understood, Colonel," came the prompt reply.

"I'll get the helo in the air," Jahan continued. "If there're headlights on a dark night other than ours, it will see them."

Whether out of stubborn pride or a lack of a good place to stop and switch drivers, Tiger kept driving through Barduk and then the twisting seven kilometers to Kuran. She kept telling herself that the narrow and curving road wasn't great for a quick swap, but she mostly knew that was a mind game to cover for her fierce control-freak and competitive tendencies.

Finally, she reached a sharp left then right switchback that she knew marked their pending entry to Kuran. In the middle of the night, she didn't feel it critical to avoid stopping in the small town to avoid any unnecessary encounters with locals, but to play it conservatively, she pulled over to the right side as far as she could. Keeping the engine running, she exited the front door as McHenry pulled in behind.

As she and Villapiano walked around the front of the Grandlion, she keyed her radio for all to hear. "Okay, boys, in about 700 meters this road comes to a 'Y,'" she said. "It's a coin flip on which way to go. Going straight or to the right will take us past the mosque, and you never know what's going on there, even in the middle of night. Let's take the left in the road to avoid it. We'll have about 500 meters of road until we get to goat paths, trails, and good ol' mother nature the rest of the way. Seven clicks to the border, where we should have the cavalry waiting for us."

"Copy that, One," McHenry replied. "Yee haw. Let's get this moving."

Just as Tiger was placing her foot on the running rail to boost herself into the truck, she heard the unmistakable thump, thump, thump of a helicopter. She pulled her earpiece out for better hearing and scanned the night sky for running lights. Not seeing any, she closed her eyes and focused on her hearing.

The sound was coming from the northeast and the direction they had come, and it was approaching.

She gazed at Villapiano and shared a silent thought. The team was no longer alone in the night.

Slipping her earpiece back in, Tiger keyed her radio again, calling out, "Sounds like we have company, Two, a helo coming from the northeast."

"That's a copy, One," McHenry responded. "Whaddya think the odds are it's just out for a nice night flight?"

"Considering this ain't exactly Teterboro airport, I'd say it's slim to frickin' none," came Tiger's sharp reply. "Let's kill these headlights."

As Villapiano turned off the headlights on the Grandlion, McHenry took a moment to think.

"One, this is Two," he called over the radio while he turned to look at Hadid. "Three's gonna bring our passenger up to you. Turn off your headlights but completely disable your taillights. You take the left in the fork in the road. Three and I will keep our lights on and visit the mosque. Lord knows we could use a little prayer."

"I don't know, Two," Tiger replied. "I like having you close by."

"Mission success centers on dividing and breaking the chase," McHenry answered back while Hadid slipped out of the car. "We'll be back covering your six in a jiffy. Besides, when have I steered you wrong?"

After a short pause, Tiger keyed her transmitter and responded, "Affirmative. Three bring up our guest and on the way back, please do us the favor of smashing our brake lights and taillights."

Walking Bo up to the Grandlion, Hadid responded, "That's a good copy, One, I'm on my way forward."

Villapiano hopped out and opened the driver's side rear door. After Tiger swept Shaheen's legs off the seat, Hadid guided Bo into the truck. "Just settle in here by our guy, sir," Hadid said to their captive. "The ride won't be long."

Closing the door, Hadid heard the chopper close by. He quickly jogged to the rear of the Grandlion and used the butt of his AK-12 to bust the truck's lights along each rear quarter panel side and the top of the tailgate. Ten long seconds later, he jumped into Atlas and told McHenry, "Go, go, go!"

McHenry floored the throttle and fishtailed the SUV around the Grandlion and down the road, headlights blazing the way, hoping to attract the attention of the helicopter. Villapiano pulled in a few seconds behind and followed.

Weaving along the road as it veered north and into the village, McHenry tried to make his vehicle as conspicuous as possible. It seemed to be working, as the noise from the chopper was louder: It was closer and lower.

"Fall back, Four," he radioed to Villapiano. "I want him to follow me. When you get to the 'Y,' you go south."

"Copy," was the calm response. "Falling back and heading south. Keep your powder dry, Two."

"See you in the woods, brother."

Jahan's radio crackled with the tentative voice of the sergeant breaking through the quiet. "Colonel, we've spotted one or two vehicles just outside of Kuran."

"What was it, Sergeant, one vehicle or two?" came Jahan's brusque reply.

"From a distance, sir, it looked like two. Closer now to the town, can confirm one, moving now into Kuran."

"Major Afsoon," Jahan radioed, "what's your location?"

"We have been patrolling north but are now circling back. We'll be at the western edge of town in two minutes."

"Sergeant, keep this vehicle in sight and guide the major in to allow him to intercept," ordered Jahan.

"Yes, sir," replied the sergeant as the helicopter banked to starboard to follow the advancing headlights 300 meters below them. "Major, the vehicle is headed toward the mosque. When you come to the road on the edge of town, head east to intercept."

"Copy that," Afsoon said in reply. Then, turning to his driver, he commanded, "As fast as you can."

He unholstered his PC-9 ZOAF pistol, checked to see that a round was chambered and that the safety was on, then rested it on his lap as the truck bounced its way back into the village. Encountering a small cluster of houses and outbuildings, they curved around and approached the road directly across from the mosque.

The driver slowed to a crawl to maneuver over a drainage berm alongside the road, not wanting to either damage the truck's suspension or his comrade manning the Dushka in the truck bed. Just as the front wheels contacted the road, Afsoon saw two headlights approaching from the left.

He tapped the driver on the shoulder and ordered, "Wait here." Together they watched as the car, a green Saipa Atlas SUV, closed the distance and then drove by, the driver and the passenger both turning their heads to look at them.

"Stop them," Afsoon ordered, as the driver accelerated and turned the steering wheel to a hard right.

Chapter 30

"Holy shit, Mac, that was a technical we just passed, two bogeys in the cab and another manning a Dushka in the back," Hadid said excitedly.

"Affirm, Sami," McHenry replied, before keying his radio and notifying the entire team. "One, this is Two, we have contact with one enemy technical." Glancing back into the rearview mirror, he continued, "They're following."

He heard Tiger respond, "Copy, we'll circle back."

"That's a negative, One," he replied. "We'll handle here and catch back up with you. Over."

Seeing the road ending 100 meters ahead, McHenry veered hard to the left in front of a cafe and bounced through the garden of a neighboring house. Past a couple of isolated sections of wooden rail fencing, he was just about to turn hard left again when his mirrors reflected the headlights of the technical.

"They're definitely following, Sami," he said to his partner as he sawed the wheel to the left, bouncing into a shallow ditch. "That Dushka will tear this truck apart, and we still need it."

Hadid held his AK-12 with the shoulder stock under his right arm, barrel pointed between his knees. Nodding toward the back of the mosque and its dimly lit gravel rear parking lot, he said, "Hard left again past the mosque and I'll roll out. You go around the front and get behind any cover you can. Between our crossfire, we'll create a kill box for the Dushka."

"That's a copy, Sami," McHenry responded as he sped faster toward the mosque and increased the distance between them and the technical. Braking late, he angled the Atlas to the left, leaving the corner of the mosque as the apex in his turn, then hit the throttle hard again.

Once around the corner of the mosque and temporarily out of sight of the technical, Hadid opened the door, illuminating the cab, then without uttering a word, pivoted in his seat and hurled himself out of the cab. Turning his head quickly, McHenry saw Hadid roll his body and land on the back of his left shoulder, facing the direction of the following truck. In a fraction of a second, he was out of sight.

Quickly, McHenry was at the front corner of the mosque, and he swung the SUV hard to the left once again, causing the open passenger door to swing violently outward, buckling at its hinges, before swinging back and slamming shut with a tremendous bang. Seeing a low stone wall at the far side of the front lot, he drove straight for it, locking up the brakes and screeching to a dusty stop just shy of colliding with it. Grabbing his own AK-12, he jumped from the truck and hopped over the wall. Crouching, he took a covered position five meters south of the still running Atlas and waited.

He didn't have to wait long.

Within seconds the drab olive-green Toyota truck slid around the far corner of the mosque, clearly unaware or uncaring that a passenger had hopped out. Hadid was in the clear, and for that McHenry breathed a sigh of relief. The bad news was that he had the business end of the technical heading in his direction.

McHenry took a deep centering breath, not only for his sake, but to provide a bit of time for Hadid to get into position. Then he poked his rifle just above the wall and with its fire selector lever on fully automatic, he pressed the trigger, sending a salvo of rounds sweeping from right to left across the front of the technical, flattening tires, shattering headlights, destroying the radiator.

Immediately he dove to his right, landing on his elbows and hustled into a leopard crawl, moving away from the parked Atlas. At the same time, the technical skidded to a stop. McHenry had just begun to hear the spray of gravel from the stopping truck when the Dushka sprang to life, punctuating its fury with a barrage of rounds into the stone wall.

Giant chunks of stone flew through the air as the wall began to crumble behind him. Then, as quickly as the heavy machine gun had sprung to action, it quieted. As McHenry continued to lay low, collecting his breath, he heard small arms fire from behind the technical. After a series of short bursts, he heard running steps across the gravel lot, then the familiar voice of Hadid shouting, "Mac, where are you?"

Still in cover behind the wall, McHenry breathed a quick sigh of relief then shouted, "Friendly coming up!" Peeking over the wall, he saw Hadid to his left, on the far side of the technical and near the Atlas.

McHenry jumped to his feet and, despite his years of experience in the field, was surprised at the destruction of the stone wall between him and the Atlas. The Dushka had chewed through the ten-inch-wide wall with no difficulty.

Stepping over the ruins, he and Hadid climbed into the Atlas. "Call it in to Tiger," McHenry instructed as he slipped the gear selection lever into reverse. No sooner had the transmission clicked into gear than the night sky was awash with the spotlight from a helicopter.

Major Afsoon struggled to come to his senses, blinking his eyes repeatedly and gently shaking his head, trying to knock loose the cobwebs muddling his mind. The cab of the Toyota Hilux was filled with smoke and dust, and the sharp, acrid smell of cordite expended from the big Dushka burned his nostrils.

In their eagerness to pursue the target vehicle, they had left their rear exposed, and they had paid dearly for it. Turning his head to the left, he saw the driver collapsed over the steering wheel, undoubtedly dead. He could only assume the soldier in the truck bed manning the machine gun had met a similar fate.

He began to recall the attack, and the searing pain he felt in his back and chest in what must have been just a few moments ago. Now, leaning left toward the center console, he felt an aching pain throughout his upper body. Eerily, he felt nothing below his waist. He also noticed his breathing was shallow and labored.

Afsoon reached for the radio transmitter with his left hand, and after depressing the talk button, he sputtered through a spray of blood, "Colonel, we have contact with the enemy. Over."

"What's your SITREP, Major?" came Jahan's reply.

"My soldiers are dead and the truck has been neutralized," Afsoon replied through a heavy breath.

"And your status, Major?" asked Jahan, his worry obvious over the radio transmission.

"I am hit, sir," Afsoon replied hesitantly. He then added, "I'm afraid this will be our last mission together."

Still holding the transmitter, he lowered his hand to his lap and leaned back against the headrest, focusing on his breathing. With his right hand, he began to explore the holes of the front of his body, looking for where he might try to staunch the flow of blood first. He stared blankly ahead, still very much in disbelief.

Over the radio he heard Jahan bark, "Sergeant, call in a medic to the scene. At the same time touchdown and drop your man off to render first aid. Recall the other three patrols and relocate them within three kilometers of the border, one click north and south from Kuran. Then get back in the air and track down that vehicle."

"Roger that, Colonel. Medics en route and touching down now," followed in reply.

Coming down from the shock of the attack and his injuries, memories flooded into Afsoon's mind. Pulling the transmitter back to his mouth, he muttered out one last message. "Colonel, I heard them speaking English. You are looking for Americans."

Heading south out of the village of Kuran gave Villapiano just 700 meters of road. When he reached the end of it, Tiger pointed west and said, "The border is five clicks that way, JV."

The terrain immediately sloped upward, and millennia of water runoff and slides had left deep channels in the rock. Even with its lift kit, the jacked-up Grandlion heavily scraped across the ground, sending shuddering vibrations across the chassis and eliciting grunts, groans, and moans from Shaheen and Bo in the backseat.

"I'm glad this ain't my personal truck," Villapiano muttered as he steered the truck from side to side, desperately seeking purchase from the tires, a task made even more difficult with the blackout conditions under which he was driving.

"Don't worry about the resale value, JV," Tiger joked as she gripped the handle above her door. "Just get us a few more clicks further and then we'll finish on foot."

In the darkness, Villapiano dropped the right-side wheels into a steep gully and the truck skidded down the slope pitched at a perilous angle. Relying on his training and experience, he resisted the temptation to stomp on the brakes and instead steered into the skid to regain control, then slowly accelerated to transfer weight to the uphill side. Steadying the truck, he straddled the low point of the gully and followed it uphill for fifty meters, where it ended at a clump of boulders and wispy trees.

Slowing to a crawl, Villapiano gently steered over, around, and through a boulder field, each jarring bounce bringing shouts of pain from Shaheen, who looked now to be extremely weak, but fully conscious. His voice fraught with worry, Bo called out, "You've got to stop!"

Tiger let go of her handle and turned around in her seat just as the truck bounced off a large rock and into a larger hole, sending her head slamming into the roof. Gritting her teeth, she said through a grimace, "I need you to hang in there for a little while longer, Massoud." Reaching back, she gripped his right hand with hers, squeezing tightly. "Can you do that, Massoud?"

Shaheen squeezed her hand in return, one long squeeze that lasted several seconds. Then he let go of her hand and wrapped his arms over his chest. One squeeze silently signaled an affirmative, a "yes."

Turning back to Villapiano, Tiger said, "Steady forward, JV, but as gentle as you can at the same time."

"Um, boss," he replied as he squinted into the dark in heavy concentration, "those would appear to be mutually exclusive considerations."

Tiger slapped him on the shoulder and said, "Do your best, brother."

He crept up another twenty meters until he came to what appeared to be a wall of brush, extending in both directions for as far as he could see in the night. Hesitant to go backward, he gently applied the throttle and moved forward, feeling his way through the dried thicket and hoping to avoid any big stumps or trunks.

After just a few rotations of the tires, the front of the truck poked through the thicket and Villapiano caught sight of headlights forty meters up the slope and twenty meters to his left. Foot hard on the brakes, he reached for his AK-12, shouting, "Contact."

Tiger saw the threat, seemingly a truck with a set of running lights on a horizontal mount above the cab to supplement the headlights. It was barreling downhill at a much higher rate of speed than they had been ascending, and its path never wavered.

"They don't see us, JV," she said.

Villapiano didn't answer her. Instead, he keyed his radio and barked, "Two, this is Four. You have another technical inbound. If you're where I think you are, you got two minutes."

All he heard back through his earpiece was a crisp, "Ten-four."

McHenry turned off the headlights of Atlas. Then he remembered the still functioning taillights of the SUV.

"Damn, Sami," he said as he crawled to a stop, the sounds of the helicopter still echoing through the night. "We didn't disable the taillights on this rig."

"I got it, Mac," Hadid said as he opened his door. As he did so, the dome light between the two front seats shined bright.

The two men looked at one another and shared a brief laugh. Hadid went to the rear and got to work on the taillights with the butt of his rifle. McHenry smashed the overhead light with the grip of his pistol.

When Hadid got back to the truck, he asked through the window, "How you want to play this, Mac?"

McHenry put the Atlas in park, grabbed his rifle and got out of the cab. "If that technical sees the truck, it's liable to light it up with its machine gun. Hit the deck here, and with a little bit of luck, they'll pass by us without contact."

"Copy that, Mac," Hadid replied as he laid down, keeping his vision uphill to look out for the approaching technical.

For his part, McHenry wanted to create distance from the Atlas, allowing him and Hadid a triangulated field of fire should they have to shoot it out with the Iranians. If they were in one position, together, the heavy Dushka would chew them apart in no time.

With his AK-12 at the ready position, he jogged slowly uphill, careful with his foot placements in the dark so as not to stumble and injure himself. Fifteen meters from the front of the truck, he saw headlights bounce over the crest of a ridge and start thundering down the hill at the rate of at least 25 km/h. At its present course, the technical would pass twenty meters to his right, with clear visibility to the Atlas.

McHenry dove to his stomach, grunting when he landed as a rock jabbed him in his lower ribs, just below his vest. On the ground, his position was parallel to the course of the technical, so he began pivoting on his left hip to ensure that his rifle was trained on the incoming vehicle.

Still uphill from him, the truck seemed to slow, then angled slightly in the direction of the Atlas. They've seen the truck, thought McHenry, but not me.

The technical slid to a stop, the billowing dust roiling in the headlights, a tense moment of silence hanging in the air. Then the Dushka erupted, spraying a five-second burst at the Atlas. After a pause of a few seconds, it sent another five-second volley into the stricken SUV.

As the Dushka stopped, McHenry took a deep breath in through his nose, held it, then fired in return. Tempering his shots to short, fully automatic fire, he concentrated on the soldier manning the Dushka in the truck bed. He didn't have a great angle, so he focused on where he assumed his legs would be.

His shots drew corresponding fire from Hadid, downhill and slightly behind him, and those reports brought an exhaling sigh of relief from McHenry, as they confirmed that Hadid's cover had protected him from the Dushka's initial shots.

McHenry continued firing into the bed of the technical, rotating his fire to the Dushka's mount and the truck's left bedside, and emptied his magazine. He could see that Hadid's fire was smashing into the technical's windshield, grill, and front tires.

Quickly switching out his empty magazine for one fully loaded, McHenry saw the Dushka begin to bark out shots, foot-long streaks of yellow flame flashing out of its barrel.

It was now or never. With the Dushka in play, McHenry knew he and Hadid were sitting ducks.

Assuming the technical wasn't armor reinforced, McHenry concentrated his fire on the bedside behind the Dushka's mount. After three more fully automatic bursts from his AK-12, he saw the flames from the Dushka's barrel shoot nearly vertically. Then the big gun fell silent.

His shots had found home, dropping the soldier in back, who held onto the trigger as he fell backward into the truck bed.

McHenry rose to one knee and pumped the rest of his rounds into the driver's door of the technical. Then, not wanting to be free of cover, ran back toward Hadid, shouting, "Friendly coming your way, Sami."

Hadid greeted him on the passenger side of the Atlas. McHenry saw that the Dushka had destroyed the SUV, rendering it completely inoperable. With the helicopter's spotlight moving toward them, he said, "We're on foot now, brother. Let's distance ourselves as far from here as we can."

With that, he took off at a quick pace, running away from the smoking ruin of the SUV at a forty-five-degree angle from straight uphill.

Chapter 31

Jahan carefully lifted his head and peered at the direction of the enemy vehicle, smoking in a ruined heap in the foreground, a small fire glowing orange in the bottom of the engine compartment. Turning his head to his left, he saw the wreckage of his own truck, better off than the enemy's but still nothing more than a steaming wreck.

When the return fire had come toward the technical, Jahan had jumped and rolled to safety. Looking back at the cab and the dead driver, slumped across the front seats, he knew it had been the correct decision.

Cautiously, he pushed himself to his knees and scanned the landscape. He couldn't see any movement, but his ears heard the faint sounds of boots scrambling over rock in the distance.

Sensing they were far and moving away, he hustled to his feet and ran to the truck bed. There he saw the second soldier on his back, his head flush along the closed tailgate. Eyelids heavy, he was writhing in a near-silent agony, a huge puddle of blood pooling underneath him and trickling out of one of the corners of his mouth.

Hopping into the truck bed, Jahan pulled his service pistol out of the holster on his hip and knelt beside his stricken comrade. Then he placed the muzzle to the soldier's chest, right above his heart, and said, "*Ba khoda boro*." Go with God.

He pulled the trigger twice, mercifully ending the soldier's ordeal.

Reholstering his weapon, he rose and grabbed the handles of the Dushka, lifting to bring the barrel down. Then, finding the trigger with the index finger of his right hand, he screamed out in anger and squeezed, sending rounds hurtling into the desert night.

Despite being mounted to the truck bed, the Dushka surprised Jahan with its kick, pulling his aim upward. He quickly readjusted, sending rounds first over the wrecked SUV, then rotating his fire up the hill. In just a few seconds, however, he had used the entire belt of rounds feeding into the right side of the weapon.

Mumbling curses under his breath, he knelt to his right and opened an ammunition box. In the dark, he fumbled around to find the front end of a new belt. Just as he found it, a bright light illuminated the truck and its surrounding area.

In his battle-focused mind, he had completely forgotten about the helicopter patrolling the skies.

He rose to his feet, shielding his eyes with his left hand, and waved his right hand furiously side to side. The light steadied on him, and he was confident that he had caught the attention of the pilot.

Sensing only the slightest of breezes from his left, he turned to his right, ensuring the wind was coming from behind him. Then, squinting his eyes into the bright spotlight, he held up both arms overhead in a shallow "V," marshaling the helicopter to land.

The helicopter backed up a handful of meters and began descending, all the while keeping the colonel illuminated. Jahan kept his arms raised overhead throughout, until the aircraft was about five meters off the ground. Then he slowly brought his arms to a horizontal plane, guiding the chopper to a soft touchdown.

Jahan jumped out of the truck bed, crouched and ran to the helicopter's starboard side, where the sliding door was open. There he met the sergeant, who had pulled away his radio headphones from one ear.

Leaning close to the soldier and shouting over the whirl of the helo's rotors, Jahan ordered, "Call in your closest truck to pick me up." He paused for a moment, looking at the flight engineer, a member of the three-person crew for the helicopter. "To pick *us* up; he's coming with me," he added. "Soldier, dismount, you're joining the fight from the ground."

Looking back at the sergeant, he continued. "Hover 100 meters above me to guide in the truck. Position the other two trucks five hundred meters from the border, due west from here, and put them on high alert."

Beginning to step away from the helicopter with his additional soldier, the colonel stopped himself and leaned in. "And one more thing," he barked, pointing up the hill and toward Türkiye. "Once my truck gets here, get over that ground and locate those Americans!"

"Damn, JV, sounds like Mac and Sami are making one helluva first impression back there," grunted Tiger as the Grandlion shook violently when its right-front tire slipped off a rock. The thunderous report of a Dushka in the not too far distance had just tailed off.

"Yeah, Tiger," Villapiano replied. "I sure hope they're alright. It's taking all I can not to hop out, run down there, and lend a gun to the fight."

"I hear you, JV," Tiger answered, "but Mac's playing it to plan, and if we split up now, we'll just complicate matters more than help."

"Copy that, boss," he agreed. "That's the only reason I'm still driving."

The driving had been slow going without headlights to light the way. The general incline was over thirty degrees, but it was crisscrossed with erosion ruts and rocky ridgelines, and loose rock everywhere meant traction for the truck's four large tires came at a premium.

Then, of course, there was the vegetation, a forest steppe collection of Persian oak, maple, pistachio, almond, and walnut trees, all twisting and turning at almost impossible angles, with the spaces between trees increasingly filled with thickets of shrubs like juniper and barberry the higher they climbed.

From the engine bay, the Grandlion's 2.3-liter turbocharged diesel engine was working at its limits on the steep slope. Villapiano was resigned to accepting "slow and steady" as the fastest they could advance.

"You know, Tiger, pickin' and placin' our way through all these rocks, trees, and shrubs, has us goin' back and forth more than up," Villapiano said. "And we're just gettin' slower as we go."

"That's an affirmative, JV," she acknowledged. "But carrying Shaheen uphill ain't gonna be an easy task."

"We're gonna have to walk sometime," Villapiano said. "Drivin' over the border's likely not an option."

"I can help," came Bo's voice from the back.

Turning around in her seat, Tiger addressed Bo. "What was that, Bo?"

"I said I can help," he replied confidently. "You know, carrying your man."

"You're volunteering to lug Massoud up this hill?" she asked incredulously as she looked at the slender engineer.

"I didn't say I could carry him by myself," he answered back somewhat defiantly. "But I carry him under one arm, with you under the other, and we can drag him up the hill."

Tiger nodded and turned to Villapiano. "JV, how many clicks you figure to the border?"

"Oh, I suppose between two and three clicks."

"Even if we might be driving slower than we can walk, get us a bit closer, JV."

McHenry trailed behind Hadid by a few meters as they scrambled uphill, running diagonally from the scene of the conflict with the technical. They had heard the massive rounds of the Dushka firing into the night. What alarmed them most was the occasional shell zipping close enough to be audible as it passed before kicking up rock debris as it hit home further ahead.

For now, the big canon had fallen silent, but they didn't know for how much longer. What they did know was that the technical was immobile, and the Dushka could only fire from where it currently sat. However, they also knew the machine gun could fire its rounds nearly two-and-a-half kilometers. They needed to create distance.

They also needed to get to cover, as they also knew the helicopter was overhead. Glancing over his shoulder, he could see the helo hovering over where they encountered the technical. While the chopper hovered, its spotlight rotated out in the distance, undoubtedly searching for him and Hadid.

McHenry shouted ahead, "Sami, the chopper is acting as a beacon to call in reinforcements. Beeline it to the shrubs and the trees. We need to get invisible, and fast!"

Hadid adjusted his angle of ascent to his left, sacrificing distance from the technical for climbing in altitude. McHenry could almost immediately feel the increased angle of ascent in his thighs as the muscles burned with lactic acid and yearned for oxygen.

McHenry felt he didn't need his hands as they scrambled up the slope, so he slipped out the ammunition magazine from his AK-12 and replaced it with a fully loaded one. Only three magazines left, he thought, just ninety rounds to get to the border. That and his pistol and a knife.

The two men trudged upward about 150 meters, and the trees became more prevalent, with gnarled trunks twisting up from the inhospitable terrain every ten meters or so. As they ran past trees, no matter how slender, they curved their path, placing the tree between themselves and where they remembered the technical was placed. It was primarily instinctive, as they were both aware that a Dushka could clear a forest of slim trees quicker than any Paul Bunyan legend. Still, it offered some sense of security behind a hostile enemy line.

As Hadid led forward and upward, McHenry turned around. Confused as to what he was seeing, he paused for a few seconds to make sure.

He turned around and called up to Hadid, "Sami, hold up!

When Hadid stopped and turned around, McHenry pointed to the sky behind him. "Stick to the trees and the shrubs and keep your head on a swivel. The helo is back on the hunt!"

Yet another modified Toyota technical slid to a stop next to Jahan and the helicopter's flight engineer. Jahan immediately recognized the four gold bars on the shoulders of the driver's uniform as that of a *sarjukheh*, a corporal.

The corporal hastily stepped out of the cab and fired off a salute, saying, "Colonel, Corporal Farid, reporting."

"At ease, Corporal, and remount," replied Jahan and he quickly returned the salute. "We're on the hunt for two, maybe three Americans who are headed east to the border." He angrily added through gritted teeth, "I want them."

"Yes, sir," he answered. "You'll sit up front with me."

"Negative, Corporal. He and I," Jahan said as he gestured with his thumb over his shoulder toward the flight engineer, "will join your man in the back with the Dushka. Do you have a rifle?"

"Yes, sir, in the cab."

"Give it to him," he said with a backward flick of the head as he moved to the side of the truck and hoisted himself into the bed using the right rear tire as a step. He then positioned himself to the left of the Dushka gunner and grabbed ahold of the rollbar with his left hand.

He went to unholster his sidearm but stopped as he glanced to his left. Losing patience with the slow movement of the driver and flight engineer, he slammed the palm of his right hand on the roof of the cab, shouting, "Now! On the double!"

The flight engineer stumbled into the truck bed with the rifle slung over his shoulder, clearly more comfortable with aircraft than all-terrain vehicles. Looking around, he decided it best to position himself to Jahan's opposite, to the right of the Dushka. Once in place he patted the roof of the cab twice to let the driver know he was set.

Jahan pointed to his left, uphill, and shouted, "Go toward the border! Stay to the left of the helicopter's spotlight. Either they'll get them or we'll get them. Look for movement of any kind!"

No sooner were Jahan's words out of his mouth than the Toyota was put in gear and headed uphill to the west. Jahan pulled out his PC-9 ZOAF pistol and rested it on the cab's roof. He widened his stance and placed his right foot behind his left to steady himself with his legs as the truck bounced along. All along he looked slightly right of center, desperate to spot his prey. It was all to play for, right here, right now, he thought. There would be no second chance. They had burned through those already.

Chapter 32

Villapiano brought the Grandlion to a full stop. Picking their way through the increasingly thick trees had slowed their progress even further. Looking forward into the dimly lit night, he thought it might be time to walk out.

"You thinkin' what I'm thinkin', JV?" Tiger asked.

Villapiano turned and answered, "If you're thinkin' 'bout drinking cervezas and chasing senoritas on a beach in Mexico, then yeah, we're thinkin' a lot alike."

Chuckling, Tiger responded with dead seriousness, "I can't promise you the senoritas when we cross into Türkiye, but I damn sure can promise you some beer, and I'm buying."

"That's a promise I'm gonna make you keep," Villapiano said as he gripped his AK-12 and opened his door. "Time to hoof it outta here, boss."

Bo was already out of the cab and walking around the back of the truck when Tiger got to the cab's rear door behind hers. "Okay, Bo, you ready to do this?" she asked.

"Boss, how 'bout I fireman carry him? Terrain has flattened out a lot, and I've carried more," Villapiano said in a soft voice barely over a whisper.

"I bet you have, JV, particularly wrestlin' around Old Misery during BUD/S back on Coronado," Tiger responded. "But you're better served for now for cutting a trail to the border and peering through that rifle scope."

"HUA, boss," he answered as he stepped in front of the truck. "When you're on my six with Shaheen, I'll head out."

"Roger that, JV," she replied while turning to Bo. "Okay, Bo, you got a preference as to which side to start?"

"No preference," he replied as he turned sideways and positioned his left forearm under Shaheen's left armpit. "I'll start here."

Before Tiger could do the same to Shaheen's right side and pull him out of the truck, Villapiano interjected. "Yo, boss, just ahead looks like a little game trail or goat trail, angling from the right to the left. Looks like we can make some pretty quick time right away." Pointing up the hill, he added, "Whaddya say I light up this truck as a diversion, sending attention here while we'll be there."

Tiger thought for a few seconds, then said, "I like it, JV, but I like it better with a head start. Let's go up twenty-five to fifty meters, and while we catch a breather, you run back and scuttle this piece o' shit."

"That's a good copy, boss. Let's do this."

Tiger hooked her right arm under Shaheen's and gently patted his chest. "On three, Massoud. This is gonna hurt for a little while, but we're gonna get you to help. *Man gul mi daham*." I promise.

Shaheen nodded almost imperceptibly and grumbled out a moan, shutting his eyes and preparing for the worse.

"One, two, three," Tiger commanded, and then pulled with Bo, sliding Shaheen out of the backseat headfirst. As Shaheen's hips cleared the seat, he gasped. It turned into a full cry when his feet fell off the seat and crashed into the ground, sending a shockwave of pain through his entire body.

"Hang in there, friend," Tiger said as she pivoted to her left and started working in tandem with Bo to drag Shaheen to safety. "Bo, step on my count. One and two, one and two. Got it?"

Bo hesitantly moved forward but quickly settled into the rhythmic cadence. Together, they fell three or four paces behind Villapiano, curving slightly to the left as they found the beaten trail.

Villapiano used the narrow trail to quickly slice through a tangle of brush and medium-sized trees, stopping at a thick oak tree, its wide, lower branches just a couple of feet off the ground.

"What say I leave you here, Tiger, and go back light the truck up?" he asked.

"Get on it. You'll know where to find us," she answered with a smirk.

Villapiano started the seventy-meter jog down the hill and thought about how he was going to scuttle the truck. He didn't have any explosives, but he did have a lighter. Once he arrived at the truck, he had his plan built.

Slipping his tactical vest off over his head, he first took off his linen shirt, then put back on his vest. After he removed the gas cap off the truck, he twisted his shirt and fed it into the mouth of the fuel tank. When it came to a stop, he twisted and pushed, screwing in the fabric deeper.

Finally, satisfied it was deep enough, if not actually touching the fuel, he pulled a disposable lighter out of a small pocket on the far-left side of his vest, under his arm. He didn't smoke, and never had, other than the occasional celebratory cigar after a hair-raising op. But, like many operatives, he packed the lighter as an optional tool for operational circumstances exactly like this.

Knowing the untreated linen was highly flammable, he didn't waste time removing a bullet from its shell casing and using its propellant, a mixture of nitrocellulose and nitroglycerin, as a primer. No, he thought, this will light up fine just the way it is.

He lit the fabric that dangled from the fuel tank and watched as it caught hold. He had one chance, and he needed to ensure it worked. Seeing it fully light and climbing all the way to the fuel tank opening, he turned and started his run back to Tiger.

This was going to make a scene and grab some attention, he thought. And when it did, he wanted to be as far away as possible.

McHenry saw the orange explosion at his two o'clock before he heard it a split second later. Just seventy meters out, he felt the flash of heat too.

The moment the flash erupted, he and Hadid had hit the deck. They had spent the previous minutes ducking from cover to cover, their egress hampered by the randomness of the helicopter searchlight probing for any sign of them.

McHenry scrambled up alongside Hadid's left and asked, "That's gotta be JV and Tiger, don't you think?"

"Affirmative, Mac," he answered. "No shots fired though, so I suspect that's them scuttlin' the truck as a diversion. Unless the truck just broke down, that means we gotta be close to the border."

"It sure feels like we're gettin' close, Sami. And while we're assumin', I suspect there's at least one more technical coming from where we disabled the second one. That fire up there is gonna attract their attention like moths to a flame."

"Which way then?" Hadid asked.

"Let's sprint due north, perpendicular to the slope and get on the other side of the fire. Once we're fifty meters past, let's turn west and high tail it to the border."

"Copy, Mac," Hadid responded. "You take the lead, and I'll be on your six, lookin' for both the chopper and the technical."

McHenry rose to his feet and slapped his hand on Hadid's shoulder. "Any sign of the enemy, find cover. With their advantage in firepower and our distance still to the border, we can't afford to engage unless it's our last freakin' resort."

After Hadid nodded in acknowledgment, McHenry lifted his AK-12, locking the shoulder stock hard to his shoulder and sighting the rifle ahead of him, and headed due north at a double-time cadence.

Jahan slapped his hand repeatedly on the roof of the Toyota and shouted for the driver to stop. Skidding to a stop in a cloud of dust, he leaned around to the driver's open window and said, "Give me the radio!"

The driver grabbed the radio transmitter, turned to his right, slid open the back window, and extended his hand out. Jahan ducked under the big Dushka, and kneeling on his right knee, took the transmitter.

Calling up to the helicopter, he asked, "Sergeant, what was that explosion? What do you see from up there?

"It appears to be a vehicle on fire, Colonel. Not one of ours."

"Did we cause it? Did we fire on it?"

"No, sir," came back the sergeant's prompt reply. "There's been no reported contact with the Americans."

"Okay, Sergeant, this was probably a diversionary tactic, but guide one of your two trucks to investigate," Jahan ordered. "Now we're looking for at least three enemy personnel, but probably more like four to six. I believe they are in two groups but might be converging into one. Concentrate your search west, between the vehicle fire and the border."

"Confirmed, Colonel. And where can we expect your patrol?"

"We'll run westerly, south of the vehicle fire, then sweep north, joining your two other trucks in a search grid," Jahan reported. "Do you copy, Sergeant?"

"That's a copy, Colonel," he replied. "Good hunting, sir."

Jahan tossed the transmitter back into the cab and asked, "Did you get that?"

"Yes, Colonel," came back the instant reply. "Hold on; we're on the move."

Despite knowing the explosion was coming, Tiger had still been startled by the sound. No sooner had the last echoes left her ears than she heard Villapiano running up the trail to their position. As he emerged from the darkness, she noticed his new look, shirtless under a tactical vest.

"What, JV," she teased, "you aiming to audition for a male stripper revue on our way out?"

Villapiano wrinkled his forehead in confusion, then got the joke. "You know us SEAL team guys, always looking to show off the muscles."

"That and write a book. Surprised one hasn't been published about this op so far," she fired off in return.

"Oh, I've been taking notes." Then in full seriousness, he nodded toward Bo and asked, "You two still good dragging Shaheen? Wanna switch up duties?"

"You still good, Bo?" Tiger asked.

"It's harder than I thought, but I can keep going," Bo answered.

Tiger thought over the situation for a moment, then said, "JV, it's gotta be either you and me on point, and you're better at that. You continue on point, get us close, and then maybe you fireman carry Massoud over the final sprint."

"Copy that, boss," Villapiano responded. "Fall in and let me know when you're ready."

Having already switched sides on Shaheen, Tiger called out, "We're ready now. Move."

Emerging out of the brush that surrounded the old oak tree, Villapiano almost immediately saw headlights far to his right, about 100 meters up and 100 meters to the side. He quickly knelt and lifted his right hand, forming a fist, signaling to Tiger to come to a stop. Bo, not understanding, walked another step, tripping himself in the process and falling to a knee, almost dropping Shaheen in the process.

"Sorry 'bout that, Bo," Tiger whispered across the moaning Shaheen. "Fist means stop. For now, we stay low and let them pass."

Villapiano whispered back, "They're going to the burning truck. They'll be back. As soon as they pass our flank, we need to double-time it to the border. As fast as we can."

"Copy that, JV," Tiger responded. Then, turning to Bo, she said, "Hard as we can, Bo. We're almost there. We need to finish this for Massoud."

Bo nodded. "I can do this."

Taking his eyes off the descending headlights, Villapiano focused his attention to the western border. Once the headlights left his peripheral vision, he lifted off his knee and said, "Forward. Let's go."

Villapiano took off at a quick pace, but not quite double-time, knowing that an untrained civilian, a slightly built engineer at that, had the hard work of dragging what was essentially dead weight.

The trail curved off to the left, south, and away from their target, so Villapiano broke from it and led the small group toward. The slope leveled out considerably, and ten minutes later the team emerged from the darkness into a wide field of brownish-green grasses and small shrubs. The trees had thinned out considerably, and the trail up had obviously been the locals' way of getting their animals to pastureland.

Into the darkness to the west, it looked like a straight shot through the grassy field to the border.

Turning around to Tiger and Bo, Villapiano said, "We're in the homestretch, boss, and the land has leveled off. I think it's time for me to carry Shaheen and we make a run for it."

Knowing daylight was coming and they'd be sitting ducks, Tiger was eager to make tracks as fast as they could. "Okay, JV, I'll swap Massoud for your rifle."

Villapiano slid his rifle sling over his head and placed his AK-12 gently by Tiger's feet. Then, taking Shaheen's right arm from Bo, he bent down and hoisted Shaheen onto his back, eliciting a sharp cry of pain from the injured man as his abdomen rubbed across Villapiano's shoulders.

"Steady, Massoud," Tiger said, compassionately holding his cheek. "A few more minutes and all this is over."

Picking up the AK-12 with her right hand, she put her left arm around Bo's waist and said, "C'mon, Bo, one last push."

They hadn't taken but ten steps when spotlights flashed, dousing them in bright lights. Shocked, they stopped dead in their tracks. Before they could take any action, a loud series of bangs barked out from behind the spotlights, streaks of flame punctuating the sensory assault.

Thunk. Thunk, thunk, thunk.

The sound of a heavy machine gun, Tiger knew, and those were warning shots.

She didn't dare lift the rifle in her right hand, for if she did, what was surely a Dushka in the back of a technical would chew them apart before she could get off a single shot.

Behind the noise of an engine, the bright spotlights moved toward her and the group. With the vehicle twenty meters out, she heard a shout of *"Harkat neknid!"* Do not move.

It stopped at an angle ten meters in front of her small team, giving her a clear sight of what they were up against. Two men were in the cab of the dark pickup truck, with a third standing threateningly behind a Dushka in the truck bed.

As the passenger door swung open, the soldier standing in the back suddenly slammed forward into the Dushka, followed a split second later, almost simultaneously, by a sharp cracking sound. The soldier's lifeless body slumped on the handle of the heavy machine gun, pulling its barrel skyward until it reached the end of its range of motion.

Confused and startled, Tiger looked first at the soldier in the passenger seat, then the driver. Both were grasping at their door handles with one hand while lifting their weapons with their other.

The driver opened his door enough to put his left boot on the ground when he, too, slammed forward into the truck's A-pillar with another cracking barrage, a billowing mist of crimson blood spraying on the inside of the windscreen.

Just now lifting her rifle, Tiger turned to her left, where she saw Villapiano walking forward, Shaheen draped over his shoulders, his right arm extended, firing his pistol at the third soldier. He meticulously emptied the magazine of his MP-443 Grach into the chest of the soldier, then turned to Tiger and Bo and said, "Let's get the hell outta here."

Tiger grabbed Bo by the shoulder and followed Villapiano, who was already moving toward the border. "JV, what the hell was that?" she shouted.

Without turning around or slowing, Villapiano answered back, "That was the business end of a Barrett Model 82A1 .50 caliber rifle saving our asses, and it signals the cavalry has come to the rescue."

On the near horizon of the crowned pastureland, Tiger saw two white lights circling, the right counterclockwise, the left clockwise. They were handheld lights, she knew, and they signaled "All Clear."

The beacons were between only 100 and 150 meters out, but with each step, Tiger felt they weren't making any progress. After twenty steps, she paused, turned around, and looked behind them, scouring the gentle slope for any more threats, and seeing none. She did, however, notice the helicopter and its lights off in the distance.

Turning around, she continued her run to the border, and with every few steps, it grew apparent they were getting closer. Both the two lights and the circles they were creating were getting noticeably larger.

Running straight for the lights, she saw the silhouetted shape of Villapiano carrying Shaheen in front of her, Bo close behind. At the last moment, Villapiano veered to the left of the lights, so Bo and Tiger followed suit.

Once they passed the lights, the Turkish soldier stopped circulating them and turned them off. Her eyes momentarily adjusting to the darkness again, Tiger heard a familiar voice.

"Welcome to Türkiye, ma'am. Let me get aid for your man." Then into a radio transmitter, the disembodied voice in the dark said, "I need a medic up here, immediately."

"Frog Greer," Tiger said through a heavy pant, "what the hell are you doing in Iran?"

Stepping forward to be seen, the US Navy SEAL said in his distinctive Kentucky twang, "Technically ma'am, I'm in Türkiye.

And as far as what I'm doin', it would seem, as my mama Dumpy used to say, bless her soul, 'I'm savin' your backside.'"

Tiger chuckled. "So, am I to assume that was your shooting a minute ago? I thought you were more of a munitions guy."

"Yes, ma'am," Greer answered with a smile. "I do enjoy blowin' stuff up, but that's more of a hobby than anythin' else."

Tiger saw three Turkish soldiers in camouflage uniforms gather around Shaheen, whom Villapiano had gently laid on the ground. Turning to Greer, she said, "Frog, tell the medics our guy has a bullet wound to the abdomen with probable internal bleeding. And see to it that our guest here, Bo Jianguo, is well looked after. I got two more guys out in the field that me and JV are gonna go after."

"That's a negative, ma'am," Greer said. "You and the gentleman over there are the mission, so you're stayin' here. I'll go with JV to get your boys back, and there ain't no arguin' 'bout it."

"Frog, you can't go into Iran," she countered.

"Yeah, maybe don't volunteer to Bravo One where I went off to if he should ask," he said with a spit of tobacco juice to the side. "Besides, it ain't like I ain't never been in Iran before."

Knowing she wasn't going to win this argument, Tiger shook her head and smiled. "Frog, it's 'ee ron,' not 'eye ran."

"Nah," he said with a smirk as he nodded to Villapiano and turned around to walk across the border, "I'm pretty sure it's 'eye ran.'"

Chapter 33

Jahan knelt, reached into the driver's open side window, and patted the driver's shoulder twice, signaling him to take a ninety-degree right turn and begin to traverse the sloping ridge in a northerly direction. On the uphill side, he saw the bouncing headlights of their paired colleagues coming in the opposite direction fifty meters to the west.

Together the two technicals were deploying crisscrossing patterns north and south across the ridge, aided by the helicopter sweeping across the entire area between the truck fire and the border. Jahan's heart beat fiercely in his chest, his anger and frustration both overflowing. This must work, he thought.

Jahan knew he had started this chase playing his cards close to the vest. He acted first on the intel received and still hadn't been completely open with all the data. He had wanted the recognition to advance his career.

Now, he admitted to himself, he was in danger of sabotaging his career. He had lost a great many resources in this fight, including most likely, his friend and staunchest ally, Major Afsoon. The only remotely acceptable way out of this mess was the killing or capture of the Americans.

Standing tall again in the back of the truck, pistol gripped firmly in his right hand and scanning his vision across the horizon, his current mood was just fine with the former as opposed to the later, killing as opposed to capturing.

McHenry laid side by side with Hadid, the younger man to his left, a fallen tree to his right. They could hear a truck relatively close by, its engine revving up and ebbing down as it navigated obstacles in its path. They couldn't see headlights directly, but they would catch swatches of illumination from time to time as the truck jostled through the dark.

"Don't know for sure, Sami," McHenry whispered to his teammate, "but I reckon we're dealing with a technical, fully loaded with a heavy machine gun, just like the others."

"I think that's the only prudent assumption," Hadid replied. "And there may be more than one."

"With that being the case," McHenry continued, "we have two courses of action. One, we try to evade the patrol or patrols, plus the helo, and sneak across the border, which has got to be less than a couple of clicks away."

"Okay, so that's one potential plan, Mac. What's the other?"

"We go on the offense," offered McHenry. "Nothing about that helo has shown us that it's armed, with either guns or missiles. That leaves us free to take the technical off the board."

"I like 'em both," Hadid said, "but you know me. I kinda like taking the offense and pushing the fight. We get caught out in the open by a technical, we got no chance. We neutralize the big gun, the odds swing to our side with us being this close to the border."

"Kinda what I was thinking," replied McHenry. "To hunt this technical, we're gonna need to split up. One of us will have its flank or rear, and that big gun can't get both of us in its sights at the same time."

"So, what's your plan?" Hadid asked.

"I'll go north, Sami," McHenry said, nodding to his right. "You take off west, circling behind it and sticking to its rear as close as you feel comfortable. In a few minutes, I'll fire at it, bringing its attention to the east. That's your cue to cut down the big gun."

"Copy that, Mac," Hadid nodded in agreement. "And once the big gun's down, we'll finish the truck, rendezvous, and make our way west together."

"That's Plan A, Sami," McHenry stated. "But if it's too dicey to find each other in the dark, just head west. I've no problem with Plan B, that being regrouping in Türkiye, if you know what I mean."

"Copy, Mac. Moving west on your mark."

While he didn't have eyes directly on the truck, McHenry could tell from the lit sky that it was slightly to the north and west of their position. "No better time than now, my brother," he said as rose to a tentative crouch, Hadid rising beside him.

McHenry turned to Hadid and placed his left hand on his shoulder. "Keep your head down, Sami. See you on the other side." Then after turning to his right, he counted down, "On three, two, one, execute."

Taking off and hearing Hadid scrambling away behind him, McHenry advanced quickly to the north. Thankful for traversing the slope rather than running uphill, he made good ground, moving faster than his prey.

Moving parallel to the truck, once he got pretty much along-side it, he adjusted his course and angled to intersect with the truck's path. Weaving between the loosely gathered trees, he stumbled behind a thicket of low brush and into a small boul-der field. He rounded a good-sized boulder and immediately dropped to a knee, the area to his left suddenly open and devoid of cover.

He could hear the technical close by, to his left, but could not quite see it, only its headlights dancing out to his right. Then he noticed the headlights veering slowly towards him.

McHenry believed he hadn't been sighted as the heavy machine gun laid silent, but he laid down and crawled backward as a precaution. He watched as the headlights continued to swing toward him and then ... behind.

The technical was turning around to now take a southerly course!

He ran the scenario through his mind. The truck was now headed back from where it came, meaning Hadid was now directly in front of it. If Hadid didn't have cover, the firepower from the truck would be overwhelming. Their roles in this plan, McHenry thought, were now reversed.

He rose to a crouch and curled around the boulder. Sighting the back of the truck through his scope, he noticed three men, one manning a Dushka, with a soldier to either side. With one, maybe two men, in the cab, it was going to be a four or five on two fight, he knew, and he didn't object to that math, but only if the big gun was taken out of the equation.

Sighting the soldier behind the rifle, McHenry pulled the trigger, sending two short bursts of automatic fire into the soldier's back. As his target crumpled down into the truck bed, he paused slightly in selecting his next target—the soldier to the left or to the right. He chose neither. Instead, he fired another burst at the Dushka itself, hoping to take it out of the fight completely.

Right-eye dominant and looking through his rifle's scope, he saw through his opened left eye the soldier on the left of the Dushka jump out of the truck bed. Wanting to slip into cover as quickly as possible, he lowered his rifle and swept another burst of gunfire at the truck's rear tires, deflating them and immobilizing the technical.

Weary of the soldiers who popped out of the truck bed, McHenry quickly, but silently, slid back behind the boulder. Behind cover, he swapped ammunition magazines. He knew he was now down to his last thirty rifle rounds.

Jahan had noticed the soldier manning the Dushka slumping down in the throes of death before the sounds of the automatic gunfire registered. Realizing the shots had come from behind, he instinctively spun around to sight a target. Unable to quickly find one, but realizing he was vulnerable, he dove to his right, out of the truck bed, and rolled away from the truck.

He yelled for the flight engineer to do the same, but he wasn't certain he had before another volley of gunfire swept through the back of the truck. The truck was now three or four meters behind him, and he noticed its rear tires were now flat.

Prone on his belly, Jahan extended both arms in front of him, sighting his PC-9 ZOAF and looking to acquire a target. In the darkness he saw nothing but a line of brush and a few fallen trees to his right. He was confident that one or more targets was behind that line to his right, and if he was on the Dushka, he'd spray it down with a lethal barrage.

He was about to spring up and get back to the truck bed when automatic fire came from behind him, in front of the truck. The driver and passenger were now engaged with the enemy in front of them. If he jumped into the truck, no matter which way he faced the fierce Dushka, he'd be exposed from the back. No, this hunt, he decided, would have to resume on foot for the time being.

To his left, he heard the flight engineer crawling over to him. As he approached, Jahan lifted the index finger of his left hand to his lips, signaling the other man to be quiet. His attention captured, the man stopped his crawl. Then Jahan used his left hand to point first to his right, the line of brush and trees, and then forward.

Together, the two men rose slowly to crouched positions, then carefully made their way forward, away from the embattled truck. As they walked, they angled their weapons to the right and the brush, looking for any lurking threat. Behind them, they heard the gunfight rage on, with repeated rounds plunking into the Toyota's high-tensile steel bodywork.

Heart pounding in his chest, Jahan readied his right index finger on the pistol's trigger. Even the slightest sound behind the thicket of brush was going to be met with a volley of rounds.

McHenry knew he had made a mistake focusing his gunfire on the Dushka rather than the two other soldiers in the back of the truck. Taking the gun out of play was one move, but taking away any personnel to operate the big gun was the better play. Now he probably had those two training their sights on him.

To be the hunter or the hunted, that was now his dilemma. It was also a task that got increasingly more complicated as he heard the helicopter advancing on his position. Now he really wished he had taken out the truck's personnel, for if he was behind that Dushka he could make short work in downing the chopper.

He heard small arms fire coming from the truck and beyond it, so he knew Hadid was engaged. To keep the two from the truck bed focused on him instead of Hadid, he decided to first become the hunted. Once he dragged them away from Hadid's battle with the truck's front seat occupants, he'd then turn the tables and go on the hunt.

Keeping a low profile on his belly, he scrambled on his elbows and knees down the slope to a fallen tree. Scooting behind it, placing the stump between him and the truck, he flipped himself into a seated position, his back pressed against the tree. Just as he was about to swivel and send some rounds downrange in the direction of the truck, the helicopter appeared over the tree line downhill, just seventy-five meters away and only fifty meters off the deck.

An even better target, McHenry thought. Instead of wasting rounds as a diversion, he'd create a diversion by targeting the helo.

He sighted the bird in the distance, then followed it in as it swept toward the technical. Well within range at under fifty meters, he gently depressed the trigger of his AK-12, firing a burst into the side of the helicopter's fuselage.

The helicopter immediately wiggled in reaction, then started to rise. McHenry reacquired his target through his scope, and depressed the trigger again, sweeping his gunfire across the helo's airframe and taking out half of its search lights.

Hit hard, the helicopter nosed up and climbed, simultaneously bailing out of the fight with a hard turn to its port side. Behind him, McHenry heard small arms fire centered on his general position

The good news, he thought, was that the chopper was off the playing field. The bad news, however, was that he was out of rounds for his AK-12.

Chapter 34

Ditching his AK-12 in the brush, McHenry scrambled on his elbows and knees down the slope, creating distance between him and the sporadic small arms fire centering on his general location. Coming to a spindly tree, he spun around it, got to a knee, and fired a couple of pistol rounds toward the gunfire.

Not only did he want to draw their attention to him and away from Hadid, but he also wanted them to follow. While the terrain wasn't his own, his extensive combat experience over the course of his career made him comfortable with his chances, even if he was outnumbered.

Paramount in getting the enemy to follow was to leave them a trail to follow, but not to scare them off with overbearing return fire. The occasional round would do, McHenry thought, not only to invite their attention, but to conserve his ammunition as well.

McHenry listened closely to determine if he was being pursued. The small arms fire coming from the technical was still going on, but it was lighter. Hadid must have eliminated at least part of the threat already. He still couldn't hear, however, sounds above him that would indicate the other two soldiers were making their way through the thicket of brush and advancing on his position.

Time to become more of a fox for the hounds, he thought. So, he raised his MP-443 Grach, pivoted around the tree, and fired four shots, moving his aim along a twenty-meter stretch of the thicket. Dropping to his stomach, he then made quite the production of being noisy, grunting and loudly scattering rocks as he crawled diagonally, northeast, further away from the technical.

Continuing to listen sharply, he heard return gunfire, both from an automatic rifle and a pistol. The soldiers were still on him. Now he hoped they followed him.

Crouching down, Jahan gazed through the brush and down the slope, looking for any signs of movement. He had heard the gunfire but had not seen a muzzle flash to pinpoint a position. Still, he knew he was on the right track.

The flight engineer clumsily came to his side, breathing heavily, more out of anxiety than exertion. "Sorry, Colonel," he whispered, "but I am a bit out of my element here."

Without turning to face him, Jahan replied, "You're doing fine, son. Stay close to me as we get through this brush. Follow directly in my footsteps." Then, moving his pistol to his left hand, he reached over with his right to lower the barrel of the man's KL-133 assault rifle so he wouldn't get accidentally shot in the back. "We'll get this dog," he added with confidence.

Jahan had been tempted to have the young aviator push through the brush first, but being untrained in such matters, he most likely would have made a tremendous racket in doing so, leaving no doubt as to their position and placing them in great danger.

He had also considered splitting up and letting the inexperienced aviator draw the enemy's fire, thus revealing their position to him, allowing him to end this once and for all. Jahan decided to save that tactic for later, after they first closed the distance.

Gingerly weaving through the brush, Jahan cut a path downhill, weaving from tree to tree to keep close to cover. Along the way, he heard the flight engineer dutifully following behind, literally in each footstep he had taken.

A reflection caught his eye as he approached a stump, and Jahan knelt to get a better look. It was a shell casing. Their target had been here, and even in the darkness, he was able to see the track of where his prey had slid away.

Keeping his pistol aimed in front of him, he turned to the aviator and said, "There's only one, and we're closing in on him."

"What do you want me to do, Colonel?"

"We're going to split up and advance," he replied. He then extended his arm along the path that had been scrubbed in the ground by the retreating enemy. "We'll use this line as a meridian. I'll go five meters to the left, you go five meters to the right, and we'll advance together at the same pace," he ordered. "Do you understand?"

"Y-y-yes, sir," came his nervous reply.

"If I shoot, you shoot, understood?"

Jahan turned to his left and resumed his hunt. "Let's put this one down."

McHenry heard the two soldiers slowly approaching, and the occasional snapping of a twig and tumbling of rocks from footsteps told him the two were advancing from different positions, looking to catch him in a deadly crossfire.

Time to turn the tables and go from hunted to hunter, he thought.

Still laying on his stomach but facing uphill, he picked up a good-sized rock and threw it to his right, then repeated it a moment later with another rock. As soon as the second rock left his hand, he scrambled on his hands and knees to his left five meters and found partial cover behind a thin tree.

Picking up another rock before standing up, he tossed it in the general direction of his previous throws, sighted his pistol, then held his breath and listened. He heard faint footsteps twenty meters away, and slightly up the hill. Running low on ammunition, however, he didn't dare fire at an unsighted target.

Switching thoughts to maybe escaping up the flank of his pursuers rather than fight it out, McHenry took a tentative step backward with his right foot. He then lifted his left foot and began to swing it backward, and when his full weight shifted momentarily to his right foot, it began to slide downhill on the loose scree.

He only slid a few inches, but knowing the extended noise foretold his location, McHenry knelt and readied his aim.

His suspicions were confirmed a moment later when automatic rifle fire swept to his right and overhead, causing him to fire four successive shots toward the muzzle flashes and then hitting the deck. Under no illusions that his rounds found purchase in the enemy, McHenry kept his pistol sighted at the threat with his right hand and used his left arm and knees to move backward and to his right.

After a couple of seconds, the soldier downrange released another volley of shots, joined by what appeared to be pistol fire from further away. Both were fired well to his right, but the muzzle flashes from the rifle, his closest enemy, were enough for him to lock in a position.

Lifting his left hand to join his right in steadying his aim, McHenry fired away with his MP-443, sending its 9x19mm slugs into two tight clusters just to the left of where the muzzle flashes had been. His gunshots still ringing in his ears, he heard the soldier hit the ground, his rifle clanking as it tumbled a short distance down the slope.

One down, he thought, one to go, as he discharged his spent magazine and inserted another, the last of his ammunition. Just seventeen rounds left.

Slowly he brought himself to one knee, keeping his MP-443 trained in the direction from where the earlier pistol shots had been fired. Knowing he was facing a pistol rather than a rifle was slightly comforting, and while he was confident in his shooting abilities, he knew that the distance separating him from the second soldier would require a heck of a shot, and likely more than one.

McHenry knew that if his enemy retrieved the fallen soldier's rifle, it would swing things in the favor of the Iranian. Instead of running away, he slowly worked toward where the rifleman had fallen. If anyone gets to that rifle, he thought, it's going to be me.

I've got to get to that rifle, thought Jahan. His airman had surely been cut down by their prey's return gunfire, leaving him now one on one in the deadliest of games with the American. And with the American seemingly reduced to just a pistol, having the rifle in his hands would tip the scales mightily in this encounter.

Keenly scanning into darkness, he walked toward where he thought the younger man had fallen. Not certain from where the American had been shooting, he kept his PC-9 ZOAF moving slowly side to side, ready to respond to any threat. Reflecting the tense situation, Jahan's heart beat so loudly in his ears it masked his own footsteps.

Finally, he made out the body of his fallen partner a few paces away, but he resisted the temptation to give his position away by running. Slowly, after another couple of careful steps, he knelt beside the body, his eyes and his pistol both trained on the darkness in a futile attempt to locate the American.

Patting his left hand on and around the engineer's lifeless body, Jahan couldn't locate the gun. Lowering his right hand to help, he leveraged his strength under the body and rolled the man over. Finding nothing, he muttered under his breath, "*La'nat bar oo.*" Damn him.

Just then gunfire erupted from about ten meters away, the shock of the noise startling him, literally causing him to jump off his knees and fall to the ground behind the body of the airman. Lifting his right arm over the head of the body, Jahan immediately fired back, moving his pattern of fire from right to left, then back again.

He stopped only when his pistol's slide locked in its rearward position, indicating he had exhausted his magazine. With skilled precision from his training, he released the spent magazine and inserted a fully loaded double-stacked box magazine, his last.

Jahan knew that if he couldn't find the airman's rifle, he had just fifteen rounds left to finish the American.

Hearing a rustle on the harsh desert landscape, McHenry had fired his weapon at the direction of the sound, a quick two-shot volley followed by another. The return gunfire had surprised him by how close it was, less than ten meters.

Dropping and rolling down the slope, McHenry discharged another two-round set, followed in quick succession by another. Hearing his opponent's shots passing overhead, he continued his roll, stopping on his belly and aiming uphill. He squeezed the trigger again, but nothing happened—no comforting recoil of a shot fired.

He immediately realized his MP-443 had jammed.

Redirecting his eyes from his target to his pistol, McHenry saw that it had a stovepipe jam, where the spent casing failed to fully eject and got caught vertically in the ejection port. It was a common and simple malfunction, but it meant that he was temporarily without firepower.

In the moment, McHenry valued cover and distance over firepower, so he continued his roll down the hill. At the same time, he calmly cleared the jam by using a well-practiced tap-sweep motion, where he firmly tapped the base of the magazine to ensure it was fully seated, then used his left hand to authoritatively sweep over the top of the slide from front to rear, displacing the caught casing, and allowing the slide to close on a fresh round.

By the time the jam was cleared, McHenry was a further three meters away and prone on his belly, ready to resume the battle. To require his target, he inhaled deeply, held his breath, and listened.

He heard the mechanical sound of a semiautomatic pistol being reloaded and a round being chambered, so he zeroed in on the direction and cautiously opened fire again, releasing another two-round series up the slope, just a foot or two off the ground.

While they hadn't killed his enemy, the shots served their purpose as they drew return fire from the Iranian, revealing his position by both sound and muzzle flash. With his target sighted, McHenry resumed fire, again dispatching a series of two-round volleys.

By his count, he had fired fourteen of his seventeen rounds. *Maybe I got him,* McHenry thought.

That hope evaporated almost before the thought had gone through his mind, as three shots echoed out through the night. Only in the movies did a blind charge at the enemy work, he thought, so he rose slightly, steadying himself on his knees with his left hand on the ground, his right aiming his weapon, and prepared to run to his left, away from the threat.

The next shot that came from the Iranian whizzed by so close that McHenry swore he could feel the slug stream past his head. Entirely too close for comfort, he fired twice more and retreated away from the battle.

Shots followed behind him and struck harmlessly in the trunk of a tree ahead, then silence followed, the only sounds registering being the sounds of McHenry's boots and those of his pursuer crunching over loose rocks. Reaching a windswept tree leaning precariously uphill from years of wind, he reached out his left arm, hooked the trunk, spun halfway around, and loosed his final bullet toward the following soldier.

Seconds later, two more shots were returned by the Iranian, both well off target. Now without ammunition, McHenry dropped his empty MP-443 and looked for cover to his evasion and eventual escape to the border.

Jahan's confidence grew with every step he took. The American coward was on the run, he thought, and this land was my land. My Iran.

He hadn't been able to locate the airman's rifle, but in death, his body had served well, taking several slugs and sheltering Jahan's own body from the American's assault. While having the rifle would be beneficial, he felt he had all he needed to finally succeed.

His training was coming back to him. It had been a long time since he had been tested in battle, but the familiar sensations were coming back to him. What had started out as nervous apprehension, even fear, had transformed to excited anticipation, even exhilaration. The hunt for this one elusive prey was concluding.

Jahan held his pistol with both hands, swiveling it slowly from side to side as he scanned for movement in the darkness. All his senses were on high alert, and his ears prickled for the slightest of noises that would give away the American's position.

He gingerly placed his feet as he moved forward, almost sliding them, the soles of his boots only centimeters above the ground, using the toes of his boots to carefully feel for any obstacles so that his eyes could stay trained ahead.

Approaching a tree on his left, he decided to round it on the right, the uphill side. As he swept around the trunk, he leaned his shoulders further to the right, allowing him a better angle to aim his weapon behind the tree.

In a flash, two hands reached out, one grabbing the top rail of his PC-9 ZOAF, the other grabbing his wrist and squeezing hard. Jahan reacted instinctively, squeezing the trigger once before feeling his arm twist and the American's shoulder jam into his chest, right below his left armpit. The next thing Jahan knew, he was flying through the air.

Chapter 35

McHenry twisted his body and used the leverage of his hips to toss his enemy down the slope. Seeing the pistol, he had desperately grabbed ahold of it, but as the slide moved mechanically when the gun was fired, his grip weakened just a bit.

The momentum from tossing the soldier caused McHenry to stumble in the path of the fallen man, and he felt the pistol break free, not only from his hand, but from the hand of his opponent as well. Whoever found the weapon first would have the clear advantage, but McHenry wasn't about to place all his eggs in one basket.

Fighting for balance on the slope, he took several steps back, his boots slipping in a battle to find traction on the loose scree. As he was coming to a stop, he unsheathed his combat knife, a Russian-made Smersh-5, from the front of his vest.

Ordinarily he would have packed one of his trusty Benchmade or KA-BAR knives, but this covert mission had required equipment that would provide plausible deniability for any US involvement. In the moment, however, McHenry didn't notice any difference holding the nearly six-inch-long blade in front of him.

He held the knife with a firm hammer grip, with all his fingers wrapped around the hilt for maximum control and weapon retention, his thumb parallel to the handle behind the guard, ensuring his wrist remained straight. He positioned the blade close to his body, between his waist and chest, and took a step toward his enemy.

After a step, he paused, seeing his opponent had found his footing and was also holding a knife, positioned in a reverse grip, with the blade facing down toward the ground, a technique McHenry had been taught for close-quarters grappling.

Clearly the soldier was trained, thought McHenry, but just how much experience did he have?

As the two men began to circle one another, McHenry used his left hand to unwrap his scarf from around his neck. He then flicked it at the groin of his opponent, causing the Iranian to quickly move his right hand, the hand holding his knife, to protect himself.

That single defensive move gave McHenry a strong indicator of his opponent's skill and experience fighting with edged weapons. Experienced fighters knew it was nearly impossible to emerge from a fight without a wound when both participants were ready with knives, and they accepted they would be bleeding by the end. The inexperienced fighter sought to escape without a wound and focused almost entirely on drawing blood with their own weapon.

While the inexperienced warrior focused on inflicting a series of wounds, death by a thousand paper cuts in a manner, the experienced soldier sought one defining, mortal blow. They'd give up a relatively minor wound for delivering a fight-ending wound.

McHenry flicked his scarf once more at the Iranian, this time up high, aimed at his face. In response, his opponent grabbed it with his off hand, his left hand, and held onto it. McHenry closed the distance and held his left forearm horizontally in front of him, parallel to the ground.

The Iranian took the bait, stabbing downward with his knife and driving the blade deep into McHenry's arm. Immediately, McHenry's vision flashed white as pain shot through his entire body.

He didn't let it stop him though.

McHenry finished his approach, stepping forward with his right leg and bringing up his right hand, underneath the Iranian's extended left arm. Fueled by the pain racking his body, he used his entire might to drive his blade between the fourth and fifth ribs of his enemy combatant.

The Iranian exhaled deeply and his breath washed across McHenry's face as he began to fall backward to the ground. McHenry kept his footing and held tight to his knife, letting his opponent slide off the blade as he fell. This fight, he knew, was over. But he was still behind enemy lines, and another fight was likely on the horizon.

McHenry gritted his teeth, and using the thumb and first two fingers of his right hand while still holding onto his own knife, he pulled the Iranian's blade out of his left forearm. Another bolt of pain ran up his arm and into his chest, and it was all he could do to stifle a scream.

Using his scarf, McHenry fashioned a bandage around his wound, and he used his teeth and right hand to finish it in a knot. Looking down, he saw that the Iranian was, in fact, out of the fight.

Time to find Sami, he thought, and get the hell out of Iran once and for all.

Eyes opened, Jahan saw the American standing above him and could have sworn he saw him give a solemn and respectful nod of the head.

He held the wound on his left side with both hands, in a futile hope to staunch the bleeding. He knew, however, it wasn't the external bleeding that was going to kill him. The knife had pierced his lung and, undoubtedly, also his heart. His breathing was already labored, and his vision was tunneling as his blood pressure plummeted.

He stared upward with his eyes, for he feared that if he blinked, he would never see again. He coughed lightly twice and felt blood trickling out of the left corner of his mouth and down his cheek.

"My lovely Azadeh," he whispered, "please forgive my hubris, my selfishness. While it has robbed us of our future, I will forever be devoted to you. *Elhamdola*." Praise Allah.

Tears ran from both eyes, still wide open, as Colonel Rostam Jahan exhaled his final breath.

With Bo safely and securely seated in the back of a Turkish military truck and Shaheen in transit in another, Tiger had been busy attempting to get her team to safety. Leaning on the front of a Otokar Cobra II armored tactical vehicle, she focused on the screen of a Getac B360 ruggedized laptop, carrying the real-time feed from a AeroVironment RQ-11B Raven B, a small, hand-launched remote-controlled unmanned aerial vehicle flying nearly 150 meters above the battleground.

Using its infrared cameras, the drone was delivering real-time, high-definition video to Tiger's monitor. She had used the feed to guide Villapiano and Greer to Hadid, and they had arrived just in time to gather him up after he had dispatched the front seat threats from the crippled technical.

Now Tiger's priority was to find McHenry and get all four men safely over the border. The complication, of course, was the final Iranian technical, one that had made a beeline from its northwest sector patrol to the vicinity where the helo and technical had encountered McHenry and Hadid.

Having redirected the drone from Hadid's group to search for McHenry, she had found two heat signatures, one man walking west from another laid out on the ground. One of those men was surely McHenry, and her bet was on the survivor who was walking away. Still, she wasn't sure.

Keying her tactical radio, she called out to McHenry, "Two, this is One. What's your SITREP?"

Her message was met with silence.

"Repeat, Two this is One, what's your SITREP?"

With nothing returned but silence, she called out to Hadid and Villapiano, "Three and Four, this is One. Be advised you have one technical arriving on the scene, with another on foot heading west toward your location, two hundred meters out."

"Copy that, One," replied Villapiano. "Any sign of Two?"

"I'm hoping he's that man on foot," she replied nervously.

Over the sound of his boots on the rock, McHenry heard a faint sound. Feeling around, he found the earplug for his radio dangling off his right shoulder. It must have fallen out during the tussle with the Iranian, he thought, and surely that faint noise he heard was a transmission

After wiggling the earpiece back in, he called out, "Bandit elements, this is Two. I've been off comms. What's the status?"

"Welcome back to the party, Two," came Tiger's reassuring voice. "You're about two hundred meters east northeast of Three, Four, and a special guest. Be advised, there's a technical converging on the scene from the north. Can you make it to Three and Four?"

McHenry knelt and thought for a moment. "That's a negative, One. I'm combat ineffective, nursing a wounded arm and with no firepower. Repeat, no firepower. You get the boys out, and when they're close to the border, have 'em pop some sort of diversion to get the technical's attention. I'll use what's left of our cover of darkness to slip around the back of the technical and cross the border further north."

The return silence was deafening, and during it, the headlights and searchlight of the technical came bouncing into his vision from over the horizon, causing him to lay fully prone on the cold ground.

Finally, Tiger's voice came back on the radio. "That's an affirmative, Two. Stay low, go slow, and stay on comms."

"Roger that, One," he replied, then began leopard crawling as best as he could with his wounded left forearm. After two days of hell, he was too close to completing this op to stop now.

"Alright boys," whispered Villapiano to both Hadid and Greer, "you heard the boss. Let's hightail it west to the border."

"Copy that, JV," replied Hadid. "I'll take point. You all keep up."

"I got our six," stated Greer.

With that, the three took off single file up the slope and to the border, three meters separating the men. Every few paces, Greer looked over his right shoulder to ensure the technical hadn't changed course and was on their tail. Not seeing headlights but not entirely trusting his eyes, he soon began performing little pirouettes, twisting full circle to scan the complete environment, causing him to slip behind the other two.

"Slow up a little, boys," he shouted. "I can't look up and down and run as fast as you two at the same time."

As Hadid slowed the pace, it allowed Villapiano to course correct. "Hey Sami, veer slightly south to get to our egress point," he offered.

As they looked in that direction, they saw three quick flashes of light, just fifty meters to seventy meters out.

"That must be the open door," Hadid said with a smile. Turning around as Greer rejoined them, he said, "Forget our six now, Frog. We got a ten-, twelve-second sprint to the border."

Overcome with their natural competitive spirit, the three men sprinted uphill in the direction the beacon had been shone. As they got closer, they heard Tiger shout, "Keep running boys, almost here."

Hadid won the race, smiling as he ran past Tiger and a small cadre of Turkish soldiers, and then took cover behind an armored vehicle. Villapiano followed close behind.

Not entirely comfortable leaving their rear unprotected, Greer had stopped twenty meters away and scanned for the technical. Seeing they were clear, he made his way to Tiger and the group.

"Got any ideas on what to do for a diversion?" she asked.

"I do, in fact," Greer answered. "I got me a couple of frags I could toss out there to make some racket, and we could follow it up with some gunfire from these here armored trucks."

"Grenades and guns," said Tiger. "That's liable to draw fire. Help me get everybody here either in a truck or behind a truck, and let's make sure all the heavy guns are manned."

"Yes, ma'am."

Working with Greer's Turkish liaison, they quickly hustled the ten men on site into the three Otokar Cobra II vehicles left on the scene. Each of the vehicles were equipped with turrets sporting either 7.62mm or 12.7mm machine guns, and all three turrets were manned with a Turkish soldier.

Once ready, Tiger stood at the rear of the command truck, and she gave a visual command to Greer to proceed. Receiving it, Greer walked to the front of the truck, pulled the pin on a M67 fragmentation grenade, and chucked it as far as he could.

Leaving no time to admire his work, he repeated the process with his second, and final, grenade.

Four seconds after he threw the first grenade, it exploded, followed quickly by a second explosion. Walking to the back of the truck, he exchanged a quick high five with Tiger, then they both squatted down, Greer peeking around the corner, Tiger looking for McHenry on her laptop's display.

Seconds after the two explosions, the Turkish commander gave orders to the command truck's machine gunner to fire a couple of short salvos into the air to complete the ruse. Then, they waited.

But not for long.

In short order, a spotter in the Cobra II on the left flank shouted he had a visual on the Iranian technical and that it was fast approaching. Everyone turned and looked as its headlights and searchlight bounced up the hill, getting ever closer. Tension was high throughout. The Turks had more than enough firepower to win this dispute, but, in the very best-case scenario, it would cause an international incident with a bordering country. In the worst-case scenario, an encounter would signal the commencement of a shooting war.

When the technical closed to within 100 meters of the border, the Turkish commander gave his order, and the three Cobra IIs fully illuminated their roof-mounted searchlights. Within seconds, all three beams were centered on the olive drab Toyota Hilux.

Startled, the driver of the technical froze it in place, and a tense standoff ensued. From her position, Tiger could make out the Iranian soldier manning the Dushka in the back, holding onto the machine gun with one hand while desperately attempting to shield his eyes with another.

It had to be clear to the Iranians that they were outnumbered, at least three to one, she thought. However, there was no way for the Iranians to know the firepower that stood just on the Turkish side of the border. For all they knew, they might think they had the firepower advantage with the technical.

For the Turks' part, displaying their firepower advantage with a few warning shots could be construed as a provocative act of war, particularly firing their weapons onto Iranian soil. So, by order of their commander, the big guns stayed silently trained on their target, to be fired only if fired upon.

The standoff continued, excruciating second after second, causing even the most battle-hardened veterans like Villapiano, Hadid, and Greer to hold their breath. As the stalemate approached thirty seconds, the sounds of an approaching helicopter pierced the silence.

The initial sounds of the chopper immediately escalated the tension among Tiger, her team, and the Turks. But they were soon alleviated when it became apparent the chopper was approaching from the west, Türkiye, and not the east, Iran.

When the helicopter was twenty-five meters behind the Turkish stronghold, it too triggered its spotlight, adding yet another beam to those collected on the Iranian technical. It also served as the final decision-making variable for the Iranian team, as moments later it turned a slow, lazy circle to the south and then continued on a slow southwest retreat.

Tiger combed her hand through her hair and breathed a long sigh of relief. She then keyed her radio and said, "All's clear, Two. Come in from the dark. We'll leave the lights on for you."

During the standoff, McHenry had quickly moved north to skirt well past the technical, then turned a hard left, west, and double-timed his escape. Knowing his knife was useless at any distance, he sheathed it and used his right hand to apply pressure to the wound on his left forearm.

He was careful with each of his hastily placed steps, knowing the position of his arms left him inherently unbalanced. Still, concentration was difficult as each jarring foot placement sent pain searing out from his wound.

McHenry slowed as he neared the border, clearly denoted at this point by bundles of concertina wire, a high-security, coiled razor wire that had been expanded like an accordion, creating a formidable, anti-climb, and difficult-to-cut barrier for smugglers, traffickers, and others looking to illegally enter Türkiye. With no visible way through, McHenry turned south and walked parallel to the wire, busily scanning for any breaches.

"One, this is Two," he radioed to Tiger. "I'm north of your position, working my way down the wire perimeter of the border."

"Copy, Two," she promptly replied. "We have you on UAV. You're 400 meters out. You'll crest a little bump and see a cluster of trees. We're stacked up about fifty meters past. You said you're nursing a wound, but you're making good time. You need us to come get you?"

While McHenry would have loved to have had a friendly next to him, he knew it was a risk that couldn't be afforded. Everyone was safely across the border. This was not the time to bring another one or two back onto the enemy's turf.

"That's a negative, One. My legs and feet are just fine. I have a knife wound on my left arm that will need some tending to is all."

"Well then hurry your ass up, Two," Tiger responded. "I figure we can all use a bit of breakfast, don't ya think?"

McHenry smiled to himself and continued his march. He was nearly at the end, but his experience told him now was not the time to let his mind wander, to lose his vigilance. Helping his cause, dawn was beginning to break on the far horizon to his left, and the emerging light was rapidly improving his field of vision. Of course, it was improving the vision of any Iranians out on the field as well.

Topping the thinly grassed bump, he saw the trees Tiger had mentioned, as well as the headlights from the Turkish forces still visible shining perpendicularly across his directional path. At the end of the concertina wire, he saw Tiger, Villapiano, and Hadid, along with two Turkish soldiers. In the background to the west, he saw a T-70 Black Hawk helicopter, the Turkish variant of the Sikorsky S-70i, taking off.

Hadid was first to greet him, stepping up and gently grabbing McHenry's left wrist. "Damn good to see you, Mac. How's the arm?"

"It hurts like a sumbitch, Sami, but I'll be alright," he answered, wiggling his fingers to prove his point to Hadid.

"All the same, Mac, we're gonna pop you in the back of a truck with our Turkish medic here," Hadid continued, nodding in the direction of the uniformed soldier to the side of Tiger.

Smiling, McHenry slapped Villapiano on the shoulder, both men respectfully nodding, communicating hundreds of words and multiple emotions, all without uttering a sound. Finally, McHenry turned to a smiling Tiger.

"You know, boss," I'm getting to be a bit old for this shit," he said.

"Shoot, Mac. I'm countin' on you just beginnin'."

Chapter 36

Eight days later, Tiger sat in front of Devin Thomas's desk in his office on the seventh floor of the Old Headquarters Building in Langley. In a frame on the wall behind him was a battered and worn forty-eight-star American flag that had once flown on a US Navy warship in World War II, the war after "the war to end all wars."

Guess we missed that prediction, she thought.

She knew Thomas, a career intelligence officer, had been the recipient of the Distinguished Intelligence Cross, the highest honor bestowed by the Central Intelligence Agency. Yet one would never know it by looking around the office.

A great many recipients of significant, but lesser, honors, like the Intelligence Star, had proudly shown their honors in prominent places in their offices. That Thomas preferred to hang a flag in honor and respect of the meritorious actions of American men and women that came before him spoke volumes of the person he was.

Thomas appeared from behind Tiger and sat behind his desk, opening a half-inch thick folder and taking a moment to peer through the reading glasses perched on the tip of his nose.

"Tiger, I've read over your full account of the Iranian shit show," he started.

"Sir, I'm more inclined to think of it as the Iranian fiasco rather than shit show," she offered in response, a hopeful attempt to lighten the mood.

Thomas glared at her over his glasses for a moment.

"Nice try, Tiger. My office. My term." Closing the file, he continued, "I think 'shit show' is the better reflection of an operation that resulted in over twenty-five deaths, over half of them uniformed service personnel, and two cops on top of that. What started as a covert operation ended up as an international incident that has barely escaped being revealed in the media."

"Yes, sir, Deputy Director," Tiger replied as she lowered her eyes and focused on the file folder.

"It's still a 'win,' though," Thomas added with a sigh. "You got the objective, the engineer, out of the country and into our hands, and he's been a font of data on Iran's nuclear operations and capabilities."

"After his full debrief, what's gonna happen to Bo?" she asked.

"We already have a new identity for him and a role at Los Alamos National Laboratory out west," Thomas answered. "He sorta pissed and moaned about his life being turned upside down, but that was mostly a negotiation ploy to get a bigger bundle of cash. The more significant problem is his girlfriend here in the States."

"Oh yeah?"

"Yeah, she has family and her own life, but we'll make it work eventually. Probably with another big check. Speaking of which, to keep the peace with the Turks, we're going to be providing a lot of financial assistance in the completion of the border wall. This op's getting more expensive as the weeks go by."

"I'm sure glad they weren't ahead of schedule on that wall," Tiger added, looking up again from the desk.

"I saw that one of your team was wounded in the escapade. Is he okay?"

"He's recovering well," Tiger answered. "You know they all go where one goes, so the three of them were flown to Ramstein so Mac could get tended to at Landstuhl Regional Medical Center. He underwent a quick and successful debridement surgery, and they caught a ride back a couple of days ago." With a smile she added, "I imagine they're putting a dent in beer inventories wherever they are."

After a short pause, Tiger continued. "There is one thing I don't know, sir, and that's the status of our asset, Shaheen."

"Funny you should ask, Tiger. He's currently in an Istanbul hospital. As you know, it was sketchy as hell, but he's going to make a full recovery. He knows he's blown in Iran, but we have plenty of reason to believe he'll be receptive to us setting him up in Baku. If he goes for it, you're going to be the agent who runs him. Got any thoughts on that?"

"I'm perfectly okay with that," she answered. "Massoud's a good man, and we can trust him."

Pushing the file over to the far-right side of his desk, Thomas said, "As far as I'm concerned, it's time to call it a wrap on the Iranian, uh, 'fiasco.' We move on to the next."

"Roger that, sir," Tiger replied. "Will part of the next include sniffing out what we think is a mole."

"On that, Tiger, we've made a lot of progress," he said as he crossed his hands on the desktop. "We've handled the investigation off books so far, and it's led us directly to the Directorate of Support."

"Jeanie Clayton Slater's team?"

"Yes, but more Clayton Slater than her team," he answered.

"What's the plan?"

"Right now, it looks like a two-way connection between Beijing and Langley, via an intermediary in DC. We're gonna close the Beijing line, but we're also going to watch her to see if she extends any new lines. We can play her for not only disseminating misinformation, but also the identification of bad actors we might not already know about."

"We're not lettin' her get away with it, are we?" Tiger asked with a tilt of her head and a raised eyebrow.

"Oh, absolutely not," Thomas replied promptly. "In a couple of months, we'll reel in the line. In the meantime, we wanna put a few more hooks on the line and increase our haul of fish, is all."

Leaving Thomas's office, Tiger found herself waiting at the elevator lobby, lost in thought. The bell marking the arrival of a car snapped her into focus.

Stepping back to let the car empty, she watched a small parade of "blue badgers" walk by, employees of the agency denoted by the blue badges they wore on their belts or on lanyards around their necks. At the back of the group, she noticed a diminutive, middle-aged blonde woman stepping out.

Smiling, Tiger pointed to her and said, "You're Ms. Clayton Slater in Support, right?"

Caught momentarily off guard, the startled woman quickly smiled and replied with a stammer, "Y-yes, yes, I am."

Tiger took another step into the car, spun around, and while pressing the button for the third floor, said, "Thank you so much for getting me and my guys everything we've needed. Our success, and safety I might add, has been dependent on your group."

"You're most welcome, dear," Clayton Slater responded with a genuine smile. "You know who I am, but I don't believe I've had the pleasure. As such, you have me at a sort of disadvantage."

"Well, we wouldn't want that, now would we?" Tiger said with a wink as the elevator door closed.

Chapter 37

Resplendent in his immaculately pressed black slacks, white Mandarin collared shirt, and spotless white apron, Samuel Tsai walked purposefully from the kitchen of the Liulin Restaurant to the dining room, expertly balancing a bottle of water, a bottle of Moutai *baijiu*, and two stemless wine glasses on a small circular tray. After over two weeks, his mission in Beijing was almost over.

Tsai, an American-born descendant of Taiwanese expatriates, was an agency operative who had been stationed in Taiwan for five years. Three weeks ago, he entered China under nonofficial cover and a forged student visa. Using connections in the Chinese underground organized crime world, he had procured a position as a waiter at the upscale dinner restaurant.

The Liulin was located adjacent to the Hongse Triumphal Arch Hotel off Maolinju West Road, just south of where it intersected with Yuyuantan South Road in the Haidian District of Beijing. It catered to upscale visitors of the hotel, many of whom had dinner meetings with officials housed in the August 1st Building, also known as the Bayi Building, across the street, facing Fuxing Road.

The offices of the building included those in the Ministry of National Defense, the most prominent and powerful member being that of the minister, Zhau Xiang, who was discreetly seated at his usual table in the back corner, facing the door and windows.

Tsai knew Zhau was a regular at the restaurant and had served him a number of times over the past couple of weeks. This time, however, he was alone, making it the first best opportunity to complete his mission.

If nothing else, Zhau had proven to Tsai to be a creature of habit. His preferred dinner was the roasted duck served with a sweet bean sauce called *tian mian jiang*, paired with delicately thin pancakes, sliced scallions, and cucumber sticks. During dinner, he drank tea. After dinner, however, he preferred a glass of still water and several glasses of *baijiu*. His pattern of behavior was Tsai's opportunity.

Tsai approached silently, for the minister was notoriously intolerant of any non-essential conversation. Across the table from his patron, Tsai placed his tray off to the side and picked up the bottle of Moutai, making a show of displaying the label to the minister as he rested it on his left forearm. After a moment, he placed the bottle on the table to the right of Zhau and accompanied it with an empty glass.

Next, Tsai placed down the other glass and filled it with room temperature water from a glass bottle, placing the bottle on the tray when he was finished. Lastly, he filled the first glass with a pour of the *baijiu* and left that bottle on the table. With a curt bow, he picked up his tray and exited the dining room. Out of the corner of his eye, he noticed the minister emptied his water glass in one big slug.

Walking through the kitchen, Tsai untied his apron and placed it by the back door. Then, with the partial bottle of water in his hand, he walked out the back door and into the Beijing night. Turning right, he traversed a darkened alley toward the Spicy Fisherman Degandian restaurant, emptying the contents of the water bottle along the way. Once he got to that restaurant's dumpster, he opened the lid, wiped his fingerprints from the bottle using a serving towel tucked in his back pocket, and chucked it into the far corner, the satisfying sound of the bottle breaking bringing a smile to his face.

He lowered the lid of the dumpster and walked to Maolinju Middle Street, where he turned left, east, and continued walking, hands in the front pockets of his slacks. At the next corner, the grate of a sewer drain greeted his arrival.

Tsai casually removed a small glass vial from his right front pocket and twisted off the lid. Waiting for the light to turn, he dropped the open vial of clear liquid, a fast-acting cardiotoxic compound built on a lab-grade alkaloid, into the Beijing sewer system.

Working his way to the next point of his exfil, the Beijing West Railway Station, Tsai afforded himself a small smile of satisfaction. Even as he was disappearing into the dark, he knew the old minister was succumbing to a sudden cardiac arrest.

Notes

Upon reading my first novel, *Outflanked*, my friend Marc Dietz asked me if I was living vicariously through one of that book's main characters, Cal McHenry (who, of course, is one of the two main characters of this book, *The Iranian Fiasco*). Marc couldn't help but notice that I was about three years older and twenty pounds or so lighter than Cal, but shared some other similarities, and was wondering if, you know, Cal was me.

Well, let me settle this right here and right now. Cal is a badass. I am not.

The character of Cal McHenry came to me when my wife, Lori, and I were watching the beginning of season two of the show, *Special Ops: Lioness*, starring Zoe Saldaña. In the premiere episode of that second season, the show's creator, Taylor Sheridan, plays a character named Cody Spears, a wizened, experienced soldier.

I immediately thought, now that's an interesting character to explore! Heroes in the thriller genre, be it in book or on screen, are typically young studs. What about the older studs, the ones who survived the battles to become old soldiers in the first place? There could be interesting stories to tell in that space, no?

And so, I began to tell that story, first with *Outflanked*, and now with *The Iranian Fiasco*. But as I started writing, I realized that the story would be so much better with another unique character, and that led me to creating Lilly "Tiger" Swanson.

I, too, wanted to make Tiger different from the cliche. I wanted to create a strong, powerful female character. Tiger is no damsel in distress. She doesn't need a knight in shining armor to come riding into the rescue. No, Tiger is fully capable of saving herself.

Again, I pulled inspiration for her character from that very same streaming series. Jill Wagner's character, Bobby, is a strong, badass character, and I built Tiger somewhat in her image. Tiger's an operative, not a soldier, but she leads by example and doesn't back down from a fight.

With regards to locations, places, buildings, businesses, equipment, and other details in the book, nearly everything is real. That motorcycle shop out in the boonies in Iran? Yeah, it's there (or at least it used to be).

As a reader, I used to love to delve into the details of a good Tom Clancy novel. I aim to provide some degree of detail to you, the reader, but at the same time recognize that readers these days don't typically read gigantic novels anymore. So, I try to walk a fine line: provide details but keep it somewhat concise and move the story along.

I've also made conscious decisions to move the storyline forward at a speed that doesn't lend itself to a really deep development of characters, Cal and Tiger included. I recognize the books would be better for some readers if there were more time and space (i.e., words) dedicated to what makes them tick. Again, it's a trade-off. Some ideas hit the proverbial cutting room floor in an effort to make the book a manageable and marketable size.

I did write up psychological dossiers on both Cal and Tiger, and I thought about including them in this book, most likely as an appendix. Instead, I put them on my website. If you're interested, please visit my blog at rayhartjen.com.

I wrote *The Iranian Fiasco* simply because early readers of *Outflanked* provided such wonderful feedback. They enjoyed reading the first book, just as I enjoyed writing it. That being the case, why not run it back? And so here we are.

Will there be a third? Yes, and I already have ideas. In fact, I jotted down a few hundred words in the beginning of an untitled third book in what's becoming a series while I was only halfway through *The Iranian Fiasco*.

Let's make a deal, shall we? You keep reading 'em, I'll keep writing 'em.

Whaddya say?

Acknowledgments

The only possible place to start is with my wife Lori. I was lucky enough to have her marry me on May 14, 1994, and even luckier that she's been steadfastly alongside me every day since. She is the kindest, most compassionate and empathetic person I've ever met, and without her, none of this journey would matter.

With Lori, we've had the honor and pleasure to bring two amazing people into this mixed-up world of ours, our daughter, Olivia, and our son, Raymond. I absolutely love watching them become the people they are, as well as the people they are becoming.

To our friends, we owe so much. They've made us smile, they've made us laugh, and they've made us cry, and when I write 'cry,' I'm referring to the grateful kind. When people in social networks and constructs face challenges, some in the circle, mostly out of not knowing what to say or do, sort of disappear. When I was diagnosed with multiple myeloma in March of 2019, our network stood up strongly and helped my family push forward. I'm forever indebted to the ringleaders of that effort, Donna and Paul Truex, as well as their daughters, Taylor and Kennedy, both of whom Lori and I consider our 'other children.'

Thank you, too, to our family, Ruth, Audrey, Eli, Sophie, Tom, Colleen, Fred, Lita, Erralyn, and Wilet. Thank you to my father, Ray, mother, Helen, and a grateful recognition of those of Lori and mine who are no longer with us: my mother, Irene, and her parents, Alice and Richard.

I may have never had the confidence to write a manuscript if it wasn't for my friend, Jeff Christensen. During the early days of the pandemic, I started writing a novel. In telling him what it was about, he expressed his interest in reading it. It turned out he liked it, or at least he said he did. I haven't finished that manuscript, but it did give me the confidence that I could write long-form content. That confidence led me to collaborating with my friend, Tom O'Lenic, to write *Immaculate: How the Steelers Saved Pittsburgh*. And the rest, as has been so often said, is history.

Finally, I want to thank you, the reader. Thank you for taking a shot and investing your time, and perhaps even your money, with me. I greatly appreciate each and every one of you. My hope is to engage with a reader a day. By all means, please hit me up on any social networking platform—you can find me with my name.

Also, now that you've finished the book, please consider leaving your authentic review wherever books are sold, even if you didn't buy it from there. Reviews are so important to a book. First, they trigger algorithms, so the book more frequently shows up in lists and as suggestions. Most importantly, they guide other readers toward decisions on whether they want to try the book or not.

I'm not pandering for five-star ratings, although if you think *The Iranian Fiasco* is a five-star read, then by all means please rate it as such! I am asking, though, for your *authentic* rating. Of course, if you think it's a one-star read, well, then, maybe let's keep that between you and me.

Ray Hartjen is a writer and musician living in Mission Viejo, California with his wife, Lori, and their goldendoodle, Quinn.

Ray has been a storyteller for most of his career, first in Corporate America, then adding his personal interests as well. Today, he blends his creating between freelance clients and the interests and passions of his own.

Diagnosed with multiple myeloma in March of 2019, Ray is an advocate for cancer patients, caregivers, and allies every day of the week that ends in a 'y.'

Connect with Ray on X (f.k.a. Twitter), LinkedIn, TikTok, and Facebook. His handle on every platform is his name, "rayhartjen."
#PunchTodayInTheFace

Other Books by Ray Hartjen

Immaculate: How the Steelers Saved Pittsburgh

Me, Myself & My Multiple Myeloma

Revenue Orchestration & Today's New Era of B2B Sales and Marketing

The Indy 500: A Year-Long Quest to Win the Greatest Spectacle in Racing

Outflanked